The Healer

Sabrina Furminger

iUniverse, Inc.
Bloomington

The Healer

Copyright © 2011 by Sabrina Furminger

All rights reserved. No part of this book may be used or reproduced by any means, graphic, electronic, or mechanical, including photocopying, recording, taping or by any information storage retrieval system without the written permission of the publisher except in the case of brief quotations embodied in critical articles and reviews.

This is a work of fiction. All of the characters, names, incidents, organizations, and dialogue in this novel are either the products of the author's imagination or are used fictitiously.

iUniverse books may be ordered through booksellers or by contacting:

iUniverse
1663 Liberty Drive
Bloomington, IN 47403

www.iuniverse.com
1-800-Authors (1-800-288-4677)

Because of the dynamic nature of the Internet, any web addresses or links contained in this book may have changed since publication and may no longer be valid. The views expressed in this work are solely those of the author and do not necessarily reflect the views of the publisher, and the publisher hereby disclaims any responsibility for them.

Cover photography by Peter Eastwood.

ISBN: 978-1-4620-4075-9 (sc)
ISBN: 978-1-4620-4077-3 (hc)
ISBN: 978-1-4620-4076-6 (e)

Printed in the United States of America

iUniverse rev. date: 8/12/2011

To Dale, Anil, Samantha, Didi, and the dogs—

You are my Circle of Light.

To Paul and Mariana—

You are my Big Loves.

Acknowledgements

The author extends her gratitude to the following individuals for their support, guidance, encouragement, and assistance throughout the creative process:

Ajit Mehra, Anil Mehra, Cheri Hanson, Dale Mehra, Damon Kiperchuk, Daphne Kiperchuk, Helen Kiperchuk, Heather Fitzpatrick, Jenny Wolfe-Binder, Jo Prescott, Kate Pattison, Krista Hill, Lindsay Drysdale, Paul Furminger, Peter Eastwood, Ronya Lake, Samantha Mehra, Stan Mehra Furminger, Stefanie Curran, and Trevor Curran.

You are rock stars, each and every one of you.

The young woman's jumpsuit stank of recent violence: blood, vomit, guts, and sweat. Other people's pain. For a moment she yearned to peel off her clothes and escape the foul stench, but the decision to change was no longer hers to make and so she let go of the desire. Instead, she stood in the centre of the tiny cell and struggled to breathe without remembering the preceding hours. *This didn't work. It never did.*

She clamped her eyes shut but the violence was waiting for her behind her eyelids, too—the torn flesh, the battered faces contorted in agony, the blood gurgling beneath her busy hands. Bile began to rise up her throat as it always did this time of night and the young woman snapped open her eyes and brought her hands within inches of her face. Still vibrating hot and cold. Still crimson with violence.

Frantically she looked from one white wall to the other, to the concrete floor and the locked door, and, finally, up to the security camera trained down upon her. *I'm as guilty as they are.* And yet she could not stop herself from participating.

"What more do you want from me? When will it be enough?"

But the security camera offered no reply to her desperate inquiry, and the young woman ground her hot palms into her eyes and wondered how much longer she could torture herself with such questions. Slowly she scraped her nails down her face. *I want a new kind of pain.*

And so she collapsed in a heap on the hard bench that served as her bed and forced her mind back to the man who was now a ghost, to the one who had lifted her to untold heights before the epic fall. She fought the impulse to weep, and failed, and wondered if she would have the courage to take her life if a knife miraculously appeared in her hands.

Maybe I'm already dead. How would I even know?

Finally exhaustion dragged her down into unconsciousness, and as she faded to black she chanced a hope that she would meet her lover in her dreams, or at the very least, dream nothing at all.

PROLOGUE

i.

After a few moments of careful examination, the old midwife wrapped the unmoving mass of blood and flesh in a towel and placed it in the waiting bassinette. "A stillborn girl," she said gently without meeting Mrs. Merchuk's frantic gaze. "I'm sorry, dear. Your baby is an angel now."

Such hollow words did little to soothe Mrs. Merchuk, who gripped the edge of the mattress and opened her mouth to scream. For at least a minute, she was too anguished to produce any sound at all.

"Not dead," she whispered finally, pale and luminous with sorrow. "Not Ivy." The name had come to her in a particularly vivid dream. "I want to meet her. I want to hold her."

"The bleeding is far too heavy," muttered the midwife, who had turned her attention to Mrs. Merchuk's spread legs. She clicked her tongue and called out over her shoulder. "It's time to call for an ambulance, Mr. Merchuk." Being of a somewhat queasy disposition, Mr. Merchuk had asked to wait out the home birth in the hallway. His footsteps echoed down the stairs and into the study.

"Oh, he should be in here with you," the midwife said suddenly and bit her lip. "I'm sorry. I could have called for the ambulance myself. You're bleeding a lot, and…"

"I want to meet her," Mrs. Merchuk repeated slowly. "I want to hold my baby… my Ivy."

"Mrs. Merchuk, we need to prepare you for the hospital."

"Bring Ivy to me, please," Mrs. Merchuk said, strong and resolute despite the many hours of labour she'd endured. The old midwife sighed and nodded. Soon the little blue corpse was in Mrs. Merchuk's arms.

"I'll give you some time together," the midwife said before shuffling to the other side of the room and bowing her head.

Oh, Ivy. Mrs. Merchuk wept as she kissed the baby's forehead and grasped the tiny blue fingers in hers. *This can't have all been for nothing.* She brought the wrinkled fingers to her lips. "I love you, sweet baby." Mrs. Merchuk clamped her eyes shut against a tsunami of tears.

And then vibration. Indiscernible to the eye but Mrs. Merchuk felt it in her fingers. *It's the baby. Her hand is… vibrating?* In an instant Mrs. Merchuk was overcome by waves of warmth and contentment, spreading from her fingers to the tips of her toes and every crevice and organ in between. Time seemed to halt in its tracks as Mrs. Merchuk hovered on the brink of unconsciousness—but she rebounded and rode a wave of golden energy. She threw her head back and laughed heartily. Her limbs were buoyant. She opened her eyes and gazed down at her daughter, who was squirming in her arms and very much alive.

"Welcome to the world, Ivy." Mrs. Merchuk laughed again. She couldn't help but laugh. She was joyous. The baby was flushed with colour. Eyes as big as saucers, as blue as the sky.

Immediately the midwife was beside the bed. "I don't… it's just… how can this be?" The midwife stammered. "She was blue. She was dead! And now she's as pink…" She peered deeply into their faces and thoroughly examined Mrs. Merchuk. "You've stopped bleeding," the midwife exclaimed, blinking and shaking her head in disbelief. "All the tears that occurred during labour are… are healed over. You're healed." The ambulance could be heard approaching from down the street.

"After what she went through, you'd think she'd be crying," the frazzled midwife clucked as she prepared the baby for the ride to the hospital. "But no, she's lying there with her eyes open, as if nothing happened."

"She's just happy to be here," Mrs. Merchuk said quietly with her eyes fixed on her baby's serene face. "She has a lot of living to do."

ii.

The make-believe world of five-year-old Ivy Merchuk was complex and intoxicating. She ruled her backyard kingdom from under her favourite oak tree with Suzy, her long-limbed black lab puppy, by her side. With her bottom lip stuck out in a defiant pout, Ivy vanquished dragons, twirled and danced with the fairies, composed songs and stories, read picture books to Suzy and the elves, and protected the backyard from nefarious alien invaders.

One sunny summer morning, the king of the elves beckoned to Ivy. "I'm going to lead a group of elves across the laneway to build a new village," he said gravely. "You need to make sure the dragon doesn't hurt us when we leave the yard."

"I don't know." Ivy's mother had told her countless times that she was forbidden to leave the backyard. "It's too dangerous."

"You have to protect us from the dragon!" The king began to cry. "If you don't, he'll burn us to a crisp! Please?"

"I need to ask my mom," Ivy replied, knowing full well that her mother would not allow her to step out of the backyard. But it was equally clear that the elves would be unable to accomplish their mission without her help.

"Okay," she said decisively. "I'll help you, but my mom can't see what we're doing." The king scurried off to prepare for his pilgrimage, and Ivy glanced towards the house. Mrs. Merchuk was watching her from the kitchen window, as she always did when Ivy played outside. *We can't go unless she leaves.*

An hour passed. Ivy was beginning to doubt that the opportunity for escape would ever present itself when the phone began to ring in the study.

"I'm just going to answer the phone, sweetie," Mrs. Merchuk called out from the window. "I'll be back in a minute." She disappeared from her post.

Ivy counted to ten, crept to the side gate, and undid the latch.

"Come on!" Ivy beckoned to Suzy and the elves to creep through, all the while on the lookout for fire-breathing dragons and Mrs. Merchuk. *So far, so good.*

The horror reached Ivy's ears before it met her eyes. The screeching of tires. A thud. Ivy spun and watched an unfamiliar red car speed off down the laneway. The elves scattered, leaving Suzy lying alone and untended in the middle of the road. Ivy dashed to her best friend. A scream escaped her throat. She fell to her knees. Suzy struggled for air. Blood poured from her mouth and an open wound in her side. Ivy scooped Suzy up in her little arms. Soon Ivy too was covered in blood.

"Don't die, Suzy!" Ivy cried. An unfamiliar vibration coursed through Ivy's body and buzzed in her ears. Her palms grew warm. Her head felt foggy. Suzy moaned in her arms. Ivy fell into a white light, and in an instant, there was nothingness.

Ivy awoke disoriented in her bed. She was in her pyjamas. Her eyelids were heavy. She was very cold. It was no longer light outside.

"How did I get here?" She reached out a heavy hand to where Suzy normally lay beside her legs. "What happened, Suzy?"

But there was no dog on her bed. She flashed back to the laneway and saw Suzy in the middle of the road. She wept into her pillow.

When her tears subsided (*I will cry everyday and I will make a new kingdom and name it Suzy*), Ivy discerned her parents arguing in hushed voices just outside her bedroom door.

"I know what you said happened, but it's impossible, Amrita, don't you see?" Her father's voice was heavy with exasperation.

"Her clothes are drenched with blood, but there is not one wound…" Mrs. Merchuk's voice trailed off. She sighed. "I saw it happen. I rushed to the gate and watched it happen. It was… surreal. Beautiful. Terrifying."

"If it's true, think how amazing this could be for our family. No one else in the world can do this." Mr. Merchuk was breathless. "Think of the money we could make."

"How can you even suggest such a vile thing?" Mrs. Merchuk's voice was low and sharp, like an angry growl. Ivy wished she understood all the words. "I'll leave you."

Here ensued a long minute of silence. "I'm sorry, Amrita. I'm sorry." Mr. Merchuk sounded incredibly regretful. "Take her to Vivian tomorrow. Get her checked out." More silence, but Ivy knew her parents were hugging. Her parents' fights were few and far between, and what arguing did occur never failed to end with a long embrace, which always soothed Ivy to behold—even if Mr. Merchuk rarely hugged her himself.

The door cracked open. Mrs. Merchuk tiptoed to the bed. "Ivy? Are you awake?" She sat down on the edge of the mattress and again Ivy's heart ached. "How are you feeling?"

"I'm so sad because of Suzy," Ivy said, nearly choking on her grief.

The dim light that spilled in from the hallway illuminated Mrs. Merchuk's confusion. "Suzy? You don't remember what happened?"

Obviously her mother didn't know everything that had transpired in the laneway. "Suzy got hit by a car and died and it was my fault." Tears pooled on her eyelashes.

"Oh, honey." Mrs. Merchuk grasped Ivy's cold little hand in hers and massaged it tenderly. "There's no need to be sad." Mrs. Merchuk whistled and Suzy bounded up onto the bed.

In an instant, Ivy's grief was replaced by unadulterated joy. "Suzy!" There were no bandages, no stitches, no wounds, no indication that she'd been ploughed down in a hit-and-run only hours before. Ivy cuddled her giddy puppy.

"You saved her, Ivy," Mrs. Merchuk whispered and stroked Ivy's curls.

"She's okay, Mommy," Ivy squealed as Suzy covered her face with wet kisses. She didn't understand why her mother's eyes were so sad.

iii.

Megan was Ivy's best friend. Megan didn't care if the boys called Ivy a geek because she liked to read books that were too advanced for other fifth-graders. Megan talked to Ivy even though some of the other girls stuck gum in her hair and tripped her during gym class.

"Megan is cool and she thinks I'm cool, too," Ivy boasted to her mother as she wolfed down her after-school snack. *Megan actually used the word 'cool' to describe me.* "Soon other kids will think I'm cool, too." Nothing mattered more than coolness.

"Why don't you invite Megan over for a sleepover?" Mrs. Merchuk asked with a big smile on her face. Ivy nodded nonchalantly and swallowed the remnants of her cookie—as she figured any cool kid would do in a similar situation—but inside, she was wild with happiness. *I've never had a sleepover before. It's nice to have a friend.*

In the beginning, the sleepover exceeded Ivy's cautious expectations. Mrs. Merchuk had purchased matching hot pink feather boas for the girls, which they wore over their pyjamas. They painted their fingernails, watched a movie, ate pizza and popcorn, and gossiped about every single student in their class.

"We're having pancakes and waffles for breakfast," Ivy announced from where she sat on the floor watching Megan jump on her bed.

"This is a really bouncy mattress!" Megan squealed.

"That's because I jump on it all the time," bragged Ivy, who in fact had never once jumped on her bed. *Is it weird that I've never jumped on my bed?*

Megan giggled with delight. "Watch how high I can go." She waved her feather boa above her head as she bounced three feet in the air.

Megan's laughter morphed into a shriek. Her ankle buckled. She tumbled off the bed and landed on her back. Her head smacked against the hardwood floor. Pink feathers fell all around her.

"Megan!" Ivy bellowed, crawling to her fallen friend. "Mom! Come quick! Megan fell!"

Even though she was afraid, Ivy put her hands to Megan's head. Blood gushed onto her fingers. "You're going to be okay, Megan," she whispered. Her tears betrayed her terror. She heard her mother's footsteps on the stairs.

Ivy gasped. The palms of her hands flushed hot as fire and began to vibrate. A loud buzzing rang through her head. She fell into a white light at the very moment she heard her mother fling open the door.

Ivy awoke on the bed with her head on a pillow. Megan and Mrs. Merchuk loomed above her. Her mother dabbed her forehead with a damp cloth.

"Why did you pass out?" Megan was incredulous. "I was the one who fell off the bed."

Ivy blinked and attempted a cool shrug. "I don't know." She coughed. She was very thirsty. Her fingers were cold as ice.

"Well, are you okay? You were sleeping for a long time." Ivy nodded. There was a chill to Megan's voice that hadn't been there before. Ivy knew that particular tone very well. The other kids used it when they mocked her. Ivy's spirits plummeted. She mustered her last few ounces of energy. *I will fix this.*

"Mom, can we make the ice cream sundaes now? With the chocolate sauce and sprinkles?" Mrs. Merchuk didn't answer. Her eyes were far away.

Megan seemed to brighten at the mention of sundaes. Perhaps the evening could be salvaged after all. Ivy eased herself off the bed. Megan's eyes widened.

"Whoa," she gasped. "Your hands are all bloody. Whose blood is that?"

Dr. Oliver was Mrs. Merchuk's oldest friend. They'd attended kindergarten together, pledged to the same sorority, and remained friends through heartbreak, weddings, baby showers, and motherhood. Mrs. Merchuk drove Ivy to Dr. Oliver's office two days after the sleepover.

"But I'm fine, Mom." Ivy sulked in the passenger seat with her arms crossed indignantly in front of her.

"We don't only visit doctors when we're sick, Ivy." Mrs. Merchuk's gentle rhetoric did nothing to shake Ivy from her foul mood. Ivy hated going to the doctor's office. The smell of the waiting room. The crying babies. The crinkle of the paper under her thighs as she sat on the examination table. The rubber hammer hitting her knee. Dr. Oliver always handed her a lollipop at the end of each appointment, but it failed to stamp out the unpleasant taste of the total experience.

They were immediately ushered into Dr. Oliver's examination room.

"Was it like it was five years ago?" Dr. Oliver cracked open her notebook and readied her pen. "Did you see it this time, too?"

"Yes, and it was almost exactly the same," Mrs. Merchuk replied decisively. "This time, she was only unconscious for fifteen minutes." Ivy stared at her mother from her perch on the examination table. *What happened five years ago?*

Dr. Oliver closed her notebook. "Amrita, I'm going to do my best for you, but I'm telling you upfront: I don't know what I'm looking for, and if it were anyone else but you, I wouldn't be doing anything at all." She leaned forward and raised one eyebrow. "I'd be referring you to a shrink."

"I appreciate it, Viv."

Dr. Oliver sighed heavily. "You say the other girl didn't have a scratch, and yet Ivy was covered with blood."

Mrs. Merchuk shook her head. "Not one scratch. She hit the back of her head. I took her to the hospital and the ER doctor told me she was fine."

Ivy's cheeks flushed. The embarrassment of the entire debacle was still fresh. Mrs. Merchuk had opted for the emergency room instead of sundaes, and Megan had barely uttered two words to Ivy since the weekend. She glared at her mother. *I'll never forgive you for destroying my only friendship.*

In the hour that followed, Dr. Oliver subjected Ivy to a gruelling examination. Blood work. Vision and hearing tests. Dozens of confusing questions about the night Megan fell off the bed. "How did you feel before you passed out? Does the sight of blood make you feel sick to your stomach? Were you scared?" Dr. Oliver pressed her stethoscope all over Ivy's body. When Mrs. Merchuk finally poured her into the car, Ivy was too fatigued for school, and spent the rest of the day in bed.

They returned the following week for the results.

"Ivy is healthy, Amrita. Very healthy." Ivy read disappointment on her mother's face. *Isn't it good to be healthy?* "I can't find anything unusual, and nothing at all suggesting any of the phenomena you described."

"You didn't see what I saw, Viv." Mrs. Merchuk was adamant. Her voice held an edge. Ivy dared not breathe for fear of missing a single word. "You didn't see the blood, the light…"

Dr. Oliver pulled Mrs. Merchuk away from Ivy to the opposite side of the examination room. "My advice is to let it go." Dr. Oliver's voice was a near-whisper. "If what you say is true, Ivy could be in danger."

"Danger?" Mrs. Merchuk seemed to repeat the word as if she did not understand its meaning.

"Yes, danger. Think of all the different groups who'd benefit from her abilities." Ivy did not understand all the words, but she knew enough to be afraid. "She'd be the star of her very own freak show." *So I'm not normal. I'm a freak. That's what they call me at school.*

Mrs. Merchuk's eyes were wild. "Vivian." Her voice was hoarse. "My daughter is not a freak."

Dr. Oliver patted Mrs. Merchuk on the arm. "Keep an eye on it, keep it quiet, and let her be a kid." She led Mrs. Merchuk to a chair. "In the meantime, do you want me to prescribe anything for you? Something to help take the edge off? You look exhausted, Amrita."

iv.

When Ivy was sixteen, Mr. Merchuk took it into his mind to repair the roof. He'd never been much of a handyman and Ivy watched him assemble his new tools with no small measure of scepticism. *I don't know why he's even bothering. He's going to give up right away.* Mr. Merchuk's eyes shone equal parts determination and confusion. Mrs. Merchuk, clearly amused, brought him a glass of lemonade.

"Do you really need an axe to replace roof tiles, dear?"

Immediately Mr. Merchuk seemed deflated. "I guess I don't," he mumbled. But Mrs. Merchuk kissed him lightly on the cheek and he brightened, gave her behind a playful swat and—already sweating profusely—mounted the ladder.

From where she reclined beneath the oak tree, Ivy observed her parents with a tinge of melancholy. The gulf between Ivy and Mr. Merchuk was gargantuan, as it had always been. Mr. Merchuk kept his daughter at a distance. Sometimes he attempted to bridge the gap with money and ridiculous gifts. *He doesn't understand me. No one does. I wish I could live in a book.* She sighed and smiled. Her wallowing gave her much pleasure. She turned her attention back to Dostoevsky's *Memoirs from the House of the Dead*, required reading for her university-level night course. Her intention was to graduate from high school a year early. *I need to get out of here. I need to be free.*

Five minutes passed before Mr. Merchuk's grumbling pulled Ivy's attention away from her book. "I should've hired someone," he muttered as he crawled back towards the ladder. "I'm a partner in a law firm, for crying out loud. That's it. I'm done." Ivy watched with increasing alarm as Mr. Merchuk felt around with his foot for the ladder, missed the rung completely, and plunged toward the patio below. He landed with a thud and a bone-chilling crack.

For a few seconds, Mr. Merchuk lay perfectly still, and Ivy, paralyzed from the shock of having watched her father fall, feared he was dead. Suddenly, he howled.

"Help! Amrita! Help!"

Mrs. Merchuk inspected his arm. A jagged edge of bone pierced the skin. "Don't worry, Nick. I'll drive you to the hospital. Back in a flash." She dashed into the house.

"Drive me?" Mr. Merchuk sounded flabbergasted. "I need an ambulance! I'm crippled!"

Ivy stood awkwardly a few feet away from her father. Slowly, she knelt to the ground and peered into his pained face. A wave of compassion swept through her. *He's so unused to feeling anything.* "Next time, let me call a contractor, okay, Dad?" At that, Mr. Merchuk managed a weak laugh.

Ivy jumped slightly when buzzing started in her head. There was something vaguely familiar about the sensation. She looked down to her hands. They vibrated and burned hot. "Dad, I feel…" White light filled her vision. She grasped her father's broken arm and keeled over beside him.

Ivy reawakened into the middle of a heated exchange between her parents. She kept her eyes shut.

"What the fuck did she do to me?"

"Keep your voice down, Nicholas." There was no warmth in Mrs. Merchuk's voice. "You broke your arm, and she healed it. It's as simple as that."

Ivy heard Mr. Merchuk plop down into his leather armchair. Ivy imagined him casting a dark glare to where she lay on the sofa. "There is nothing simple about any of this," he fumed. "This just doesn't happen. She's a freak."

Ivy cringed. *I've felt this before.* She flashed back to the disastrous sleepover with Megan. And before that, there was Suzy, in the laneway, blood pouring from her mouth. Her past self had been uncritical—a child—and she'd left these confusing scenarios unquestioned behind her. But now Ivy was nearly university-bound. *There is something fundamentally wrong with me.*

Ivy's eyes snapped open. "I want to hear everything, Mom." There was shock on both their faces. She pulled herself up on her elbows. Her head was heavy, her hands ice cold. "I have a right to know."

Mr. Merchuk stormed out of the house without uttering a word to his wife or daughter. He left his tools scattered all over the yard and didn't return until the following morning, reeking of smoke and whiskey and the backseat of his Mercedes.

Ivy and Mrs. Merchuk sat at the kitchen table. Steam danced off their tea cups. Ivy pressed her cold hands against the china. The chill refused to relinquish her fingers. "You say I healed them with my hands." She turned her cold hands over on the table. There was no answer in her palms. "How is it possible?"

Mrs. Merchuk was very quiet, and had been so from the very moment Ivy had demanded an explanation. When she did speak, she seemed to select her words carefully. Ivy was left with the impression that her mother placed a great deal of import on this conversation. She sat up straighter in her chair.

"You have a gift, Ivy. I don't know how or why, and I'm not sure that anyone in the world can explain it, but I do know that it is beautiful." A dark cloud touched down upon her brow. "You need to be careful."

Ivy heard Dr. Oliver's voice. "Danger," she said flippantly, recalling her long-ago visit to the paediatrician's office. Her eyes rushed back to her mother's. "Danger? From this? Isn't being able to fix people a good thing?"

Mrs. Merchuk's sigh was exceptionally deep. Ivy sensed years of concealed weariness. *Maybe she'd hoped we'd never have this talk.* "Your ability is a good one, but many people aren't good. This could be used against you. Oh, Ivy. Be careful with this gift." Her eyes were imploring. "Promise me you'll keep it quiet."

There was something so surreal about the entire conversation that Ivy couldn't quite believe it was actually occurring. Did she really have the power to heal fractured bones, cracked skulls, broken dogs? *This doesn't happen in real life.*

"Ivy," Mrs. Merchuk begged. "Promise me."

I'm freakish enough already without this. "I promise."

It would be the first of only two times they would discuss her unique skill.

The second time was three years later, as Mrs. Merchuk lay dying in a hospital bed. Cancer had tightened its icy grip in the course of six short months. She lost her hair, struggled with agonizing pain, and wasted away. When she could no longer laugh her signature tinkling laugh, she smiled, and her smiles were full of endurance.

Day after day, while perched on a stool at her mother's bedside, Ivy waited for the healing powers that through her had mended her father and friends to devour her mother's cancer. *We've tried everything else.* But nothing happened. Ivy watched the laboured rise and fall of her mother's chest and her heart ached with mounting self-recrimination.

Mr. Merchuk no longer spoke to Ivy. When Ivy chanced to pass her father in the hospital corridor, his eyes bore into hers with barely contained blame. *He's wondering why I'm alive and she's dying. He's wondering why I can't save her. I'm wondering the same things.*

"He loves you, Ivy," Mrs. Merchuk whispered, hoarse from pain and cancer drugs. "He's scared. He's always been scared of love. It's difficult for him to express it, but he does love you."

"I don't know any different," Ivy admitted dejectedly. *I'm failing her.* She adopted a cheerful tone. "I'm sorry, Mom. I'll reach out to him."

Mrs. Merchuk's eyes fluttered shut and what was left of Ivy's heart shattered in her chest. *She's almost gone.* "I never told you about the night you were born." Mrs. Merchuk was far away. "You were dead, Ivy… At least, the midwife thought you were dead. I knew better." Ivy massaged her mother's hand, just as her mother had done when she was a little girl. "I grasped your cold little hand in mine… your fingers were so tiny… and suddenly you were alive. You healed my wounds. I knew you were going to do great things." Tears streamed down her sunken cheeks. "I'm so proud of you, Ivy."

Ivy fought down a sudden burst of rage. *I am nothing to be proud of. I'm a freak.* "You're the strongest woman in the world, Mom," she choked. She wished she could float away. "I am nothing like you."

Mrs. Merchuk smiled sadly. "Oh, Ivy. I'm so sorry. I'm sorry for making you promise to keep your special gift to yourself. I'm sorry for making you scared of life." She squeezed Ivy's hand with what little force she could muster. Ivy thought of her university life. No meaningful connections with other human beings. "Don't be scared of life. Don't close yourself off from your gift, from… from other people. Live every second. Be happy."

Mrs. Merchuk died the next morning. Her body had been wheeled away to the morgue by the time Mr. Merchuk arrived. Ivy slumped on the stool beside the empty bed. She was numb to the world.

"You changed her," Mr. Merchuk seethed. "You broke her. It was never the same after you. What good are you?" His eyes were wild. He expected an answer. She had none for him. He stormed out and collapsed in the hallway. *I am an orphan.* Two nurses led him to a chair. She heard his bitter tears. She had none left to shed.

THE
AWAKENING

CHAPTER 1

The morning bus reeked of sweat, cheap cologne, bologna, and weed. Ivy juggled a book bag and coffee cup and struggled to stay on her feet between an overweight postal worker and a Korean exchange student. The student giggled into a pink phone. *Far too perky for this hour of the morning.* The bus hit a bump and lurched forward. A small drop of coffee spilled onto the postal worker's shirt. He didn't notice. She said nothing.

Ivy's eyes wandered aimlessly. She never knew where to focus her eyes during the morning commute. They fell onto a plastic twenty-something in a polyester suit standing a few feet away. Likely a financial type at the beginning of his career. *His hair is too perfect.* He winked at her and pulled his lips into a shit-eating grin and revealed teeth that were far too white to be natural. Ivy averted her gaze and focused instead on an ad for erectile dysfunction medications plastered above the window.

Would it really be so bad if I smiled back? Her eyes drifted back to the young man's tanned face. He'd been staring. He blew a kiss. Quickly, her eyes returned to the spot of coffee on the postal worker's shirt. *Tomorrow I'll save the bus fare and drive.* Her stop couldn't come soon enough. She pushed her way through the groggy masses and was relieved when the banker didn't follow her off the bus.

Try as she could to avoid it, people stared at Ivy wherever she went. "There's something about you," strangers would say. "I can't look away." They approached her on the bus, in the library, at the produce market around the corner from her apartment. "You should be a model," they'd utter in amazement. Ivy couldn't see what they saw. She saw average: a big mass of curly brown hair, blue eyes, her mother's nose and lips. Sometimes she'd stammer out an awkward thank-you, but for the most part she'd hurry off and pretend she hadn't heard them. Her mother had handled similar interactions with tact and warm smiles. *I wish I was invisible.*

Ivy didn't date. Didn't have friends. Seven years had passed since her mother's death, since she'd put 3,000 miles between herself and her father, with no complaints on either end. She lived a quiet life in a small apartment in Vancouver's crowded West End. She worked, read, ran along the beach, and ate alone. Rinse and repeat. Each day she strove for invisibility.

Ivy was attempting to fit her lunch into the overstuffed employee fridge when Janet—her eternally exasperated boss—burst into the break room.

"A busload of eight-year-olds... within the hour," Janet reported breathlessly. Clearly this was crisis time. "Colleen will lead them through story-time. Stand by with the vacuum cleaner and a garbage bag. And make sure none of the little bastards ride the book carts."

"Would you like me to choose some books...?" But Janet was gone before Ivy had a chance to finish her sentence. Janet rarely remained in a room long enough to confront a question or a dissenting opinion. Ivy sighed and headed to the supply closet for the vacuum.

"Not what I had in mind when I became a librarian," Ivy mumbled as she hauled the ancient contraption out of the closet. She sighed, closed her eyes, and pictured the pile of books awaiting her on her bedside table. The image gave her pleasure. *I'll take five minutes with a good book over a prolonged conversation with another person any day.* Books were free of judgment. Books couldn't hurt her. Books accompanied her to restaurants, on bus rides, to bed. Books ushered along the hours so that Ivy could collapse into a deep sleep without once having to speak to herself.

But sometimes, books failed her, as they did sixteen hours after the frenzied onslaught of hyper third-graders. In the uncomfortable space between wakefulness and sleep, her repressed instincts began speaking up for themselves. *Is this it for me? Will I always sleep alone?* The chatter rose to a fever pitch. Her mother had begged her to knock life off its axis. *I'm barely scratching the surface of life. I'm a freak. I can't shake my truth.*

Her thoughts strayed out of bounds, to the incident with the homeless man a few weeks previous. He'd been a daily sight, lounging under a tree near her bus stop. He'd never once begged for money. Often, he'd smiled at her, a toothy, ageless smile that reminded her of the jack-o-lanterns her mother had carved with such precision.

One morning, Ivy had arrived at the bus stop and noticed a large red puddle on the sidewalk where the grass met the pavement. Slowly, her eyes had drifted from the puddle to where her homeless man lay sprawled under his tree.

"Are you okay, sir?" She'd received no reply as she moved towards him. Only when she was four steps away had she realized the seriousness of his condition. His skull had been smashed in. Eyes closed. Breathing shallow and uneven.

I can save him. The thought had been unexpected. Heavy with uncertainty, she'd closed her eyes and implored her hands to vibrate. Nothing. She'd strained. *Okay, I'm ready. It's time.* Again, nothing.

Defeated, she'd called 911 on her phone, and looked on forlornly as the paramedics wheeled her homeless man away. She'd sat at the bus stop for two hours. Bus after bus had passed her by. He had yet to return to his spot under the tree. She didn't know if he'd survived his injuries.

I opened Pandora's Box and found—nothing. Dust and disappointment. She pulled the pillow over her head. *Maybe I've outgrown it. I'm a freak either way.* Her heart cried out into the night.

Ivy took her work home with her every night. Leaning against her Jeep (a farewell-and-don't-come-back gift from her father), she balanced a stack of books on her hip and searched her purse for her keys. Last night she'd led herself through several academic journals documenting aberrations in human evolution. This weekend she planned to return to her favourite subject: anthropology. *Looking to explain myself away.* The air was damp and crisp, typical September weather for the Pacific Northwest. Perfect night for a run, and then a sweet surrender to wine and books.

Or I could go clubbing and pick up a guy for a one-night stand.

A smile danced across her lips and faded fast. Those experiments, few and far between as they were, always left her feeling empty and angry.

A crash of shattering glass shook her from her reverie. She froze. Indistinct sounds of scuffling and shoving poured out of the alley down the block from her car. Feet kicking meat. Male laughter. Groans. Despite the laughter, there was nothing funny about the groaning.

Alarmed, Ivy surveyed the empty street. *Do I run? Do I call the police? If so, what do I say? That I heard a loud noise?* Frantically she turned to her instincts for guidance and was informed that, in this instance, the police would arrive too late to save a life. *Better to actually see what's going on and be a reliable eyewitness.* She swallowed her fear, placed her books on the pavement, and crept into the alley.

"This isn't a game, Victor," boomed a male voice, deep and unaccented, from fifty yards away. "You're out of your league."

Ivy kept to the shadows. Her eyes were slow to adjust to the dim light. Eventually she identified four male silhouettes: three standing, delivering the kicks, the other on the ground. The piece of meat. One of the standing silhouettes swung a baseball bat. Ivy pulled further back into the darkness and pressed her body against the wall.

The deep-voiced man crouched next to the man-meat and poked him roughly. "Are you listening to me, Victor? I want to make sure you hear this." Another groan. The crouching man brought his face into a shaft of moonlight and revealed Asian features. "You've crossed the line from amusing to irritating. Cross it again, and you will die a death so brutal, you'll wish I'd killed you tonight." And with that, the crouching man leapt up and strode past Ivy, out of the alley, and into the street. The scent of expensive cologne tickled her nose. The two other suits followed close behind. A car started and pulled away quickly. Finally the alley was silent—until the injured man resumed his groaning.

"That's one helluva warning." The figure on the pavement began to stir. He attempted to prop himself up on his elbows, but immediately collapsed. "Shit. Ribs. Shit." More muttering. A misty rain began to fall. With much effort, the man—Victor—rolled onto his back and examined his hands. Ivy spied chunks of broken glass lodged in a deep cut. She didn't have to see his chest to know that several ribs were poking through the skin.

"Fuck. What now, Victor?" He asked no one in particular, and Ivy unintentionally.

Stop cowering in the shadows like a loser. He needs your help. Ivy took a deep, steadying breath and crept into the light. Victor jerked suddenly at her footsteps, which led to more cursing and groaning.

"Please don't move," Ivy implored gently as she dropped to the ground beside him and fumbled in her purse for her phone. "I'm going to call an ambulance."

Wet hand on her wrist. She looked into Victor's face for the first time and inhaled sharply. A handsome face, mid-thirties, dark features, contorted in pain. A bloodied urban cowboy. "No hospital," he croaked. Their eyes locked. Now it was Victor's turn to gasp. His chest constricted and the pain from the broken bones and traumatized organs seemed to overwhelm him. Ivy's heart ached in empathy. "Luminous," he drawled. "You're glowing." His eyelids fluttered shut. His hand fell from her wrist.

"Stay with me, Victor, please." Bewildered, Ivy picked up Victor's hand and stroked it gently while she considered her options. Sketchy dealings aside, the poor man had been the recipient of a brutal beating. He required immediate medical help. He didn't want a hospital. *Aren't there off-the-grid clinics that could treat him? How can I locate one at this time of night?*

"Hmmm," he moaned dreamily while her thoughts raced. "Wanna have dinner with me? Champagne? Lobster? Pudding?" *He's delirious.* Suddenly it dawned on Ivy that her palms were vibrating. Then came the buzzing in her head—a sensation she'd all but forgotten.

Not now. I can't pass out in this alley. What if those men come back?

"Come home with me, Ivy." And in an instant she was blinded by the pure white light, and she fell into his pained dark eyes. Immediately before the descent, she remembered that she hadn't yet told him her name.

CHAPTER 2

The clanking and sputtering of a nearby train jarred Ivy into consciousness. Disoriented. Head in a fog. Palms ice cold. She awoke curled up on a corduroy couch with a musty afghan draped across her body. She rubbed life into her eyes and surveyed a cavernous room bathed in daylight: brick walls, high-beamed ceilings, sparse furnishings, concrete floors, numerous windows and doors, books piled high against one wall. A mud-splattered Harley Davidson parked in the middle of the floor. An indeterminate workshop cloaked in shadows. An unmade bed. She raised her wrist to her face to check the time. Eight in the morning. It was then that she noticed the blood on her hands. Flashed to blood in the alley.

Run for your life, Ivy. Run!

But before she had a chance to stand and flee, the injured man from the alley—Victor—entered the loft carrying two coffee cups. His footsteps echoed throughout the massive post-industrial space. From the couch, Ivy appraised his face: rugged and chiselled with a slight damaged quality. *Like a timeworn statue of a Roman warrior.* His boot-clad strides were broad. No limp. He was obviously no longer in pain. The deep gashes on his face and hands and muscular arms had been replaced by pink scars. He seemed to sense her eyes upon him and stopped in his tracks. He turned to her. A smile spread across his face.

"Don't be scared," he said quickly as she jerked in surprise and nearly tumbled off the sofa. "I couldn't leave you in the alley, so I brought you home with me. Your car keys are on the table, although

I hope you'll stay for breakfast." He peered at her closely as her eyes darted to her keys. "Are you okay?"

A torrent of stammered words fell out of Ivy's mouth. "I passed out on you, didn't I? In the alley, I mean? Sorry about that. Blood makes me squeamish. Some help I turned out to be!" Forced laughter. *He'll never buy it. His healed wounds tell a story.* "Your name's Victor, right?"

"Victor Morgan," he replied. She tried not to squirm under his piercing gaze. "Are you a crime fighter? Or a superhero?" There was no edge to his voice. A lilt, perhaps. His eyes were deep pools of green. She turned his question over in her mind. *Maybe he thinks I'm dangerous.*

"I'm a librarian," she managed finally. "I work in the building next to the alley." She trembled as he moved towards her.

Victor dropped onto the sofa and set the coffee cups on the floor. Ivy's eyes trailed along a string of words that had been tattooed onto his tanned forearm: *To understand is to forgive.* "Do all librarians rush to the aid of injured men?" He searched her face. "You healed me." Pause. "How did you do it?"

She forced out a tinkling laugh and hoped it rang out as carefree as her mother's. *No need to panic. There's no subtext. He's just curious.* "Maybe you weren't as badly hurt as you thought you were," she said. She affected a yawn and stretched her arms towards the ceiling. "Is one of those coffees for me?" *I'm going to have to do better than that.*

He cocked his head. "What's your name, Florence Nightingale?" His voice was deep and hoarse and gentle. Her palms grew warm.

"Ivy. Ivy Merchuk." *You said it last night. You don't remember. How did you even know?*

A look of recollection flashed in his green eyes. "I'm going to start on breakfast now, Ivy Merchuk. Enjoy your coffee. You've been asleep for fourteen hours."

Victor recounted the events of the previous night while he sliced red peppers for an omelet. He'd awakened strong and happy with Ivy collapsed on top of him. Pain vanished. Wounds healed over. No more blood, except for what had already drenched his shirt and jeans.

"I was laughing, if you can believe it," he said jovially. 'It's been a long time since I've felt that... *light*." Ivy nodded coolly while scrambling to conceal the ball of anxiety forming in her chest.

According to Victor, he'd hoisted her up, identified her Jeep by the pile of books on the pavement, fished her car keys out of her purse, and driven them both to his loft, located in Vancouver's gritty Railtown district. He'd been awake and energized ever since.

Bacon sizzled in the frying pan. Victor was relaxed and conversational, as if the surreal events that had flung them together had been normal, everyday occurrences. Ivy perched on a barstool and sipped her coffee. Her eyes strayed to a computer streaming video from a security camera trained on the exterior door. *Well, that's odd and troubling. Am I in danger?* Leaving had crossed her mind for a second, but then she resigned herself to her instincts. *Stay put—at least for the moment.*

"You want it spiked?" He nodded towards a half-empty bottle of whiskey on the counter. She shook her head. "Are you sure? You had a rough night." He poured several shots into his own coffee.

They ate in comfortable silence side by side at the breakfast bar. Arms barely touching. Ivy took sidelong glances at her dining companion, glimpsed dark memories in his face, and looked away quickly. *I should go. I don't know what will happen if I stay.*

"God, you're luminous." Victor broke the silence. Ivy turned to face the green eyes. He'd been staring. "And magical, evidently."

"Magical?" There it was. Ivy went cold. "Magical" could be just another word for "freakish." "Victor, there was nothing magical about it. You were beaten, I fainted from the blood, and you recovered quickly."

Victor smiled. "I had at least three broken ribs. Gashes on my face and both hands. Before you arrived, they pummelled me with steel-toe boots and a baseball bat. Not the sort of experience you bounce back from in five minutes." Ivy sat frozen. Victor leaned in. She could smell the whiskey on his breath, wondered what his lips tasted like, and immediately chastised herself for the ill-timed thought.

"Something remarkable happened to us, and I want to understand it." Victor's voice was low. His hand fell to her wrist. "Why are you so afraid? What are you hiding?" There was no threat in his voice.

She opened her mouth to object, then exhaled deeply instead. There was something about this man that made her want to cast off the rusty armour that had long since fused with her skin. *It's time to share the burden.* She reached for the whiskey bottle, took a long swig, swivelled on her stool to face the green eyes, and poured out a story that didn't belong to her alone anymore.

"Can you cure diseases? Cure cancer?"

"No," Ivy said emphatically, and then reconsidered. "Well, I don't think so, anyway. It's more like emergency surgery. When there's been trauma. I can't cure something that's part of the body." *Mom.* "It doesn't work every time." She told him about the homeless man. "And I've never healed injuries as severe as yours."

It was mid-afternoon. They'd moved from the kitchen to the couch and, finally, to a rooftop patio where they lounged on mismatched deck chairs, looked out over the industrial rail yard, and tossed back tequila shots in the Indian summer sun. Ivy had taken a break to shower off the previous night's dirt and blood and change into one of Victor's old shirts. Otherwise, they'd been drinking and talking all day, but Ivy didn't feel drunk. Comfortable, yes. Victor evidently had a high tolerance for alcohol.

"What am I supposed to do? Follow cop cars and ambulances? Show up at car crashes and elbow my way in and say, 'excuse me, I might have the power to heal you?' I'd be arrested or…" She shuddered. It was the "or" that always scared her. Nightmares of research labs, probes, needles, specimen jars. Dissection. Suspicion and distrust. "I'm trying to live my life and avoid calling attention to my… skills."

"You called attention to your skills last night." Ivy's eyes darted to Victor's face. The grin that accompanied this statement of fact was warm and devoid of judgment. Ivy shrugged and managed a small smile.

Ivy had started her story right from the beginning, from her remarkable birth, and loped through her childhood, her mother's death, all the way up to her life in Vancouver stacking books by day, devouring them by night.

"I'm lonely," said Ivy, who then surprised herself when she followed her earnest admission with a throaty chuckle.

"What's so funny?" Victor asked. "There's nothing funny about being lonely. I speak from experience."

"I just feel…" Ivy hesitated as she struggled to make sense of the conflicting emotions she was experiencing. "Relief. I'm telling you stuff

I haven't had the courage to admit to myself. I had no idea how tired I was of… of living a lie." She looked out over the inlet and felt Victor's eyes boring through her.

Occasionally, Victor asked a question, unobtrusively and seemingly free of judgment and scepticism. Some of his questions perplexed her.

He wanted to know what happened to her body when she was healing someone's injuries. "What does it feel like?" His inquiry was nearly drowned out by a noisy train five floors below. "What does it look like to the outside eye?"

I should know the answers to these questions. The train blew its whistle and raced towards the horizon.

"I can't answer your second question, because my only witness died before she could give me a blow-by-blow account," she replied after a pause. "First my palms burn, then I hear a loud buzzing in my head, and I see a white light, and then I'm unconscious. I have no idea what happens to either body when I'm… doing whatever it is that I do." Ivy sighed. "I wish I could ignore it, or control it, but it seems to have a mind of its own."

Victor handed her another full-to-the-brim shot glass and sat down on the arm of her deck chair. Ivy could smell the sun on his skin. "It's not an 'it,' Ivy," he said softly, brushing a disobedient curl out of her eyes. His hands were coarse against her skin. Her palms burned from the closeness. "It's who you are. It's a gift."

"It's a headache," she tossed out, weak from booze, sun, non-stop conversation, and unchecked, unfamiliar arousal. "More harm than good." *Please kiss me now.* Victor did not oblige, and instead stood and surveyed the North Shore mountains.

"I'm living proof that that's not the case." His voice trailed off. He fixed his gaze upon a pair of birds soaring high over the inlet. He turned. His sad eyes brightened. "Hey, I haven't given you the grand tour yet. Would you like to see my palace?"

Victor made his living as an independent metal worker. "I forge, solder, weld, and play with fire," he announced proudly as he led Ivy through a maze of tools and machines that she half-expected to spring to life and begin drilling, cutting, buzzing, and grinding away at any moment. "As long as it involves steel and high temperatures, I'm happy to show up for work." Not that he had too long a commute: Victor rolled out of bed and right into his workshop, which took up half the loft. Clients were always referred, he explained. Custom art pieces. Industrial fittings.

"Is metal work your passion?" Ivy nearly tripped over an unfinished brass lamp base as she scrambled to keep up with her tour guide. He appeared to be leading her toward a door, only one of three in the loft space; the others led outdoors and into a spacious concrete bathroom.

"My passion? Hell no," he said as he pushed open the heavy door and felt around for a light switch. "That's all a means to an end. *This is my passion.*"

Ivy peered through the door and into a second loft. It was windowless and much smaller than the first. With a flick of a switch, a dozen light bulbs erupted to reveal an unexpected sight. Dozens of swords, suspended on wrought iron racks. An urban armoury. Ivy gaped. Her wide eyes danced as they took in row upon row of sheathed swords and a small workshop in the corner. *I probably should be shocked by all this, and yet standing here feels like the most normal thing in the world.* "You could arm an entire platoon with all these swords!"

"Mostly katanas," corrected Victor as he strolled into one of the aisles and removed a slender sword from one of the racks. Slowly, he drew the long, curved blade out from its red lacquer sheath. The polished steel glimmered in the low light. His touch was solemn and reverential. "Samurai swords." He sliced the air. The vibrations from the blade echoed through the windowless warehouse. "The real money is in custom orders for battle-ready katanas." Ivy flashed back to the previous night. The man from the alley.

"Joji is my biggest customer," Victor said as he placed the katana in Ivy's outstretched hands. She was surprised by its substantial weight. "I've made swords for his entire crew. I etch each tsuba"—he indicated the brass sword guard—"with family characters. He considers me a cultural pirate and resents my skill in this Japanese art. Fact is I have no other skill, and he's happy to exploit me so long as I keep my mouth shut." He grinned. "I refused to make him a Musashi sword. Hence my broken ribs."

"What a pair we are," Ivy said, mesmerized by the cold steel blade and the kimono-clad figures on the tsuba. "Your gift inflicts injury, while mine heals them." She regretted the words the moment they passed her lips and looked up with a start. *He's been so kind to me.*

Victor didn't seem to take offence. "Bullshit," he said breezily. "Violence with baseball bats and guns is crude and easy. Samurai is art, custom, and style; the power is in not using it. Samurai—which Joji is not, by the way—were governed by Bushido. The way of the warrior. For the true samurai, it goes hand in hand with the blade." He looked her square in the eye. "I will make you a sword. You've got more honour than any Yakuza."

Dusk. Victor balanced on a ladder and searched the highest stack of books for a volume of Bushido teachings.

"I bet you'll love samurai lore." He was mere inches from the ceiling. *Will I be able to heal him if he falls?* "My life changed after one reading. It's intense."

Ivy rested on a stool at the breakfast bar and wrestled with an oppressive weight of reluctance. *Soon I'm going to have to leave this place and go back to my fake life.* Every fibre in her weary body commanded her to stay. *Don't break your connection with this man.*

Despite the gruesome violence of the previous night, and the many pints of alcohol he'd consumed during the day, Victor radiated energy and adrenaline. He leapt from the ladder with the leather-bound volume in hand.

"The Hagakure," he announced as he handed her the heavy book. "Translated from the Japanese. All the teachings of Bushido are in here."

Ivy slid off the barstool. "It's getting late, Victor. I think I should be going." Her voice was barely a whisper. The words were hollow and mechanical. "I'm sorry to rush off." She averted her eyes.

Victor's face darkened. "What are you rushing back to? The library books? The lies?" His words were daggers; Ivy reeled at the truth of them.

"You're right," she said quietly. "It's all a lie. My life is a lie."

The storm passed suddenly. Victor's eyes shone regret and sadness. He pulled her into his arms. She melted. Her palms burned hot. His lips found her head, her face, her mouth. "I'm sorry. I'm so sorry." Ivy heard the desperation lodged in his throat. "This is crazy. I feel like I've known you forever."

Ivy clung to Victor's lean body and struggled to keep up with her racing thoughts. *Yes, this is crazy. Today has been crazy. Falling in love under these circumstances is crazy.* She choked on the word. It was undeniable. There was unformed love between them. An old love in its earliest stages. Tears rushed to her eyes. Her wandering fingers found a medallion on a chain around his neck.

"If I don't leave now, I never will."

Victor gripped her tightly. "Then don't leave."

CHAPTER 3

"Are samurai allowed to have sex?" Ivy disentangled her naked body from the sheet and ambled into the kitchen for a glass of water. Her palms burned hot long after the throes of passion. The water replenished her.

Victor reclined against several pillows and sketched in a spiral-bound notebook. His brow was furrowed. "Sex? Samurai were spiritual, but they weren't monks. Samurai wives were great warriors." He looked up from his book. His eyes roamed over her nude form. She revelled in this unfamiliar vulnerability. A smile spread across his face. "And love… all samurai felt that dying in love was the highest form of love."

A wave of goose bumps washed over Ivy's body. She scurried back under the covers and burrowed against her lover. She strained to catch a glimpse of the sketch that occupied his attention, but he snapped the book shut and tossed it onto the floor. "Your sword," he said simply and planted a kiss on the top of her head. "I'm toying with some ideas. You up for Chinese food? There's a great hole-in-the-wall in Chinatown that's open 24/7. They make a mean Peking duck."

Ivy sat up abruptly. A nagging thought, discarded earlier in the day, pushed itself to the forefront of her mind. "I don't know anything about you," she exclaimed. She was genuinely alarmed. Her complete trust in her instincts had led her to this man's bed, but in truth she knew very little about him. He knew far more about her. *He could destroy me.* Her contentment shattered.

Victor grimaced. "You know everything you need to know." The tension in his voice sent chills rippling up and down Ivy's spine.

"Victor…" Ivy looked deeply into Victor's troubled face. His green eyes were pools of sadness. Heartache seemed to simmer beneath the surface. *There's no danger here.* She longed to burrow into him once more.

"We connected today, right? You like what you see? Evidently, yes, because you're still here." His eyes fell to where his hand nervously twisted a corner of the sheet. "But once I lay it all out there, will you stay? Or is this where it ends?" Victor's eyes returned to her face. Now they were desperate and imploring. She picked up his hand and kissed it gently.

"I trust my instincts," she said decisively. "My instincts told me to stay here with you. Please trust me."

The lovers returned to the rooftop. Dirty urban birds cawed and cackled overhead. "Jesus Christ." Victor raked a hand through his unruly dark hair. "Where do I even begin?" He frowned and took a swig from a dented flask. Suddenly he looked much older than Ivy knew he was. *The world is heavy on his shoulders.*

"Treat this rooftop like a confessional," Ivy said gently and shielded her eyes from the setting sun. "I won't judge you."

Victor snorted. "That's easy to say. You don't know what I've done."

Ivy caressed his thigh. "I know you're a good man. Fill in the blanks. Tell me who you are."

"I'm a jerk." *His burden must be as heavy as mine.* "Before I was a jerk, I was just a regular kid."

Victor had never known his father. When he was old enough to note the absence, his mother had told him he'd been killed in military combat. The reality, which Victor had learned as a young teen, was that his father had been a thief and a drunk who'd been killed in a bar brawl. "When I thought he'd been killed in combat, I was proud. But a drunken brawl… shit." Victor sighed. "So what does the kid of a dead bum and an over-worked single mom do with his life?"

"Rob banks?" Ivy retorted playfully. "Run wild in the streets?"

"Close," Victor said dryly, and grinned. "He becomes a cop."

Victor had entered the police academy right out of high school. "I was going to save lives and uphold the law." Each word dripped with sarcasm. "I was a swaggering know-it-all." Upon graduation, his mother had presented him with a Saint Michael medallion, Saint Michael being the patron saint of police officers. "I felt like I'd made up for my father's fuckery. I was going to be the hero he never was."

One night, while out on patrol, Victor had stumbled upon a fellow cop raping a teenage runaway. "I pulled him off her, and he proceeded to beat the shit out of me." He took a big swig from the flask. "He was close with a lot of the higher-ups. Made my life miserable after that. I did my job, but no one cared."

Victor's beat had been the area bordered by Chinatown and old Japantown, ground zero for Asian gang activity in the city. One night he'd uncovered an illegal gambling operation, but before he'd had a chance to call it in, a well-dressed Asian man appealed to his baser instincts. The man was named Tetsuro. He was Joji's father.

"Tetsuro had a gift for identifying weaknesses." Victor's eyes glowed hot as fire. "He saw the rot in me, and he exploited it."

Before Victor knew what was happening, he was accepting pay-offs to keep the location of Tetsuro's gambling dens secret, and dumping the cash back into high-stakes card games that often ended minutes before he went on duty. Tetsuro's goons plied him with cocaine until he was hooked on that, too. Soon his debt load was so huge that Tetsuro refused to pay him another dime.

"There was no need," Victor scoffed, and again Ivy recognized the self-hatred in his eyes. "Tetsuro owned me outright. I had to move in with my mom." He began to steal from his mother in order to feed the beast.

"One day, I woke up after a big binge, strung out, covered in sweat, thirty pounds lighter than I'd been six months before, and I knew it had to end. It couldn't go on. I was a bigger mess than my father had been." And so he'd gone to Tetsuro and announced that he was finished. Tetsuro had laughed, patted Victor on the back, and sent him on his way. "I should have realized then that it wasn't over," spat Victor. "You don't just walk away from a man like that. He's got too much bloody honour."

Victor had arrived home to a wall of flames. He'd dashed inside the burning house and discovered his mother dead on the kitchen floor. Her throat had been slit. "She was gone before I had the chance to beg for forgiveness." His voice was hoarse. Ivy wrapped her arms around his neck. Finally the sobs escaped from his chest. He shook in her embrace.

"Oh, baby," she whispered. She was dizzy with emotion. *There are some wounds even I can't begin to heal.* "She forgives you. You've got to forgive yourself, or you'll never be free." They held this position until dawn, looking out over the rail yard, no words passing between them.

In the morning, they ate, made love, and wandered along the tracks, revelling in a second consecutive day of unseasonable sunny weather. Victor spent an hour in his sword workshop while Ivy reclined in a chair on the rooftop patio and pored over the Hagakure. Each brief chapter contained a lesson for the honourable warrior: *Cut Down the Gods if They Stand in Your Way. Die Every Morning in Advance. Burn with Mad Death. Fall Seven Times and Get Up Eight. Conceal your Wisdom.* This copy of the Hagakure had an inscription: *Victor, It's time to live the way of the warrior. Bill.* The dedication, written in spidery ballpoint and dated five years previous, caught Ivy off-guard. She'd pegged Victor as too wounded for friends. *At least someone got through.*

Victor continued to drink throughout the day and never once seemed all-out drunk, which Ivy silently interpreted to mean that he was a functional alcoholic. *After last night's confession, I can't pass judgment. I'm happy he's alive.* Her palms burned when he drew near.

Late in the afternoon, Ivy drove Victor over to her apartment to load up on clothes and essentials. Victor was clearly awed by this delicious access to the mundane details of her other life. He lingered over a framed photo of her and her mother lounging in the sun.

"You've always been luminous," he remarked playfully. She blushed, pulled the picture off the wall, and dropped it into her overnight bag.

On the Monday, she phoned in sick. It was an act of disobedience that was completely out of character.

"I don't think you've ever taken a sick day." Janet's voice overflowed with concern. "It must be serious."

"Something is working its way through my system," Ivy croaked. *That's not entirely untrue.* "I'll give you an update tomorrow." She coughed, cut the conversation short, and hoped Janet hadn't heard the passing train rattling the windowpane.

In the early hours of Tuesday morning, she clung to Victor's sleeping form and allowed her thoughts to touch upon her present and future. *Everything is different now.* Something had shifted within her the moment she'd stepped into that damp alley. She couldn't return to her old pattern, and even if she did, she knew there would be no easy resumption of the anonymity she had once enjoyed. *I wish time would stand still so I could figure this out.*

She ran a finger lightly over the tattoo on Victor's arm. Understand. Forgive. He'd told her the saying was a riff on a Buddha quote: *To understand everything is to forgive everything.* Victor didn't seem concerned with general forgiveness. Forgive himself, perhaps? Forgive Joji's family? He stirred in his sleep. *I know my future is intertwined with his.* She kissed him softly and rolled onto her back to stare at the high-beamed ceiling. *Before I can even begin to understand him, to heal his deep wounds, I have to understand myself.* She hoped that time would stand still just a little longer.

It was early afternoon. The temperature rose to stifling levels. The lovers sought relief from the humidity in the relative coolness of the armoury. Victor rifled through a stack of papers on top of his workbench while Ivy paraded up and down the aisles, admiring the craftsmanship of each weapon. She didn't know anything about swords, but she knew these were works of art. No sword had been crafted flippantly or half-heartedly. Her thoughts returned to Victor's work for Joji.

"Why do you work for Joji after what his family did to yours?"

Victor seemed to hesitate. *Perhaps he doesn't know why.* "I'm keeping my enemies close at hand." She wasn't sure she believed him.

Though Victor had described him otherwise, Joji was hardly a customer. Years had passed since his mother's senseless murder, but Victor had yet to pay off his debts to the Yakuza's satisfaction. When Tetsuro had died two years after the fire, Joji took over the family business. "Joji said he had big plans for big money, but I had no desire to know any of the details," he said, and averted his eyes. *I need to help him shake his shame.* Joji now demanded custom swords instead of cash. "My debt to Joji has no end. This is the Hell I've created for myself."

The night of the beating—*has it only been a few days?*—Victor had been ambushed by Joji and his goons as he'd loped home from a local bar. He'd climbed into Joji's Mercedes quite willingly—"even though I knew the journey would end with broken bones." They'd argued. Joji had demanded respect and commanded him to complete the Musashi sword as requested. Or else. "I called him a gutless brat unfit to carry the sword of a legendary warrior," Victor said. "The car ground to a halt and—well, you know what happened next."

"Why didn't you fight back? You're easily stronger than they are."

"I deserve the pain."

"Not from them. Stop punishing yourself." Ivy ran her warm palm over his tattoo. *To understand is to forgive.* "You need to read yourself sometime."

She glanced down at a book lying open on the workbench. From the yellowed page, a uniformed samurai—Miyamoto Musashi—stood defiant against the passage of centuries. "Are you going to finish Joji's sword?"

"Should I? Can I, even?" He was clearly frustrated. "I don't want to. Making a sword like this takes a lot out of me. My heart has to be in it. I don't think I can do it anymore." He smiled wryly. "How can I be the man you deserve and also his punching bag? I think this part of my battle is coming to an end."

So he's been feeling it, too.

"Let's go on a date," Ivy blurted suddenly, then blushed a deep crimson. *What poor timing. What's wrong with me?*

But Victor seemed to brighten at the suggestion. "You're brilliant," he said as he pulled her close and kissed her neck. "I could use the fresh air. How about that farmers' market on the North Shore?" He tossed her a helmet. "But this time, I'll drive."

In those few brief hours at the market, Ivy came as close as she'd ever come to carefree abandon. With hair cascading over her shoulders, she spun in her summer dress, gripped Victor's hand and pulled him from vendor to vendor. The reds and greens and yellows of the vegetables and fruits were especially vivid and the afternoon sun especially bright, as if the hues had been artistically rendered to reflect the couple's joy. They piled sacks of fresh vegetables onto the bike. *I didn't know I could be this happy.* The roaring of the engine drowned out all worries and fears.

Victor stopped briefly at the crest of the North Shore mountain range. The city spread out beneath them. "Such a small city, when you look at it from up here." He clutched her fingers in his gloved hand. "You'd think we would have found each other before now."

"You don't really seem like the library type," she giggled. Her fingers toyed with his Saint Michael medallion.

"You're my family now." Victor choked on the words and brought her fingers to his lips. Ivy could hear the pain in his voice. "I will never fail you." He revved the engine and set the bike in motion, but Ivy's heart was already clocking a thousand beats per minute.

A black Mercedes idled in front of the warehouse. Victor stiffened and rolled the bike to a stop some forty feet away. Joji leaned against the car. He looked Victor up and down and raised his eyebrows. "Apparently we didn't work you over as well as we thought we did." Joji sidled towards them with his hands in his suit pockets. There was movement within the car. "I was sure I was going to find you drunk and paralyzed." His eyes traveled over Ivy's body, sending a chill speeding through her despite the evening humidity. "Why don't you ditch the loser, sweetheart? I'm sure I could find some work for you." Ivy swallowed her disgust and swung the sacks of groceries over her shoulders.

Victor blocked Ivy from Joji's view. "Eyes off, Joji," he seethed as he whipped off his sunglasses to reveal a man possessed. "I wasn't expecting you. What do you want?"

Joji grinned. "Down, boy." Ivy marvelled at his relaxed shoulders and even keel. *He's the king of his world.* "Is that the way to speak to your oldest friend?" Victor continued to stare. Ivy felt him holding back. "As a matter of fact, I've come to collect my sword." He glanced at Ivy and smirked. "I guess you've been too busy to finish it."

"I'm not going to finish it."

Joji sneered and threw his hands up in the air. The head of a dragon tattoo peered out from under his left sleeve. His right hand was missing its pinkie. "Victor, Victor, Victor. We've been through this already." A tinge of venom seeped into his measured tone. Ivy detected hatred boiling beneath the conceited veneer. "We should have offed you years ago. My old man was too fucking sentimental. One of the reasons I killed him."

Ivy didn't see it coming. With one lightning-fast movement, Joji pummelled Victor in the stomach. Victor staggered forward. His hands went to his abdomen, to the blood spreading across his shirt. Ivy hadn't seen Joji produce the long dagger that was now lodged in Victor's stomach. The wound had been delivered with precision, intended to be deep, debilitating, and deadly. There would be no recovery this time around.

"Time for harikiri, motherfucker."

Victor, eyes desperate and locked on Ivy, fell first to his knees, then onto his back. *Not so soon. Not like this.* The sacks of groceries crashed to the pavement. She rushed towards him. Joji caught her around her waist. "Guess we'll have some time together after all." He dragged her to the Mercedes and slammed her against the car. He resisted her struggling with little effort. He ripped her summer dress, mauled her breasts, scratched her back with his manicured fingernails. All the while her eyes remained locked on Victor's body. "I hope you're watching, Victor," Joji mocked mercilessly. He pinned his defiant conquest to the Benz while his two grinning goons jumped out of the car. "I always regretted that you never got to see the fun we had with your mom." He unzipped his trousers.

I am always powerless. Ivy's palms burned scalding hot. Street lamp after street lamp burnt out along the empty street. She ground her palms against Joji's face. Her fingers dug into his right eye. Crackling electricity sprang from her palms. The stench of burning flesh reached her nose. Joji shrieked, tumbled backwards, and buried his scorched face in his hands.

The goons were slow to react. One caught Joji before he fell to the ground, while the other, apparently unsure as to precisely what had transpired but knowing Ivy responsible, pounded one fist into Ivy's jaw, another to her abdomen. She didn't defend herself and chose instead to collapse to the pavement. She felt no pain. *This is all a waste of time.*

Joji yelped and screamed. "Get me out of here!" The goons poured Joji into the Benz and sped off.

Weak and winded, Ivy crawled over to Victor. He'd grown so quiet. She knelt in the expanding pool of warm blood. He was almost a ghost. His eyes fought to stay open. "I'm not… I need…" Blood flowed from his wound. Ivy flashed back to the homeless man and sobbed. *This can't be how it ends.* She gripped Victor's arm with one hand, yanked the dagger out with the other and flung it to the side. The rush of blood accelerated.

"Victor. Victor, I love you. Stay with me."

He raised his head slightly. Smiled with his eyes. "A lifetime in a weekend. Worth dying for." His head slammed back against the pavement. His eyes were empty.

The world spun. Her hands burned. Ivy fell into the white light scared to the core that it was already too late.

CHAPTER 4

Even before she opened her eyes, Ivy knew that the room that held her was small. A thin layer of blanket separated her from a concrete floor. Ice coursed through her veins. Her head pounded as if in a vice grip. She found her eyelids far too heavy to crack open, and so she kept them shut. *Joji must have come back for me.* There was no sense of urgency, no drive to flee, not that her body would have cooperated with any dash for freedom. She lay frozen and immobilized. A shallow-breathing corpse.

Though she lacked control of her body, Ivy retained her emotional faculties, and within moments of tasting consciousness, she hurled herself into a bottomless well of grief. *Let me rot until I am mold. I hope the grief never ends. I'm already dead.* The thought flashed through her mind that she might already be so.

With eyes clamped shut, she raced back to those agonizing moments in front of the loft. She heard the clattering of the dagger as it hit the pavement behind her. Victor's eyes had been oceans of calm in death. Like her mother, he'd gone gently into that good night. "Worth dying for," he'd said. *He was the only one who believed that to be true. Why couldn't Joji kill me, too?* In that instant, a tidal wave of wrenching sadness swept her away. For the first time since waking, she moaned, and cried, and slammed her fists against the cold concrete.

There was movement within the small space. A shuffling of feet.

"Ivy? Baby, are you waking up? Ivy?"

How could it be? His eyes were empty.

She wrenched open her heavy eyelids. Victor crouched beside her, his tired features bathed in shadows and dim blue light. His bloodshot eyes were lined with dark circles but as full of life and fire as they'd ever been. Her mind raced to process this vision. She sobbed. He scooped her up in his arms, pressed her trembling torso against his, and planted gentle kisses on her crown.

"You've been unconscious for two days." His voice broke. "I was terrified you weren't going to wake up."

Ivy's watch inched towards 1:00 AM Friday morning, almost one week since her first meeting with Victor behind the library. They'd been holed up in a defunct cold storage room in the smaller loft since shortly after the stabbing. Victor reported that he had not slept for more than 48 hours. As he had in the alley, he'd burst from his near-death experience joyous and energized and utterly stupefied that he'd survived. "I walked into death with my eyes wide open," he recalled, holding a bottle of water to her chapped lips. "Next time around, I'm not giving up my life so willingly." She smiled weakly from where she lay on the floor. She'd never known such a chill. Her jaw throbbed where she'd been punched days before.

After he'd carried her into the loft and bolted the door, Victor's jubilance had morphed into panic. Something was different in Ivy's skin and breathing when compared to her post-alley slumber. "You were so cold," he shuddered. "And pale. And you wouldn't wake up."

Within hours of the stabbing, Joji's goons had returned to dispose of the corpse and finish off Joji's attacker. Via the security camera, Victor had watched the dumbfounded men survey the blood on the concrete, the dagger ("I made that dagger for the son of a bitch"), and the bloodied footsteps leading away from the pool of blood to the warehouse door. They'd pounded on the door, but their fists were unable to penetrate the reinforced steel, and they'd sped off shortly thereafter. Victor had known he had only a handful of minutes before they returned with the tools and manpower required to seize and conquer his industrial palace.

With Ivy vulnerable and the clock potentially ticking down to the second bloodbath of the day, Victor had carried food, water, the laptop, and his sleeping beauty into an old walk-in freezer in the armoury. Its windowless door was obscured by shadows and boxes of sword parts.

The wireless laptop continued to pick up the signal from the security camera, and it was from this vantage point that Victor had witnessed a dozen Yakuza goons tear through the loft. They'd entered the armoury, prowled the sword aisles, decided Victor and "the whore" had skipped town, and, before departing, helped themselves to as many swords as they could carry.

By this point, Ivy had yet to come to and reassure Victor that she was going to make a full recovery, and so he'd been hesitant to move her from the flash freezer. "We'll leave as soon as you're well, but we've got to stay discreet, because they might be watching the building." He sponged her forehead with a damp towel. His eyes were indecisive. "Are you still cold? What do you need?" Ivy felt his concern. Colour had yet to return to her cheeks, and a paralyzing cold held her in an icy grip. She was worried, but she didn't want him to worry about her.

I need you to stay beside me. "I'd love a hot bath." Ivy aimed for cheerful, but her voice remained a whisper. Her answer seemed to satisfy him; the tension in his face lessened slightly.

"I'll whip up some dinner, too, because you must be starving." He hesitated. "While we're eating, I've got something to show you. The security system recorded the entire incident with Joji. You can clearly see what happens when you heal me."

Ivy's limbs were far too stiff, her stamina far too depleted, to amble into the deep claw-footed bathtub unaided. Victor drew the bath and lowered her into the tub, and hovered and fussed like an old aunt.

"Are you comfortable? Is the water okay?" His eyes bore through her as if he didn't quite believe she was real.

"I'm fine," she sputtered and forced a smile to her lips. *If I say it enough, maybe it'll be true.*

Finally Victor seemed satisfied enough to depart and prepare the midnight feast. He wore a sheathed sword at his side. Despite his outward confidence, his actions screamed that he had little doubt that they remained at the top of Joji's hit list.

Ivy couldn't get warm enough. She shivered in the hot water. *I probably should be worried about myself right now.* But self-care was not a priority at that moment. Her grief over Victor's brutal murder now quieted, her tired mind replayed the bloodthirsty rage she'd unleashed upon Joji.

Victor had made no mention of Ivy's attack on Joji. She pondered this omission. Maybe he hadn't seen it. Maybe he didn't consider this new manifestation worth mentioning. Maybe he didn't know what to say and didn't want to worry her while she appeared so weak and hobbled. But for Ivy, even the memory of the attack made her sick to her stomach. *I've never hurt another living being before.* This emerging ability, the polar opposite to her pre-existing affliction, had sprung up suddenly, and she had no idea how to wield it, if it was possible to control it at all. What if she harmed an innocent? Harmed Victor? *Who am I to inflict injury? I'm no better than Joji.* She wept.

Victor returned. "I'm chopping the vegetables we bought at…" His voice trailed off. His eyes shone horror. He scooped her out of the bath and folded her into a large towel. "Are you hurt? Any burns?" She shook her head, confused by his extreme reaction. He ran his hands under cold tap water.

Blinking, Ivy processed the scene before her. A thick steam engulfed the room. Water in the bathtub had reached a boiling point and was bubbling over the sides. The tap had been off since Victor had drawn the bath. *The high heat must have come from me.* One of the light bulbs had exploded. Glass floated in the water. Her limbs were red and glistening. She'd felt nothing.

"I don't know what's wrong with me, Victor," she confessed, utterly exhausted and too tired to contemplate any additional unexplainable phenomena. "I'm so cold."

They returned to the freezer for their midnight picnic. Victor's concern and Ivy's frailty were illuminated by candlelight. Ivy struggled with each bite. The mere act of tasting food required more energy than she could muster. She cocooned herself in layer upon layer of clothing and huddled against her lover.

"Hold me closer," she begged. "Squeeze me until we fuse."

"We can't stay here, Ivy." Victor shoved his plate away. "You need medical help, and the longer we stay here, the more likely it is we'll see Joji again. I refuse to take any more risks with your life." His voice, though brave, was fraying. Ivy sensed the magnitude of his love and grief in his words. *He's nearing his breaking point.*

She ran her icy fingers over his cheek and down his neck. Her fingers found his Saint Michael medallion. "Victor, I've never felt more secure than I do now." Though she couldn't see Victor's face, she felt his body respond to her words. "I walk with you with my eyes wide open. Joji is a wild animal." She smiled wryly. "You might even say that, without Joji, we wouldn't be together right now."

"I'm not ready to thank the bastard just yet," joked Victor, though Ivy heard the barely concealed hatred. *Only one of them will survive their next meeting.* He pulled away and searched her face. "Do you need a hospital?"

Ivy considered the question as honestly as she could. Her instincts had always kept her away from the medical establishment. "What's a hospital going to do for me? What doctor in his right mind is even going to believe my story?" The tears collecting on her eyelashes surprised her. She begged her instincts for guidance. They replied in kind. "I just want to rest. I want to curl up in your arms and sleep for days and days and get my strength back. I want to get warm. And I don't want to be afraid that Joji is going to bust down the door at any moment."

Victor nodded. "Then our only option, as I see it, is to head to Bill."

It took Ivy a few seconds to remember why the name was familiar to her. "The inscription in the samurai book." *The one who got through.*

"Bill's my old trauma counsellor," Victor said. "He's a retired shrink—and a Reiki master."

"Reiki." Ivy narrowed her eyes thoughtfully. She knew all about Reiki, a Japanese technique for stress reduction in which healers purported to direct the flow of energy through their clients' bodies using their hands. Reiki—unlike whatever it was that plagued Ivy— was a socially acceptable form of energy healing. *I'm anything but socially acceptable.*

"Bill used to treat cops suffering from post-traumatic stress, and he was damn good at it," Victor said warmly. Clearly Bill meant a great deal to him. "His methods were pretty wacky—Reiki, vision quests, hypnosis—but he got results. The city paid for me to see him after my mother... well, before I quit the force." He paused and, for a moment,

Ivy knew he was somewhere dark and lonely. He cleared his throat. "Bill's a good friend. We can trust him."

They would pile into Ivy's Jeep shortly after dawn and drive a long, circuitous route to Bill's remote rural cottage. Factoring in a couple rest stops, Victor expected the entire journey would take them straight through to dusk. "Are you sure you're up for this, Ivy?" He rubbed her frozen hand. She felt a faint buzzing in her palm and forced a smile to her lips.

"I'm leaving myself in your hands, Victor. I'm not afraid." Ivy hesitated. From the moment they'd returned to the freezer, the thought of confronting the footage had filled her with dread. Victor had yet to mention it. Panic mingled with the cold coursing through her veins. The moment would soon arrive. "I'm not ready to watch myself," she announced suddenly, then fell silent, unable to provide any further explanation.

Victor nodded. "We'll bring it with us to Bill's." He kissed her head and eased her onto the floor as he moved to prepare for their escape from Railtown. "It'll be there for you when you want it."

The Jeep was soon bursting with books, clothes, tools, and half a dozen swords. Ivy yearned to assist Victor with his packing and planning, but the strength simply wasn't there. She faded in and out of consciousness, while the chill tightened its grip on her bones. Shortly before dawn, Victor wrapped Ivy in several blankets and carried her to the passenger seat. His touch was tentative and gentle, as if he were handling priceless porcelain.

"Never thought I'd have to escape from my own home under the cover of darkness," he observed as he pulled away from the loft. There was no regret in his voice. Ivy fought a losing battle to keep her eyes open.

In an instant, she was seated on a wooden stool by her mother's hospital bed. Mrs. Merchuk was pale and skeletal, a shell of her former, full-figured, luminous self. Whispers wafted over the curtain. Footsteps echoed down the corridor.

"Is there anything I can do for you, Mom?" She gripped her mother's bony hand and implored her body to send the healing power to her hands, to kill the cancer and restore her mother with life, blood, her tinkling laugh. *I am useless. I am nothing. Make time slow down.*

A peaceful smile spread across her mother's face. "You're my miracle, Ivy. You'll do many great things. Just be you." Mrs. Merchuk's eyes fell empty. Her chest ceased its unsteady rise and fall. Ivy sobbed, fell onto her knees, and took her mother's face in her hands. Joji's face sneered back at her. His cheeks and forehead were a mishmash of blistered, mangled flesh. His right eye was clamped shut. His skin bubbled and sizzled.

"I'm going to kill you, you fucking freak," he seethed. His one good eye flashed with rage. He wrapped his nine fingers around her throat. Ivy awoke with a scream on her lips.

The sun shone big and fiery above the highway. They were an hour out of the city. The treed landscape was interrupted occasionally by berry farms and factories. Victor pulled into the crowded parking lot of a roadside diner. "We have a ways to go before we get to Bill's. Traffic is light so we should make good time. Do you want a coffee? Or breakfast?"

She nodded. "Yes. God, yes. Coffee."

Ivy pushed her head back against the seat and prayed the hot coffee would warm her frozen organs and limbs. There would be no more sleep on this journey. She rubbed her neck where she still felt the pressure from Joji's mutilated hands.

Bill's cottage was set far off the rural road and obscured by a row of hedges. He'd foregone a grass lawn in favour of granite rocks. The stark landscape was punctuated by a smattering of Japanese maples and a cement sculpture of a pagoda. No weeds poked up through the stones. Several well-tended bonsai flourished in a small garden. Behind the cottage, golden fields of wild wheat stretched towards the horizon, halted only by a distant snow-capped mountain range. No other homes or farms could be discerned from where Victor and Ivy stood on the front porch.

"You've got nothing to worry about," Victor said, sensing Ivy's wariness. He propped her up beside him. She remained unsteady on her feet. "I trust Bill completely. Hell, I trust him with you."

Bill opened the door before Victor had raised his hand to knock.

Ivy was underwhelmed. Bill was a diminutive man in his seventies, with grey receding hair, a wrinkled face, and eyes twinkling beneath tortoise shell glasses. Decked out in a sweater vest, plaid shirt, and corduroy slacks, his feet swathed in worn moccasins, Ivy mused that Bill hardly looked the part of a master energy healer—until he shook her hand in greeting, and a current of electricity passed between them.

Victor jumped at the crackling. "Holy shit."

Ivy pulled her hand away quickly. All her inhibitions fell away. "That's never happened like that before. Did you do that?"

Bill laughed. His laugh was full and warm, as if it bubbled forth from a source of contentment deep within. Ivy had the sudden longing for Bill to be her father. "I have no idea, but clearly there's much to discuss," Bill said jovially. His accent held a whiff of maritime air. "Please, come in. I've just put the kettle on for tea. Victor, if you want something stronger, there's an unopened bottle of something or other in…"

Ivy didn't hear the rest of the sentence. She collapsed into darkness.

CHAPTER 5

Ivy awoke in a ray of sunlight and lazily consulted her watch. Just after 7:00 AM. She was alone in a bright, white bedroom. For a moment she struggled to recall the events that had brought her to this bed, but she gave up almost immediately. She stretched out like a cat, sighed happily, and searched for Victor. There was a dent in the pillow beside her. Victor had slept by her side. She had a faint memory of his arms wrapped around her and kisses on her shoulder. She sunk further into the fluffy pillow and gave the rising sun full reign to replenish her. The cold had vacated her bones. Her mind was quiet. It had been days since she'd been visited by this level of peace. Again she fell into dreamless unconsciousness.

When she emerged a second time, Victor was in the room, towelling off after a shower. Ivy took a moment to peruse his muscular body. Prominent among the tattoos and scars was a large pink gash on his stomach. Ivy shuddered. *I came so close to losing him.* Victor turned his back to her, unaware that he was under her microscope.

She crept up behind him, leapt onto his back, and pulled him backwards and down onto the bed. "All better," she giggled. Victor smelled like shampoo and peppermint soap. The dark circles under his eyes had vanished with the night.

"I think you need a second opinion." He grinned. "Dr. Morgan is going to examine you." They luxuriated in each other's limbs. Ivy's palms pulsed and vibrated against Victor's skin.

"It's essential to begin each day with a nutritious breakfast." Bill pulled eggs, milk, strawberries and a loaf of bread from the fridge. He'd waved aside their offers of help and instructed them to sit while he whipped up a hearty feast. "Well, breakfast is the second most energizing thing you could do to start the day. But you young people already knew that." He winked at Victor, who burst out with a hearty laugh. Ivy turned a deep shade of crimson.

The kitchen was the most spacious room in the cottage. Its functions were not solely limited to food preparation and dining. An old stone fireplace ate up one wall. Framed photographs of a much younger Bill and a handsome, smiling woman—atop the Eiffel Tower, in front of a golden Japanese temple, on safari in Kenya—lined the mantelpiece. On another wall, two large bookshelves contained lofty works by Dickens, Tolkien, Tolstoy, and Shakespeare, as well as dusty volumes boasting titles like *Tao Te Ching*, *The Journey to Here: A Comprehensive Guide to Unity Consciousness*, and *Essential Reiki*. *Do any of these books hold definitive answers to my impossible questions?*

The kitchen appliances were old but exceptionally clean. On the counter, a stack of empty egg cartons climbed towards the ceiling. A dining table vast enough to accommodate twelve people dominated the room. Sunlight poured in through two giant bay windows. The entire effect was disarming. Ivy's embarrassment faded fast. *This feels like home.*

Bill reassured the runaways that they could remain concealed on his property for as long as they so desired. "I'm grateful for the company," he said simply. Ivy did not doubt his sincerity—nor did she doubt that, while she'd been comatose, Victor had shared enough of her back story to pique the interest of the aged Reiki master.

Victor's admiration for his old friend was contagious; over breakfast, Ivy wasted no time in sharing her story with Bill. Empathy and compassion radiated from his sincere eyes.

"You ever heard of anything like this, Bill?" Victor asked as he gently massaged the small of Ivy's back. He'd lifted his shirt at the appropriate moment to display his souvenir from his most recent altercation with Joji.

Bill shook his head. "This is very, very different from Reiki. It took centuries but Reiki is now an accepted practice. There are thousands of Reiki healers around the world and not one of them can claim to do anything like this. No, there is indeed something miraculous about you, Ivy."

Ivy grimaced; "miraculous" was as distressing a word as "magical"—a candy-coated "freakish."

Bill evidently noticed her discomfort and rushed to clarify himself. "I don't mean miraculous in a divine sense. You're channelling the energy of the universe, something healers strive to do each day. In your case, the results are extreme, tangible, and, yes, miraculous."

"I don't want it. I didn't ask for it." *I'm tired of repeating the same old refrain.*

Bill's smile reminded Ivy of that of a dolphin: optimistic, warm, and otherworldly. "But you have it. It's been part of you since birth." He took a sip of steaming green tea. "The challenge for you is learning to control it. Once you stop permitting your animal instincts to dictate when and how you use it, you'll be able to harness it, and you will do many great things."

Ivy heard her mother's voice in Bill's words. Her stomach churned. "I seem to be branching out from healing lately." She had no desire for Bill to romanticize her abilities. She recounted her assault on Joji's face. The aroma of burning flesh. The boiling water and exploding bulbs.

"You met Victor recently too, yes?"

Ivy fought to rein in a sudden burst of indignation. "Are you saying that Victor is turning me into a violent freak?" She glanced at Victor. He shrugged.

Bill pushed on. "Have you ever been in love before?" Ivy blushed and shook her head. Victor stirred in his chair. "Energy and emotion go hand in hand. My own healing reached new heights when I met my wife, and I would guess that your feelings for Victor pushed your abilities to new levels. Even in harming Joji, you were saving Victor, and that is neither evil or, to use your word, freakish. Frankly, I don't think there's anything freakish about you."

Ivy knew Bill was bang on with his diagnosis. This new love with Victor was of the oldest kind. *Can it really be as simple as that?* She squeezed Victor's hand under the table.

But the chill? The boiling water? "Your body is like a computer system trying to come back online after a power surge." Bill paused. "I can help with that."

Victor could not be still. "It's been days since I've had a drink, and everything is way too clear," he confessed to Ivy as he laced up his boots. It was the first time he'd spoken of his newfound sobriety. Ivy was proud of him. "I need to walk." He kissed her cheek, grabbed his leather jacket and whistled for Milo, Bill's gargantuan Golden Retriever. Ivy mused that any passing truck driver who chanced to catch a glimpse of the urban samurai, with a sword on his belt and an overweight dog by his side, would wonder if his eyes were playing tricks on him.

Timidly, Ivy entered the small parlour that Bill had designated as a healing room. She heard the clanking of dishes in the kitchen and knew that Bill would soon arrive to lead her through the promised Reiki session. Her anxiety perplexed her. *What do I have to fear from Bill?* The furnishings were sparse, save for a blanket-covered massage table and a small desk crowded with scented candles, incense, crystals, Catholic prayer cards, a small Ganesh figurine carved from sandalwood, and a battered stereo. A diminutive statue of an angel with large wings gazed down at Ivy from a shelf high on the wall.

Though retired, Bill offered Reiki sessions to his rural neighbours. Like the urban police officers before them, these farmers and labourers crept into the healing room quite warily but left relaxed and grateful. Bill had said he considered himself a frontier-town healer with a solemn duty to guide and restore that unseen life force energy upon which Reiki practice is based, and as such refused to accept any payments.

"If you are blessed with the ability to heal psychic traumas, or to enrich people's lives, it's immoral to accept payment," he'd explained after offering the treatment to Ivy. "Police officers, farmers, even librarians"—here his eyes twinkled—"all require healing along the way, and I'm happy to help." Many of his patients gifted him with eggs, vegetables and homemade bread, all of which Bill graciously accepted.

Tacked onto the wall was a sheet of rice paper listing the principles of Reiki. Two sentences immediately leapt out at Ivy. *Just for today I will not worry. Just for today I will not be angry.* She closed her eyes and inhaled deeply. Anger and worry had been constant companions for many years. *Could I ever live like Bill and offer up my abilities to strangers?* She chastised herself for entertaining such a folly. Bill was an experienced psychologist and Reiki master in full control of his faculties. Ivy was a biological aberration, unpredictable and potentially dangerous.

"This will only work if you believe." Bill stood in the doorway. He juggled a pitcher of water and two glasses in his weathered hands. Ivy backed away from the wall and bumped into the massage table.

"I have no reason to doubt the power of Reiki," she stammered, embarrassed for the second time that morning. "My life is already unbelievable. I'm open to anything."

He set the water and glasses down on the cluttered table. "You must believe in yourself." He emphasized the last word. His eyes sparkled. "Believe that you possess a great gift. Believe that you are capable of wielding it." Ivy said nothing, and instead climbed up onto the massage table. Bill covered her torso and legs with a blanket and explained that his hands would hover over areas of her body where he sensed energy blockages. She could stop the session at any time.

"I'm ready." Wracked with doubt and gloom, but ready. She'd felt so alive, so in tune with the universe when she'd first awakened in that big bed in the white bedroom. But now, fear—yes, that was fear gnawing at her heels. Bill fiddled with the stereo and soon a scratchy recording of a Japanese flute wafted through the room. Ivy closed her eyes.

At the very moment that Bill pressed his fingers to Ivy's crown, a wave of vibrations spread through her body. She floated above her consciousness, suspended in space, in time, in warmth. She fell away from Bill, from the plaintive wail of the Japanese flute, from the massage table and the scented candles and the Principles of Reiki, towards the familiar white light that usually heralded the end of consciousness but, in this moment, was the start of a long corridor of bursts of light and swirls of colour. She looked to her palms, her stomach, and her chest. All emitted a soft glow. She raised her hands until they were but inches apart; a white orb of light danced and bobbed between them. She swung the ball of light down the corridor. She felt no fear. *I've been here before.*

Her mother stood before her. She was draped in light and a thousand times more luminous than she'd been in life. The reunion was the most natural thing in the world. Ivy was not surprised to see her.

"You're almost there." Mrs. Merchuk's voice echoed in her head. She took Ivy's hand in hers and pulled her towards the wall of white light that signalled the corridor's end. Her eyes shimmered. "This is the moment." A tinkling laugh emerged from behind the unmoving lips. Ivy passed through the white and into nothingness.

Ivy awoke gasping for air. She was once again in the healing room. The CD was skipping. Hail pounded against the window. She thrust off the blanket, swung her legs over the side of the bed, and raised her hands to her face. A glowing orb of white light danced on each palm. She pressed her palms together and then slowly pulled them apart, dazzled by the manner in which the orbs responded to the movements of her fingers. When the lights faded away, she laughed joyously; she would find them when needed. She still didn't know how to heal on command, but now she knew how to draw this strange, beautiful light to her palms. *It's a start.* For a moment, she had felt her connection to the universe. Her head snapped to where Bill leaned against the wall. "I'm a believer, Bill."

Bill was drenched in sweat. The room was unbearably hot. The pitcher of water had boiled over.

Victor stood in the doorway. His face reflected awe.

"So many energy blockages," Bill gasped. "So much wild energy beneath the surface. I've never experienced anything like it." His legs gave way. Victor caught him and eased him onto the floor.

"You unlocked me, Bill," Ivy beamed as she leapt off the massage table and crouched down in front of her weary healer. "I think I can find the energy without falling unconscious. At least, I know how to start practicing."

Bill's smile was weak. "Those were the most intense two hours of my life." Milo peeked into the room and sniffed cautiously. "Can you grab me that bottle from the cellar, Victor?"

Victor and Ivy huddled together on the front porch. The hail had ceased and night had unfurled a giant canvas dotted with countless twinkling stars.

Bill had taken to bed shortly after the Reiki session. Ivy was beside herself with guilt. "He's an old man. I burnt someone a few days ago. I should have known better than to expose him to my... dammit." She groaned and buried her face in her hands.

"Don't you do this to yourself, Merchuk." This was the third time

Victor had expressed this sentiment since they'd sat down on the porch. "Bill knew the risks. He was thrilled to help you today. Today changes everything."

Ivy considered her breakthrough. She pulled her hands away from her face, willed the energy to her palms, and smiled when they emitted a soft white glow. Milo lay at the foot of the porch steps and followed the white orb with suspicious eyes. She pressed her right palm against Victor's leg. He arched his back and purred. "You're making me vibrate again," he moaned. "I hope I never get used to that."

She drifted back to the corridor of light, to her mother's angelic glow and cryptic words. "Was it all a dream? Was it the afterlife? Was it my subconscious kicking my ass to the next level?" She sighed and switched off her light. "I don't know what else I can do. I don't know how to get from here to wherever it is I go when I heal people." She wrapped her arms around her and leaned her head against Victor's shoulder. "So I'm a nightlight. So what?"

"So you need to train," Victor said decisively. "You need to grab this opportunity to figure out what you're capable of. Figure out how to control it. Then figure out how you want our life to unfold from here." *Our life sounds good. I like the singular of a shared life.* Victor would set up a workshop in the shed and tackle some personal projects while Ivy sharpened her skills. *I'm glad he has a plan. Without him, I wouldn't know where to start.* She gazed out into the darkness and felt very small.

Victor opened his mouth to continue, then stopped and sighed. Ivy poked him playfully. "Spill it, Dr. Morgan," she chided. Reluctance remained on his brow. He glanced at her, and relented.

"Today wasn't the first time I saw your nightlight trick, baby."

This admission puzzled Ivy. "If it's new to me, how is it not new to you?"

Ivy read vacillation in his green eyes. "The footage. From the night Joji stabbed me."

"I think it's high time I watched it," Ivy said lightly as she stood. "If I'm not ready after today, I'll never be."

Victor powered up the laptop. The kitchen was in darkness, save for the glow of the screen and the intermittent light from Ivy's palms. In the space of twenty-four hours, Ivy's fear of the footage had been replaced with anticipation. "You've seen it already," she remarked as he searched for the video file. "What did you think?"

Victor had been rather quiet since the healing room. *Bill said this is happening because I love him. I hope he's able to derive some joy from this. I know I am.* He appeared to consider her question and smiled. "I've always said you were luminous. The footage backs it up."

Though soundless, static, and black-and-white, the footage nonetheless captured the horror of that distant evening. A bird's-eye view of a familiar scene filled the screen; Ivy and Victor were in frame, but Joji's car was not. Joji skulked towards them. Ivy battled a wave of nausea and inexplicably remembered the bell peppers and zucchinis in her grocery bag. The flash of the dagger. Victor rewound and paused the footage at the moment the dagger cut through his flesh. "Son of a bitch had it tucked into his pants," Victor muttered. "Where's the fair play in that?"

On the screen, Victor crashed to the pavement. Tears rushed to Ivy's eyes. "I can't watch this all unfold again," she cried. Victor sped through the footage; in seconds, a pool of blood flooded out from his wounds. Soon Joji stumbled into the frame with his hands to his face. Ivy heard his silent scream. She watched herself crawl over to Victor's motionless body. She recalled his empty eyes and gasped.

"I'm still here, baby." He switched the footage back to its normal speed. "Okay, here we go."

Ivy leaned into the screen and grasped Victor's shoulders. *Deep breaths, Merchuk. This is a rerun. We both know how it plays out.*

For two minutes, Ivy's body remained where it had fallen across her wounded samurai. Slowly, over the span of ten seconds, her torso lifted from Victor's almost-corpse. She arched her back, stretched out her arms, and raised her palms to the sky. Her unseeing eyes snapped open to reveal shimmering pools of liquid silver. Light flowed from her palms, chest, and stomach. A sudden wind swirled and whipped around them. She seemed to be straining, pulling the weight of the world down upon her and into herself. In the video, Ivy laid her hands on Victor's chest. Her palms pressed down against his heart. His body shook violently at her touch. Steam poured from his wound. For at least a minute, Victor levitated inches off the bloody concrete, and the video Ivy pressed him to the ground; watching it now, Ivy knew that, without her hold upon him, Victor would have been lost to the rushing wind.

And in an instant, it was over: the wind, the light, the levitation, the strain of the universe—all gone. Victor floated gently to the ground. Ivy collapsed on top of him. An abrupt end to a surreal spectacle.

Victor stopped the footage. "We lay there for fifteen minutes," he said. "It's a wonder no one walked by." He turned to her expectantly. "Well?"

Ivy didn't yet know how to respond. *Is that really me? How did I know what to do?* She longed to hear the sounds, feel the wind against her skin, to relive the healing instead of merely witnessing it. But despite the gaps, it was enough. It was more than she'd had before.

"Seems like I've been putting on quite a show." She pulled his face to hers and kissed him on the lips. "Next time it happens, I want to be wide awake. I want to feel everything."

CHAPTER 6

It was the tail-end of the long day. Ivy clung to Victor and commanded herself to sleep, but her thoughts were loud and relentless. *What do I do now? How should I use my power if I'm ever able to control it? Should I heal everyone, or just people I know and love?* She imagined Joji's fingers around her neck and shivered.

"Do you believe in God?" Ivy blurted out the question before she'd asked it of herself. Her night-time thoughts had not yet formed the word "God."

"Heavy stuff for the dead of night, Merchuk," Victor murmured and rolled over to face her. His eyes remained closed. Ivy felt him teetering on the brink of sleep.

"No better time to bring out the big stuff, Victor," she replied. There was truth in this: the black of night had long been her confessional. "Are you a believer?"

Victor rubbed his temples and cracked open his eyes. "I spent years in Catholic school, but I guess that doesn't automatically make me a believer." Ivy saw the sadness in his smile. "I tried not to think about God for a lot of years. Hard to nurse murderous thoughts one minute and pray to the man in the sky the next, you know?" He reached for her hand and stroked her fingers. "Now I believe that things happen for a reason. Miracles happen. Guess you could say I'm starting to believe in a higher power."

His answer left her wanting more. "Do you think I should heal someone—save someone's life—who doesn't deserve it? Save Joji?"

Victor shrugged. "Is someone asking you to do this?" He paused and grimaced. "I sure as Hell didn't deserve it." The statement ended with a choke.

He still doesn't know his worth, not after everything he's done for me. Quickly she straddled his prone body, pressed her hands against his shoulders, and called the orbs of light to her palms. "Let's say I'm able to heal on command," she soldiered on as she felt his body relax. "Who gets healed? Who doesn't? Who am I to make that choice?"

Victor ran his hands down Ivy's back. "You've always known when and how to use it, and that's not going to change." Her skin tingled under his roving fingers. "What does your heart say?"

Ivy sighed. "I've always looked at it like it was a curse. After today, I'm humbled." Victor's wandering hands massaged the back of her thighs. He was wide awake now. "I'm not going to figure this all out tonight, am I?"

"'Fraid not, baby," he purred. "And there's no rush. I can think of other ways to cure your insomnia. What does your body say?"

Bill awoke from his lengthy slumber rejuvenated and talkative. His dreams had been, in his words, extraordinarily moving. "I recalled sounds and sights and moments from my life that I thought had been lost to the past," he told Ivy breathlessly before emptying an entire cup of hot tea in one gulp. "I held my wife again. I ran my fingers through her hair." He sighed happily and scurried off to prepare the healing room for a mid-morning session with a local farmhand.

Victor spent most of the day establishing his workshop in the shed. Sawing, banging, and the occasional curse word wafted up to the cottage as he worked. Ivy unpacked, dealt with laundry, and fussed around the bedroom. *I wonder what Janet will say when I don't show up for work again.* She set the framed photo of her mother on the dresser. This was home, at least for the time being. Home was with Victor. *Our shared life.* The wail of the Japanese flute poured out of the healing room. Ivy suddenly felt quite heavy. She fell back across the bed and stared at the high ceiling.

Ivy knew that Victor's suggestion—that she immediately immerse herself in intensive training—was the only option open to her. *Where do I begin?* In all her years poring over library books in search of answers and allies, Ivy had not once uncovered any reports of situations remotely resembling her own. *There's no Hagakure to address my kind of*

healing. No time-tested principles spelled out on rice paper and tacked onto the wall. She brought her palms in front of her face and sighed.
I'm stuck.

"I don't want to chase ambulances or hang around emergency rooms to try to figure out how to heal on command. That seems so gory." Ivy and Bill sat together at the kitchen table. Lunch had come and gone and Victor had yet to leave his workshop. "You have a lot of experience with energy and healing and—well, this kind of stuff. Is there any way for me to figure out how to use this power, and how to use it ethically and responsibly?"

Bill's eyes shone bright with concern, and Ivy was touched by his empathy. "If yesterday is any indication, I think that you already know how to use it, and I think daily practice will further connect you to the energy. I'm happy to help you." *Of course he's happy. His well of contentment is bottomless.* "You mentioned ethics. What brought that into your mind?" Ivy recounted the barrage of questions that had taunted her in the night.

"In my experience as a Reiki practitioner, the healing arts aren't just about healing," Bill said after several long moments of rumination. "Healing is a step on the path to enlightenment."

Ivy raised her eyebrows. *What a load of mumbo-jumbo.* Immediately she chided herself for the thought. *I'm so ungrateful.*

Bill seemed to read her mind, and smiled. "What I'm trying to say is your situation is unique to you alone, and you'll forge your own path when you're ready. Take your time."

Ivy nodded, but her agreement was half-hearted. A nagging inner voice—her loyal instincts, perhaps—whispered that this tenure at Bill's cottage was only a rest stop. *The sooner you get a grip on your abilities, the better for everyone. This is the moment.*

The next morning, Ivy awoke determined to train. She watched Victor head to his shed, and Bill to his garden, with bittersweet envy. *I need to be as disciplined as they are.* But she didn't know where to begin, and so she kicked off her day as she always had: she brushed her teeth, shampooed her hair, went for a jog, and gulped down a big mug of coffee. Her time-tested routine fully executed, she was surprised to find herself rudderless. Her resolve waned. She plopped into an armchair and scanned the titles in the bookcase. *Maybe this will be a Tolkien kind of day.*

"It's lovely outside." Bill stood in the doorway. He grasped a pair of pruning shears in his gloved hands. "I could meditate for hours under the endless sky."

Ivy grinned sheepishly. "You're not very subtle, Bill." She pushed herself up, strode out the door and into the sun, and inhaled the crisp, fragrant air. "I'm going to need your help."

Bill chuckled and patted her arm. "Let's get started."

Soon Ivy was seated cross-legged on a large flat slab of rock in the middle of the yard with her spine as straight as a pin.

"Close your eyes," Bill called out from where he knelt pruning his bonsai. "Quiet your mind."

I close my eyes and all I see is Joji's mangled face. "It's impossible," Ivy complained before cringing. *I sound like a whiny child.* "How am I supposed to think of nothing at all?"

"Picture yourself breathing through the top of your head," Bill said patiently. "Focus on the breathing and listen for the healing energy. It's always been with you. It should be as familiar to you as your heartbeat. You can control it."

"If you say so, Bill," Ivy said as she stretched towards the sky, shook the doubt from her limbs, and resumed her previous meditative pose. *I am in control of this. I am in control of this.* Her new mantra gave her strength. Time slowed. Finally she felt at peace, and a small smile began in her heart and surfaced on her lips. *I am in control...*

In an instant a light as bright as the sun exploded behind Ivy's closed eyelids, and she tumbled off the rock and onto her back. But she felt no pain. Instead, she basked in the swirling stream of light she'd discovered within her: sound and heat and colour and vibration intermingling in a single undulating beam. *This is the energy that heals people.* And she knew it had always been there, humming just beneath the surface, just as Bill had suggested.

"I found it, Bill!" Ivy cried triumphantly as she leapt to her feet and brushed the dirt off her yoga pants. "I found..." Frantically she searched for words that would accurately describe the torrent of healing energy she'd located within herself. "I found—the energy stream!"

"Let it go, and find it again," Bill said calmly without raising his eyes from his gardening.

After two training sessions, Ivy could hear the stream of healing energy humming inside her at all times. She learned to shoot it out of her hands with the strength of a gale force wind while silver light shone from her eyes, chest and stomach—and pull back until the energy was reduced to soft glowing white orbs bouncing on her palms. The daily practice left her fatigued and rejuvenated. *I love this. Is this what it means to have a calling?*

Sometimes Ivy abandoned her slab of rock and yogic breathing to toil and sweat alongside Bill in his garden. As she pruned the bonsai or pulled at impetuous weeds, she experienced a humility that connected her with the cycle of things. *I'm not a freak. I'm a child of the Earth.* She'd lift fistfuls of damp mulch to her face and inhale deeply, intoxicated by the smokiness of the dirt, the immortality of Earth.

Days rolled into one another. As time marched on, Ivy observed a shift in Victor. At first, the changes were subtle: he woke before dawn, laughed throughout breakfast, smiled easily, and approached his tasks in the workshop—which he deigned to keep private for the moment—with an enthusiasm bordering on maniacal glee.

"Why are you being so mysterious?" Ivy quizzed him one evening as he slid under the covers. "Why can't I visit you while you work?"

"Can't a man have his secrets?" He pulled her close. He smelled like smoke. His hands were rough and callused. "All will be revealed in time, Merchuk. Trust." He kissed her passionately and ceased all discussion for the night. *I've never seen happiness like this. The darkness is lifting.*

At first Ivy attributed Victor's new positivity to his divorce from booze, but she soon decided that the root cause was far more interwoven with her own journey. *He's forgiving himself. He's becoming a samurai.* Indeed, Victor seemed intent on achieving samurai status; when he wasn't holed up in his shed, he was outdoors with his katana.

Victor wielded his blade with force and mastery. He balanced on one foot for ten, twenty minutes at a time, sword pointed straight ahead, arm unwavering. He charged through the field of golden grass with his sword raised to the sky. He sliced through logs as if they were made of butter.

From the kitchen window, Ivy admired his razor-sharp focus, and the utter control with which he commanded his glistening muscles and deadly blade. In the midst of the violence, Ivy sensed peace and calm, power and strength.

"Impressive, isn't he?" Bill relaxed in his armchair with a cup of tea.

Ivy nodded. *Impressive. Heroic. Beautiful.* "Did you train him?"

"Victor is completely self-trained." Ivy heard the pride in Bill's reply. "The swords are extensions of his hands and his mind."

She tore her eyes away from her samurai and settled in the chair opposite Bill. "Is Victor a samurai?"

Bill took a long sip of tea. "What is a samurai? Victor strives to live by a code of honour. He tried to do that on the police force, at least at first. Honour is the measure of the samurai." He leaned forward in his chair as if about to divulge a state secret. Ivy moved to the edge of her seat. "The difference between now and then, or even two weeks ago, is that he has something to live for. To put it in Victor's words, he finally gives a damn."

Ivy leaned back in her chair, gazed across the room and through the bay window to where her urban samurai trained in the yard. "I know how he feels," she replied from deep inside her contentment. "I finally give a damn, too."

CHAPTER 7

"I am one hundred percent stir-crazy, Victor."

It had been weeks since Ivy and her samurai had stepped onto Bill's rural oasis. There had yet to be any reason to leave. The trio (and Milo) was self-sufficient and self-contained, and the world seemed to end at the foot of the driveway. After weeks of training and meditation, Ivy longed for a change of scenery.

Ivy and Victor stood shoulder to shoulder at the kitchen sink. Victor washed the dishes while Ivy dried. "How about a night on the town?" Victor splashed a handful of soapy water in her direction. A chunk of soap bubbles landed on her nose. She giggled and splashed back. *I could stand here beside Victor forever and revel in domestic bliss until I rotted away.*

"There's a town?" Her surprise was genuine.

"Tumblestone. It's got a diner, a bar, a general store, a post office, and a stoplight." Victor wiped the bubbles off her face. She crinkled her nose. "It's a regular bustling metropolis." He pulled her to him. His soapy hands pressed against her back. "Or we could skip dinner and stay in."

"For once, I'd like you to buy me dinner first," she answered playfully before pulling away and heading for their bedroom. She called out over her shoulder. "Can you finish washing up on your own? I've got to pull together an outfit for our big date."

Hours later, Ivy found Bill and Milo lounging on the back porch. The early evening sky was a tapestry of oranges and reds, purples and yellows. The autumn sun poured into the distant mountain range, itself a sleeping giant on the horizon. Ivy's heart swirled and soared at such sunsets. As she did every evening during these brief moments of multi-hued wonder, she wished she could paint.

"You look lovely this evening, Ivy." Bill's smile was tinged with melancholy. Ivy had dressed in a gingham summer dress for the occasion. She'd combed her hair off her face and secured it with an antique comb. She looked the part of a country girl heading out on a first date with a worldly man from the big city.

"Would you like to come with us, Bill?" She thought of the framed photos of Bill and his late wife. Bill often gazed upon those photos with that same sadness in his warm smile.

Bill shook his head. "Tonight I'm immersing myself in the soot and grime of 19th Century London." He patted the leather-bound volume of Dickensian prose balanced on his knee. His eyes darted up to hers. "I almost forgot: Victor would like you to join him in the shed."

Ivy raised her eyebrows. "This is a big moment, Bill. This is the first time I've been invited into the shed. I should dress up more often." Her laugh was carefree and tinkling. For a moment, she heard her mother's laugh, and realized with a start that her mother must have been passionately in love with her father to laugh with such abandon. She recovered quickly from the revelation, bid Bill adieu, and headed to the shed.

Ivy swung open the wooden door and stepped into a steamy cave. Thick sheets of tar paper had been tacked over the windows. Victor sat in the middle of a perfect recreation of his Railtown sword workshop. Ivy discerned five swords resting on makeshift wall racks. Even from a cursory glance, she knew that these new swords were far more intricate than his previous creations. *Likely far more dangerous, too.* She lingered in the doorway and observed her samurai in action.

At the moment his attention was locked on a katana that lay secured in a vice grip. He etched into the blade with tiny tools that reminded Ivy of medical instruments. His touch was delicate and deliberate. Finally satisfied, he removed his protective goggles, rubbed the blade with a single sheet of oiled rice paper, and beckoned Ivy to the workbench.

"Damn, you're beautiful." He whistled as she moved into the

light. She blushed, ducked behind him, and slid her arms around his shoulders.

"Bill said you wanted me to meet you here."

"That's a fact." He removed the sword from the grip and raised it into the light. "I've finally finished your sword."

She leaned in closer. "It's stunning," she exclaimed as she ran her fingers over the Japanese kanji that Victor had etched so skilfully into the blade. "What do these characters say?"

"They're from the Hagakure," he replied lightly. Ivy heard gruff tenderness beneath the levity. "*You Cannot Tell Your Own Strength.* It means that it's impossible for each of us to know our own worth." He looked up to her. His face was awash with pain. "So if you doubt yourself, look into my eyes and you'll see your greatness staring back at you." He stood and passed the sword onto her waiting hands. "Dammit, it kills me that you don't know how special you are." Ivy gripped the cord-wrapped handle. Both Victor and the blade were indistinguishable through her veil of tears.

"Thank you, Victor. I love it. I love you." Her hushed voice was solemn. "I don't say it enough, but I feel it all the time."

Victor said nothing. Ivy watched him searching for the words. Finally he grinned slightly, his eyes glistening.

Ivy turned her attention to the katana. She raised her arm until she held the sword at eye level.

"The handle is called the tsuka, and this point" (Victor indicated the rounded tip of the sword) "is the kissaki."

"Who is this on the guard?" Ivy peered at the detailed figure on the brass sword guard. The figure's eyes were defiant. "Is it a woman? Is that a female samurai?"

Victor nodded approvingly. "That figure is Tomoe Gozen, the most famous woman in samurai history. Most of the female samurai you read about were the wives of famous samurai, but Tomoe was a general who served under Minamoto Yoshinaka more than a thousand years ago. Greatly respected. Very beautiful." His eyes sparkled. "Tomoe and Yoshinaka were lovers, but she could never stay behind when danger called like a good samurai wife should."

Ivy's palms began to vibrate, just as they had a few weeks previous during her first weekend in Victor's loft. But instead of stopping in her palms, the energy surged and coursed through the katana. The steel blade vibrated. Fascinated, Victor held his hand millimetres away from the blade and looked to her in amazement. "It's hot."

She shrugged, inserted the sword into its wooden sheath, and pressed her body against his.

"I don't feel like much of a warrior," she admitted. "I've always felt so powerless."

"I'd follow you into battle, Ivy. I'd follow you into Hell, if that's where you needed me to go. If that's not power, I don't know what is."

Ivy and Victor dined at a small Chinese restaurant. It was the only dining establishment open in Tumblestone that Sunday evening. They were the sole customers. They held hands across the greasy tablecloth and smiled stupidly at the novelty of this impromptu date. Their order was taken by an ancient Chinese man and barked out to an equally ancient Chinese woman, who seemed to be hosting a boisterous family gathering in the kitchen. Dean Martin crooned from a countertop stereo.

"I think we're on an actual date, Mr. Morgan," Ivy mused as she toyed with her noodles. She felt inexplicably shy. "Seems like it was only yesterday that I fell on top of you and moved into your loft."

"Why waste time when it's right?" After weeks of intense training, Victor's features were especially tanned and chiselled. The effects were not diminished by the restaurant's harsh fluorescent lighting. "We haven't really done things in the normal way, have we?"

"There's nothing normal about us, and that's just how I like it." She grinned. "Who wants to be like everyone else anyway?"

Victor chewed thoughtfully and rubbed Ivy's leg under the table. Ivy knew he was thinking that, after a lifetime of constant self-doubt, her rhetorical question was a thrilling deviation. She could see herself in his eyes.

Ivy was delighted to discover that Victor's tongue-in-cheek description of Tumblestone had not been far off the mark. Besides the eating establishments, general store, post office, and exalted single stoplight, there was also a gas station, a combination fire house-medical clinic-police department, a church, a school, a dozen homes, and a community gathering place which, judging from the flyers taped to the notice board, served as a movie theatre, dance hall, swap shop, exercise studio, and meet-up spot for Alcoholics Anonymous and the Tumblestone Quilting Society.

They strolled arm in arm along the moonlit boulevard. A dog barked. A grandfather clock struck 9:00 PM. Inside one of the old clapboard houses, a middle-aged couple argued loudly and energetically, their obscenity-laced insults reaching every corner of the town.

Victor cringed. "I can't imagine us ever being like that," he muttered. "That level of venom. What a waste of time."

They managed to walk the entire length of the city proper in less than fifteen minutes without encountering a single soul. As they pivoted on their heels to return to the Jeep, Ivy's ears caught hold of a slight whimpering, like the coo of a dove. She halted in her tracks, closed her eyes, held her breath, and strained to isolate the whiff of sound.

"I hear it." Victor scanned the darkness. "Over there." They hadn't walked twenty paces before they discovered a teenage boy passed out beside a tangled mess of splintered bicycle tubing and busted wheels. His freckled face was illuminated by the full moon. He reeked of beer and weed. Blood trickled into his eyes from a large gash on his forehead.

"The fencepost is dented," Ivy said as she nearly tripped over a bicycle pedal. "He probably crashed his bike and smashed his head on the road. Look at all the gravel in his wound."

"Rough night, kid?" Victor pried open the teen's eyelids and peered into his pupils. *He knows exactly what to do—like any good cop would.* "He's still with us." Victor stood up, looked to Ivy, and grinned. "Ready to get to work, Merchuk?"

Ivy balanced on her haunches beside the barely conscious adolescent. "It's alright, honey," she whispered gently. "I can help you." His eyelids fluttered. He murmured a string of garbled, unintelligible words, and belched.

Ivy beckoned the healing energy to her hands, and it arrived, as she knew it would. The buzzing rocked her compact frame. Energy and light burst forth from her hot palms, her stomach, her chest, and her eyes. Wind whipped around her. She raised her arms to the sky and called forth the universal healing energy that Bill often described with such affection. When the white light arrived, she pushed through and fought to remain conscious.

Suddenly she faced a maze of organs, blood, tissue, muscles, and bones. She was both outside and inside the boy's damaged body. Her instincts led her to the areas in crisis, to the regions of the body where the pain dwelt: swelling on the brain, a sprain in the left arm, a lesion in the neck. She harnessed a wave of light and warmth, first flooding the injured areas with neutralizing healing energy, and then repairing everything that had been torn and damaged in the fall.

Ivy could taste the wind in her mouth, smell the torn organs and muscles and skin fusing and searing together. Her hands remained steady on his chest, directly above his heart. When he rose off the ground, she pressed him back towards the gravel. For a split second, she felt her true place between the gulf stream of the universe and Mother Earth, and she realized she belonged to both.

Eventually, Ivy could no longer see the organs and blood and tissue in front of her eyes. The wind ceased. Her work was done. The boy fell gently to the ground. He snored happily. The orbs of light upon her palms extinguished. Exhilarated and exhausted, Ivy fell back on her ass, turned to look up at Victor, and gasped at the startling sight that met her eyes.

A small crowd had gathered. Women in house coats and men in white undershirts seemed to jockey for a glimpse of the diminutive woman at the centre of the light show. Small children clutched their mother's hands. Some gawkers carried flashlights. Everyone present gaped with their mouths open. Even now that the show was over, they continued to arrive. Soon fifty people crowded around Ivy, Victor, and the unconscious teenager. An eerie silence reigned.

"It's Benjie!" A bleached blonde in her fifties pushed her way through the crowd and stopped just short of the teen. She glanced warily at the prone boy, as if she were scared to touch him, before locking her angry eyes on Ivy. Ivy felt Victor positioning himself between herself and the woman. "Who are you? What did you do to him?"

All of Tumblestone seemed to await Ivy's reply, and she found herself awash in desperation. Her training and hypothesizing had not prepared her for this scenario.

"The boy was injured." Victor's gruff voice was particularly aggressive. "We were helping him."

At his explanation, the town exploded into loud, insistent chatter.

"We saw the light. It came from her body."

"He was floating above the ground! He was on fire!"

"She was at the centre of a tornado!"

"She was hurting him."

"Is she the Devil, Mommy? Or a witch?"

No! No! The crush of condemnation was deafening. Ivy, now on her feet, shrunk into herself. *I don't know how to stop this.* She gripped Victor's arm. His body was steel. She watched his eyes dart for an escape route. She followed his gaze to a rifle swung over the shoulder of a grizzled farmer.

"Fuck, no," Victor muttered. "Just try me." His hands moved to his back pocket, to a carefully concealed dagger. His fingers wrapped around the handle. An icy chill rippled the length of Ivy's spine.

Benjie stirred. He pulled himself up on his elbows and opened his eyes. The entire town fell silent and stared back at him. "Oh, shit!" He jumped up and tripped over the sad remains of his bicycle. "Shit! My bike!" He reached up and rubbed the pink scar on his forehead.

The woman with the straw hair rushed to his side. "Benjie! What happened to you? Are you hurt?"

Benjie scratched his head, cocked it to the side, and looked from Ivy to Victor to the townsfolk. Confusion was stamped all over his dirty face. "Dunno," he said finally. "What's everybody doing here? What happened to my bike?" The crowd erupted in shouts.

A statuesque middle-aged man in a formal dressing gown and leather slippers stepped forward. His appearance had an immediate dampening effect on the citizens of Tumblestone. "It smells like you've been smoking marijuana again, Benjamin," he observed sternly. His accent was clipped and professorial. Benjie stared at his feet and mumbled incoherently.

The straw-haired woman delivered a hard whack to the side of Benjie's head. "Look at Father Owen when he's talking to you, Benjamin. Show some bloody respect. You've caused enough trouble for one night." Benjie cringed, and shuffled his feet.

The middle-aged man studied Ivy and Victor's faces intently before continuing. "It appears that you owe these kind strangers a thank-you for pulling you out of trouble, Benjamin." His voice was commanding. "If they hadn't come along when they did, you might have been attacked by a pack of coyotes."

Father Owen reached out his hand to Victor, whose fingers fell from the dagger. They shook hands like old friends, though Victor's eyes were guarded. "Thank you for your trouble," the priest said loudly before shaking Ivy's icy hand. Upon contact, he leaned in and murmured under his breath, "You're staying with Bill, correct? I suggest you head home now. This gathering needs to come to a speedy conclusion." Victor nodded curtly. Ivy, numb from fright and fatigue, could only blink and swallow.

The collective voice of the curious crowd returned to its previous fever pitch. "I think it's high time we all headed back indoors," Father Owen announced. "Obviously there's nothing more to discuss, although expect a lengthy sermon on the perils of drug use next Sunday morning."

Slowly but steadily, the townspeople returned to their homes. Some cast suspicious glances at Ivy and Victor as they dragged their feet away from the scene. Father Owen bowed deeply in their direction before ushering off the last of the stragglers. Ivy focused on her breathing, on the energy coursing through her veins, on Victor's arm around her waist as they practically flew back to the Jeep. *I was trying to help, but those people were so afraid—so angry. Am I truly a monster?* She fell into a dreamless sleep the moment Victor turned the key in the ignition.

CHAPTER 8

Ivy awoke into the dead of night. She sensed Victor sleeping beside her in the darkness and resisted the temptation to wake him. Instead she faced the gnawing thoughts that had pulled her out of sleep, and felt very much alone.

Ivy whipped between extreme emotions. *I healed the boy. I stayed awake. That's been my goal from the start.* For a brief moment, she was angry at the crowd for raining condemnation down upon her, but this was quickly eclipsed by shame and despair. *How could I have been so reckless?* The voice of a frightened child echoed through her head. *Is she the Devil, Mommy? Or a witch?* She saw the man with the rifle, and Victor's hand wrapping around the handle of the blade. *How quickly this could have turned to violence.* At that moment panic flooded from her toes and up her back, until it sat at the front of her face and she could only see the fear.

She wept, and banged her fists against her legs, but the panic remained. Hyperventilating and shaking uncontrollably, she flung the blankets aside and moved to rise from the bed, but her legs couldn't carry her far and she crashed onto the floor. She sobbed where she sprawled on the carpet. The fibres were coarse against her cheek.

Within seconds, Victor was beside her, on her, holding her, rubbing her back. Ivy could barely feel his hands on her body. *He is so very far away.* She was alone in her fog of despair. She trembled and sobbed.

"Listen to my voice," he whispered gently. "Just breathe, baby. Focus on your breathing." There was nothing he could utter to rid her of her sadness and fear, but he kept at it, and soon Ivy was exhausted. Eventually, the storm passed, and she cried herself to sleep.

In the aftermath of her panic attack, Ivy alternated between hazy semi-consciousness and violent night terrors. In one nightmare, her mother stood with her face to the wall, refusing to turn around no matter how much Ivy begged. In another, Joji screamed words she could not understand. His flesh bubbled and sizzled. And in a particularly vivid one, a bullet pierced Victor's forehead while the Tumblestone mob cheered and laughed. Following this final nightmare, she struggled to remain awake, and ultimately drifted into a restless state of unconsciousness.

Breakfast was already in full swing when Ivy—numb and far from hungry—plopped down onto a chair at the kitchen table. Bill and Victor kept the conversation to trivial matters, like the health of Bill's Japanese maple and the fierce storms that were expected to descend upon the region later that day. Ivy swirled the coffee around and around in her mug, unable to stomach one swallow. Finally, she could no longer bear their well-intentioned sidestepping.

"I failed." Immediately Ivy's cheeks flushed hot with shame. *I sound so melodramatic.*

"How exactly did you fail?" Bill asked cheerfully. His good humour only served to send Ivy's spirits further into despair. "From what I understand, you healed someone on command and stayed awake the entire time. The reaction of the crowd was unfortunate, but no one was hurt and everyone made it home. I wouldn't call that a failure."

Ivy detected a hint of challenge in Bill's affectionate eyes. *I'm sure he means what he says, but he wasn't there.* Ivy could see the mob as clearly as if it loomed in front of her: confused, angry, and afraid.

"I let them see me, and I assure you they didn't think they were watching someone performing a good deed." Victor gripped her hand. She could barely feel his touch. "They saw a freak—a monster. They were so close to turning on us." She spun to Victor. "That man could have shot you."

"But he didn't," Victor replied confidently. *What does it feel like to live without fear?* She wished he could peek inside her night terrors and understand the magnitude of the horrors she'd witnessed. "You need to move on from this, Ivy, and be proud of what you're accomplishing." He tightened his grip. "I'm so fucking proud of you."

She started to object, but gave up. Bill and Victor were family in the truest sense of the word. *They will never see me the way I see myself.* Their support far surpassed anything her father had ever offered her. *At least Dad recognized me for the freak that I am.* She gazed out the window as the rain began to pour.

From his usual spot on the floor by the fireplace, Milo growled—or at least emitted a moan that could be interpreted as a growl. He hoisted his massive body up on unbelievably supportive legs and padded to the front door with a low rumble in his throat. The trio watched this uncharacteristic display with some amusement, which for Ivy turned to fear when someone began knocking on the door.

"A-ha, an uninvited guest," declared Bill as he rose. "Although I expect the face won't be entirely unfamiliar." Ivy could barely hear him from inside her dark mood.

"Are you up to talk to Father Owen?" Victor whispered. "He'll have questions." Ivy shrugged and nodded. Perhaps Father Owen would supply a fresh perspective. *There's nothing left to lose.*

The front door opened and closed quickly. Father Owen did not pause to remove his boots. "Have you come to exorcise me from Tumblestone? You've been threatening it for years." Bill's voice was jovial. Ivy didn't have to look into his face to know that his eyes were twinkling.

Father Owen entered the kitchen with an expression of disdain, as if setting foot in Bill's cottage required an exorbitant amount of effort and sacrifice. He was dressed all in black, except for the telltale collar of his calling and a diamond-encrusted crucifix that Ivy thought to be quite garish. He removed his tan raincoat and set it on the back of a kitchen chair before addressing Bill.

"I did not come here to suffer your insults," Father Owen retorted as he lowered himself to the very edge of the chair. "I've come to speak with your guests. I'm sure my appearance is not a surprise." He pulled his thin lips into something resembling a smile. The smile, Ivy noted, did not extend to his eyes.

Bill threw his hands up in mock offence. This was obviously not their first encounter. "Allow me to give you some privacy." Bill settled into his armchair and flipped open a heavy book. Ivy knew his ears remained at the table.

Next Father Owen turned his grave attention to Victor, who did not budge. A staring contest of sorts ensued. Father Owen reminded Ivy of a Siamese cat, proud and cryptic and mindful that eyes were upon him at all times.

Victor broke the silence. "What brings you by?"

"I've come to inquire after your health, Miss…" Here he floundered.

"Ivy." Her voice was tired. She felt like she would crumble into a pile of dusty debris at any moment. *If I break, don't rush to put me back together again.*

"You seemed quite distraught after last night's… gathering." He rolled the "r" in "gathering." "Are you recovered from your ordeal?"

"I'll be okay," she replied, and, with much effort, attempted to appear hopeful and relaxed. *Fake it till you make it.* The conversation hit a roadblock. No one uttered a peep for at least a minute. Victor took a big gulp of coffee. Under the table, Milo sighed heavily. Father Owen seemed to be ruminating on something vexing. When thunder rolled over the fields, the trio perceptibly jumped in their seats.

"Is there anything else?" Victor inquired, politely but impatiently. "We've got a full day ahead of us."

Father Owen's eyes lingered on Ivy's hands before speaking. "Last night, I witnessed a miracle." His voice was both breathless and cold, and Ivy, who did not have a great deal of experience with members of the clergy, found the absence of warmth surprising.

"A miracle," Ivy repeated lightly. She was still undecided whether or not to confirm what Father Owen's eyes knew to be true. "I'm not sure what you think you saw, Father Owen, but it was certainly not…"

"I'm not to be patronized, young lady," he interrupted, and Ivy's stomach churned. Victor's eyes darkened. "I am not from these parts. I know precisely what I saw. You have been touched by our Lord, and you have an obligation to help His church."

Victor cleared his throat. "Get to the point." His tone was a hair's breath away from threatening. "What do you want from us?"

Father Owen raised his eyebrows. "From us? Do you possess this power, too?" His sweet tone failed to conceal the mocking.

Victor refused to take the bait. "We're a package deal," he said and grinned.

Father Owen narrowed his eyes disapprovingly and returned his focus to Ivy. "Your path is clear to me, as I'm sure it is clear to you," he announced decisively. "You must travel to Rome and meet with the proper authorities. There is a protocol for this type of phenomena." He glanced at Victor. "You obviously have no idea what you're doing."

Victor slammed the table. "Now wait just a damn minute. Who the Hell..."

Ivy placed a hand on his arm. "Victor, I can handle this." She spoke with quiet assertion. She wasn't afraid. Victor nodded. She turned to Father Owen and smiled sweetly. "Father Owen, thank you for your advice, and your concern, but there's no place for me in your church."

Father Owen stared. He was obviously unused to encountering any objections to his directives. "I beg your pardon?"

Ivy pictured herself floating above her body and looking down in disbelief at the farce playing out around Bill's kitchen table. "I'm no miracle worker. I guess I believe in a higher power, but..."

"You are not a person of faith." Father Owen delivered his statement slowly, as if that particular combination of words was inconceivable to him.

"Not really."

"You're not a Catholic."

"I'm sleeping with a Catholic. Does that count?" Ivy knew her uncharacteristic sarcasm teetered on the brink of rudeness, but the situation was becoming increasingly ridiculous. A chuckle wafted over from Bill's armchair.

Father Owen didn't seem to register Ivy's sarcasm. "Miracles are only visited upon believers of the greatest faith."

"That's not me, Father Owen. I'm a librarian." *I'm a freak. I'm a monster. I don't know what I am.*

Father Owen fell silent. From the deep crease in his forehead, Ivy knew that Father Owen was frantically attempting to process something that was quite unpalatable to his rigid sensibilities. Finally, his eyes snapped from Ivy, to Victor, and back to Ivy, and his face erupted into a sneer.

"Then the Devil is working through you!" His eyes were bright with rage and excitement. Ivy's cheeks burned hot. She'd never before been this close to unadulterated fire and brimstone. *Amazing. I went from saint to Satan in less than ten seconds.*

"That's it. We're done here." Victor scraped back Father Owen's chair, but not before Father Owen had uncorked a small vial of water and hurled it in Ivy's direction. The water hit Ivy on the cheek. She covered her face with her hands.

"The Devil is here with us now, in this room!" Father Owen's voice rose in shrillness. Victor grabbed Father Owen by the scruff of his neck, pushed him through the kitchen, and shoved him roughly out the front door. "God help us all!"

"Fuck off!" Victor slammed the door and raced back to Ivy's side. He knelt in front of her. Ivy knew he feared another panic attack. "He's a nut, okay? So many of them are. It's either their way or the highway to Hell. It's bullshit."

She dropped her hands to her lap and revealed a broad smile and sparkling eyes. She laughed. She laughed until tears leaked from her eyes and mingled with the holy water already on her cheek.

"Are you losing it, Merchuk?" Victor rose and dropped onto a kitchen chair, clearly confused.

Bill joined them at the table. "I think Ivy's response is most appropriate."

Ivy wiped the salty moisture from her face and hiccupped. She'd wanted to laugh from the moment Father Owen had dragged the Devil into the kitchen. "We should be grateful to Father Owen. He exorcised my fear," she said finally and hiccupped slightly. "I was unprepared for his reaction, and for the town's reaction, but that won't happen again." She turned to Victor, whose eyes were wide with concern as they often were when they looked upon her. In Victor lived her protector, her samurai, and her lover, but for a brief instant, Ivy saw the relationship as completely one-sided. *I take and take from him and give him nothing but worry.* A pang in her heart. She pushed aside the self-loathing. "I'm not always going to rush to hide behind you, Victor. I'm going to figure out how to be proud of this." She raised her palms and brought forth two barely discernible orbs of white light. She smiled warmly at Victor, and then at Bill, and then threw back her head of brown curls and laughed heartily. Her tinkling laugh was infectious. Soon the men were laughing, too.

"Poor bastard," Victor remarked sardonically and shook his head.

"He's probably got his head out the car window, screaming about Lucifer all the way back to Tumblestone."

Ivy propped her chin on her hands, rubbed her eyes, and yawned. In her moment of clarity, her sleepless night and empty stomach had finally caught up with her. She devoured a blueberry muffin in less than a minute and wondered if it was too early in the day to sink into the big bed for a long nap.

Another knock at the door. This time, Milo barked and attempted an uncoordinated dash that vaguely resembled a run.

Ivy's eyes bulged in disbelief. "He wouldn't come back, would he?"

Victor charged towards the door and flung it open mid-knock. "If you've got anything else to say…"

But it wasn't Father Owen with his tan coat and diamond crucifix on the doorstep. Instead, Ivy, Victor, Bill and Milo stared open-mouthed at a small, pale-skinned young woman sporting a gruesome black eye. Her red hair was pulled back into a clumsy ponytail. She gripped the hand of a young version of herself, no more than four-years-old. Both sets of eyes were wide with terror.

"I'm sorry," Victor back-pedalled and took a couple steps away from the threshold. "I thought you were someone else."

The woman seemed on the brink of turning on her heel when her eyes located Ivy standing behind Bill. "You." Her dusty voice was full of wonder. "I saw you last night, what you did for Benjie." She began to cry. "Can you help us?" She lifted her left wrist, which rested awkwardly in a homemade sling. "My husband… it's broken. If I go to the doctor, to the police… Everyone knows everyone… He'll know I'm leaving him… Please, I can't do anything for my daughter like this." She wept, and the child began to sob, and Ivy found tears gathering behind her own eyes, too.

Ivy pushed forward. "Yes, of course, I can try." The words floated out without passing through any filter. As mother and child shuffled indoors, and Bill took their plastic raincoats and Milo sniffed their rubber boots, Ivy heard her own mother whisper softly out of the past. *You'll do great things.*

Ivy knelt in front of the little girl. "Don't be afraid, sweetheart." The girl's little hand rested on Milo's bowed head. "Your mommy has a small hurt and I'm going to take away the pain." But as she attempted to pour her positive energy into the eyes of the traumatized little girl, she realized that there were certain wounds she couldn't reach with her energy. *She's at the beginning of a long journey.*

Gently and delicately, Bill directed the mother to the healing room and led the child to one of the big chairs by the fire. Milo was now glued to her side. Ivy remained for a moment in the open doorway. The rain fell in heavy sheets and clear vision was virtually impossible beyond a few metres. Victor embraced her from behind.

"You're a remarkable woman, Ivy Merchuk." He rested his chin on her shoulder. His voice was thick with unspoken words. "Are you sure about this?"

"Yes," she replied, again without thinking. In the light of the stormy day, she recognized the healing of the previous night for what it was: a defence of life in the face of grievous injury. Such a defence should never be second-guessed. "I'm a healer. This is what I do. Heal first, think later." *And I'll keep figuring this out as I go.*

Victor kissed her hair. "You're too good," he observed with a lilt and a wink as she pulled away and headed to the healing room. "Saint Ivy of Tumblestone County. That's got a nice ring to it."

CHAPTER 9

The young mother was the only resident of Tumblestone to turn up on the doorstep, but she wasn't the only one interested in Ivy's abilities. After weeks of occasional, intermittent ringing, the phone now rang a dozen times a day. On the other end of the line were curious citizens seeking confirmation that their eyes hadn't played tricks on them, and that a young out-of-towner had laid her hands upon Benjie and healed his wounds. Bill took the calls and managed to answer the questions without actually confirming or denying anything. Some even called to inquire about Ivy's rates.

"Rates?" Ivy gasped when Bill related the message over dinner. *As if I could ever sell my body like that.* "What comes next? Billboards? Commercials? A media tour?"

"People want access to the divine," Bill said solemnly. "News of a beautiful young woman with an extraordinary ability won't stay confined to Tumblestone for long."

"This town is getting too small for us," Victor muttered darkly. "Something needs to change." But he didn't expand on this statement and instead glared at the plate of spaghetti in front of him. *Tell me what needs to change, and I'll make it happen. Just don't shut me out.*

From the moment the phone had begun to ring off the hook, Victor seemed to wrestle with giant thoughts. His nights were restless. The calm and positivity that had characterized his katana training evaporated. A couple times, he left in the Jeep without mentioning to Bill and Ivy that he was even leaving the property, only to return hours later with a heavy brow and unsatisfying explanations—"I just needed to drive"—as to his whereabouts.

The stormy weather did not keep Victor from his daily practice, but now when he slashed and thrust his sword through the rain, Ivy saw a fiery anguish in his eyes. In quiet moments, she would feel him staring at her, and when she'd meet his gaze, she glimpsed a man in crisis. He would mask the sadness immediately, but she'd seen it, and she was unsettled.

In night's confessional, Ivy attempted to break through. "Share your thoughts with me, Victor." She cocooned herself in his arms. "That's what I'm here for. We're the same person." Silence. *He's become a fortress.* "You once spoke of our shared life. Share it with me, whatever's going on. You shouldn't have to struggle alone."

Victor sat up, switched on the light, and looked upon Ivy with an expression so tortured and urgent that she was instantly nervous and reached for his hand.

"What are you thinking?" She was surprised to hear desperation in her hushed voice.

"You deserve to have the best possible life," he began forcefully as he gripped her hand. "There is no life in the shadows."

Ivy was confused. "My life is with you." Her eyes fell to the Saint Michael medallion. "I'm alive wherever you are. What are we debating exactly?"

For a few moments, Victor said nothing. He raked his fingers through his hair. The seconds dragged on. Panic began to lap at Ivy's toes.

"Victor…" Ivy's head was light as air.

"I want to settle it with Joji." He spit the words out. "We can't keep running like this. It's time to have it out. We shouldn't have to live in fear. Now that people know what you can do, he's going to hear about us sooner than later. Better we find him before he finds us." He seemed relieved for a moment, until the colour began to drain from Ivy's face.

"Why would you want to charge back into the lion's den?" She felt Joji's fingers around her neck. Smelled his sizzling flesh. "It's suicide, Victor. He doesn't want to negotiate with you. He wants you dead. Why would you risk it? Why would you risk destroying us?" Tears poured from her eyes. She stood on the precipice of another panic attack. *I am fragile without him. I am porcelain.* Her palms burned hot. Victor scooped her up in his arms.

"It's okay, baby," he cooed as he rocked her. "Don't worry. It's okay. I'll figure it out."

When morning arrived, Victor was gone. Ivy rose and stretched and rubbed life into her sleepy eyes. She glanced through the window, noted that her Jeep was absent from its usual spot, and rode a wave of apprehension without fully understanding why.

As Ivy showered, she flashed back to her bathroom in Vancouver, to the cracked floral tiles that had stared back at her day after day as she'd shampooed her hair and conjured up the courage to walk out into the world. In her previous life—she'd lived another lifetime in the intervening month—her ability had been a disability. *I will never go back to the complacency of my old life. Complacency is death.* But there seemed no danger of complacency so long as she could hear the energy coursing through her body and see herself in Victor's eyes.

Ivy towelled off and pulled on her yoga gear. She knew this morning's meditation session would be particularly gruelling. *Too many frantic thoughts rattling around inside my head.* There was no easy route around the fear that Victor would continue on a quest that would almost certainly end with death. She sensed a wall between them. *He needs to be able to rely on me without being afraid that I'll break.* Ivy caught a glimpse of herself in the mirror. There was a hint of defiance in her eyes. *Perhaps I am stronger than I think I am. Perhaps I could be as brazen and fearless as Tomoe Gozen.* The toned woman in the mirror smiled slightly.

As Ivy touched her fingers to the handle of the bedroom door, she heard loud footsteps on the front porch, footsteps so heavy and out of place that she dropped her hand and retreated backwards into the middle of the room. Fingers frozen, palms hot. Then came a brutal pounding on the front door, followed by a crash and a rush of loud male voices. She stood paralyzed and as straight as a stick, unable to make out much beyond the rapid beating of her own heart.

"Who are you?" Bill's outrage impressed Ivy despite her fear. "Get out of my house!" Milo began to bark with such ferocity that Ivy's heart swelled at his heroism. Milo's outburst was cut short with a thud, followed by whimpering, and then a long second of thunderous silence. Footsteps echoed through the house.

This is someone else's life. I can't feel my legs. I've forgotten how to breathe.

Ivy managed a silent dash to the window and, trembling, peered outside. She saw but couldn't compute an imposing black SUV in the driveway. A well-dressed man emerged from its dark interior. He carried a black attaché case. And then her brain processed the fact that the man was Joji, in oversized aviator sunglasses that barely obscured the disfigurement she'd inflicted upon him only a few weeks previous. She knew that there would be no negotiating with this monster. For a moment he paused, surveyed the scenery, and allowed himself a deep gulp of country air. Even from this height, Ivy knew that he was congratulating himself on a job well done. *He doesn't know that Victor isn't here.* This thought filled her with courage. She would make Victor proud. She would be fearless. She leapt away from the window and pressed her shaking body to the wall.

Her mind pulled her to the en suite bathroom. She pictured herself crawling out the bathroom window and escaping across the fields. *But where is Victor?*

Bill continued to shower the goons with arguments and objections. "What do you want with me? What are you looking for? There's no one here but me and my dog!" He spoke loudly and deliberately. Ivy knew he was prompting her to make a dash for help.

"Shut up, old man." The younger voice was irritable. "If you're not going to help us, we'll help ourselves."

Ivy had only moved two steps towards the bathroom before the bedroom door flung open and a well-dressed goon stormed through. He smiled broadly when his eyes fell upon her. It was the same thug who'd decked her in the jaw. She dove for the bathroom, but he caught her arm and slammed her face-first to the floor. He yanked her arms behind her back and, after some struggling, slapped handcuffs around her wrists and pinned her to the floor with his knee. She tossed and attempted a turn, kicked and flailed, but he continued to sit on her and grip her roughly around one arm. His hand was sheathed in thick leather gloves. Her wandering gaze passed over Victor's jeans folded on a chair and brushed against her sword leaning against the wall. A training session with her samurai had yet to materialize. Even if she could reach the katana and wrap her fingers around the handle, the confidence and mastery of Tomoe Gozen remained far out of grasp.

"Careful, Yuki." She recognized the frosty voice booming from the doorway. "Avoid her hands. This bitch plays dirty." Joji strode across the room and knelt down in front of Ivy. The tip of his alligator boot rested an inch from her eyeball. He grabbed her chin and wrenched up her face so she had no choice but to look into his. His glasses were off. Ripples of pink and purple mottled flesh ate away most of his face. His right eye was swollen shut. It was as if he'd stepped out of her nightmares. He slammed her face into the carpet. The goon pressed his knee into her lungs. Breathing became impossible.

"So nice to see you again." Joji stood and Ivy heard him drop something—the attaché case, Ivy guessed—onto the bed. "You underestimated me, you stupid bitch. You have no idea what we've got in store for you." Ivy's palms vibrated. She gasped for air and choked on a cough.

"Don't damage the merchandise, Yuki." Joji fumbled with the contents of the bag. "Remember what Mariko said. She's worth more to us in one piece." The goon decreased the pressure on Ivy's back. Still she could not pull in enough air to speak. She could see all the words she wanted to say. *Leave us alone. Let us live our life in peace. Victor will destroy you when he finds you. He's stronger than you could ever hope to be.*

In the hallway, Bill's yelling increased in pitch and volume. *I'm okay, Bill! I'm still alive!* Ivy struggled under the weight of Joji's henchman. *Where is Victor?*

"He's annoying me," Joji called out over his shoulder to the goon in the hallway. "Take care of him."

A gunshot rang through the cottage. Bill's shouts ceased. The world melted away and Ivy was alone with her horror and shock and powerlessness. Her lungs allowed a small scream into the carpet. Tears streamed from her eyes and formed a small pool underneath her face. *Victor will never forgive me. Everything is my fault. Oh, Bill!*

Once again Joji's boot tip filled her field of vision. "Your arrogance is staggering," he remarked casually as he dropped onto the carpet. "You thought you could live without paying for what you did." Here he giggled gleefully. "You're about to start paying."

"Victor will come," she croaked through laboured sobs.

The goon twisted Ivy's left arm and slapped her bicep a couple times. "I actually feel a little sorry for you," Joji sighed as he stabbed her arm with a hypodermic needle. She didn't flinch. "Victor isn't coming, sweetheart. He delivered you right to us." Ivy fell into immediate blackness.

THE FALL

CHAPTER 10

Ivy crashed into consciousness with her eyes wide open. There was no transitory dream-state, no smooth wave lifting her gently as she broke through the surface. She emerged from the unfeeling darkness into overarching panic, cold sweat, and the blinding light from a fluorescent bulb suspended a couple feet above her face. Damp air slashed at her limbs like a million little katanas.

It was impossible for Ivy to discern much beyond the light and deafening rush of her internal energy flow. She assessed her body as best she could. She lay on her back with her exposed skin pressed against cold metal, and guessed she was still dressed in her skimpy yoga gear. Her legs, waist, wrists and head were strapped down with unseen restraints. Both hands bound up in fists. A tube in her arm. Ivy could see nothing but the fluorescent bulb and the lattice-like shadows cast by unseen wires and pipes on the concrete ceiling. She pulled against all the restraints but managed to shift only a fraction of an inch before collapsing back in frustration. *He wasn't there.* Ivy closed her eyes and struggled to bring her breathing and rapid heartbeat under control. Her palms burned and buzzed within their bindings.

Victor isn't coming, sweetheart. He delivered you right to us.

Joji's voice struck out at Ivy from her recent memory. The words were more painful to Ivy than any blow to the face.

"Never!" Ivy cried out into the circle of light. Her throat was dry. "It can't be true."

Ivy's thoughts strayed to Victor's days of distraction and anxiety, his unexplained absences, and the sadness in his deep green eyes. Could

Victor have led Joji right to their bedroom? Was the freedom he craved for him alone? Her memory took her to the loft, to his wide smile and sun-soaked skin, to his hands on her back, to those golden moments where he pulled her out of time and space, where there was nothing else in their universe but their intertwined limbs. *You're my family.* His voice cut through her inner chaos and panic. She was once again perched on the back of his motorcycle. He was overwhelmed by the enormity of their newly discovered old love. *I will never fail you.* She felt his lips against her fingers. Tears gathered behind her eyes.

Can't believe it. Won't believe it. Victor wouldn't have risked us like that. She heard the gunshot that had silenced Bill and fought a descent into grief. *I've got to focus on staying alive.* And yet the sense of betrayal lingered in her throat and crushed her heart. She felt the premature loss of their shared life.

A door opened and closed. Someone shuffled into the room. The newcomer remained in the shadows and out of Ivy's limited field of vision. Ivy heard the clanking of bottles and the pouring of liquids. The movements were slow and displayed no sense of urgency. Ivy strained to catch a glimpse. "Release me, please," Ivy implored as she struggled against the restraints. For a split second, the unseen person seemed to halt in their movements, but then resumed their tasks at the same unrushed pace. "I want to speak to Joji. Where is Joji?" Perhaps she would stumble upon a way to talk herself out of the situation.

A young woman emerged into Ivy's circle of light. The woman was Japanese and shockingly small-boned, a delicate little bird sporting a Mickey Mouse t-shirt and an expression of indifference. Her distant eyes seemed to shoot right through Ivy. She checked the IV tube in Ivy's arm and fussed with the connecting fluid-filled bag without so much as an indication that she'd heard Ivy's calls.

"Joji," Ivy repeated, increasingly desperate. "I want to see him. I don't need to be strapped down. I'm not dangerous. What are you doing?" Her pleas remained unacknowledged. Ivy was invisible. With a jolt, she realized it was not the first time her unlikely nursemaid had dealt with someone in Ivy's position. The little bird plucked a small bottle from a nearby tray and released the milky contents into the IV bag. Her fingers seemed even too small for the miniature bottle.

"Can you hear me?" Ivy shook all her limbs in a vain attempt to grab and sustain the woman's attention. "What's in the IV bag?" No flicker of recognition. Ivy wondered if the young woman was herself a captive. *She's a corpse. There's no walking away from here.* The cold sweat on her brow began to pour into her eyes. Every hair on her body stood up and screamed. She yanked up on the leather restraints and felt them cut into her ankles, wrist, and forehead. She prayed for unconsciousness to yank her back into its safe haven and silence the rapid thud of her heartbeat. She began to wail. Her palms flared a searing heat. The smell of burnt leather reached her nose. The fluorescent bulb above her face flickered and pulsed. *Victor wouldn't send me here, would he? Did I mean nothing to him? Is this the cost of his freedom?*

The panic ceased suddenly and Ivy felt nothing. Numb. Couldn't move her limbs or turn her head from side to side. Her voice stopped in her throat. She was paralyzed inside and out. The anxiety was replaced by empty acceptance. Her eyes remained open, and though she could blink, the act sapped her remaining strength. Her palms buzzed slightly before falling still. Even the hum of the internal energy flow was subdued. *None of this is natural.* Ivy was trapped beneath an imposing, invisible mass of air, time, and space.

The young woman peered into Ivy's face, pulled Ivy's eyelids to and fro and stuck her fingers against her neck before standing back. Ivy detected a small, satisfied smile on her otherwise blank face. Task performed, the little bird and her Mickey Mouse shirt padded back into the shadows and departed through the unseen door. Ivy was left suspended in purgatory. *I've been pumped full of indifference.*

Hours, or maybe minutes, passed, but Ivy's nurse did not return. Sleep proved unattainable, and Ivy, both lulled and listless, found herself waiting for something to happen. Stupefied, she attempted to pull together a mental picture of the room. The woman's footsteps had echoed. Ivy's screams had bounced off the walls. *This room is cavernous.* There were pipes on the ceiling, a damp chill in her bones, no windows providing natural light. She sniffed the air and recoiled from the bleach and sterility. *I'm in a clinic.* But sniffing and guessing could only take her so far, and frustration mounted with each passing second of futile detective work. *Is this what Joji has in store for me?* She sighed inwardly. No, Joji's plans would be far more invasive. *He wants to hear me scream.* She vowed not to do so again, and wondered how many of her vows she'd be able to keep as she descended further into Hell.

Ivy's thoughts dragged her back to the little cottage that had so recently become her home, to fat Milo, to wise Bill and his bright smile and unending well of contentment, to the heroism they'd both displayed when they'd raged against Joji's henchmen. She wondered if the bullet had killed Bill instantly, if he'd died a slow death, if he might have survived without her there to heal him, if she could even contend with a bullet wound. She wondered if Victor had ever returned, if he'd been surprised or horrified by the bloody mess. If he missed her. If he'd ever loved her at all. She wondered if her father would cry when her corpse was fished out of the sea.

Ivy managed a groan so slight it failed to cross her teeth. *If I keep on like this, I'm really going to lose my mind.* She returned to waiting for something to happen, and attempted to clear her mind and breathe through the top of her head as Bill had taught her to do. *Poor Bill…*

The door swung open, and Ivy's ears picked up the rise and fall of footsteps. This time, the footfalls were heavier and more confident in their intent. Ivy felt little panic or fear as the footsteps neared her table. Resignation, yes, and a tiny grain of gratitude that something was finally happening.

A grinning face popped into the circle of fluorescent illumination. The newcomer was male, in his late twenties, with a hint of Asian in his features. His face bore a well-kept goatee and mischievous eyes. He looked somewhat peculiar in his navy blue suit, as if it was the costume of a serious grown-up and he wasn't quite serious enough for it yet. Altogether, the upbeat young man was not what Ivy had been expecting to stride through the door.

"Good evening," he chirped conversationally. The young man displayed a sparkle that Ivy thought better suited to a car salesman or a hotel concierge. Unabashedly, he ran his eyes up and down her prone, paralyzed body, and whistled. "Has anyone ever told you that you could be a model?" Ivy rolled her eyes. "Oh, she's given you sedatives. Sometimes she'll double the dose when the patient is really dangerous. But usually we're talking 300-pound assassins. Anyway, the drugs will rob you of your tongue for a while." His eyes rested on her leather-bound hands and he frowned. "I've never seen fists bound up like that before. Not sure why they felt the need to strap you down. You look harmless enough." He chuckled. "Guess you have a lot of fire in you." Ivy wanted to smack his face, give him a rough shake, and laugh; such were the effects of his inappropriate jocularity. She could only hope her face reflected a sneer.

The young man appeared to admire her for another moment before seemingly remembering that he had a job to perform. He darted out of Ivy's field of vision and bounded across the spacious room, all the while whistling a jaunty tune that sounded to Ivy like the theme song to a television game show. In less than a minute he was at Ivy's side once more, this time pushing an unoccupied wheelchair.

"Your carriage awaits," he quipped as he slid the IV tube out of her arm. "We're heading out on a field trip. Are you happy about it? I'd be happy if I were you." He glanced up and around him and shivered. "This room gives me the creeps. I avoid it at all costs. I'm taking you to much nicer surroundings." He moved down her body and untied the straps around her wrists, stomach and legs. He did not squeeze her breasts or molest her in any way, which Ivy noted with relief. "I mean, I suppose rooms like this aren't meant to be cozy. They serve a purpose. But sometimes I feel like they went out of their way to make some of these rooms horrible. Would it have killed them to throw up some bright paint or a couple plants when they were furnishing it all? But then again, the whole place came together really quickly, and… oh, I almost forgot your head." He unsnapped the strap that held her head against the metal table. Ivy was now completely unrestrained and, were it not for the powerful sedatives weighing down every pore, she would have been free to stand, stretch, and make a run for it.

He loaded her onto the wheelchair with no small measure of difficulty. "This isn't my regular gig," he offered by way of an explanation as the wheelchair skidded across the floor and he struggled to support Ivy's body against his own. "I'm more of a desk guy." He was leaner than Victor, and nowhere near as muscular. His scent reminded Ivy of her father: a combination of menthol cigarettes, black coffee, and pricey cologne. He poured Ivy into the wheelchair. Her head rolled forward, then to the side. Though she felt more like cargo then a human being, Ivy was now afforded her first glimpse beyond the circle of fluorescent light.

Ivy had been correct when she'd surmised that she was in a medical environment. A dozen identical metal tables were distributed a few paces apart throughout the large room. Adjacent to each table was a tray displaying shiny medical instruments: scissors, scalpels, retractors, and other sharp, intimidating tools for which Ivy could only guess their functions. A darkened fluorescent lamp hovered above each tabletop. With a start, Ivy realized she'd awakened on an operating table. *Why does Joji need an operating room?* Along the walls stood glass-fronted cabinets housing bandages, cotton swabs, blankets, and hundreds of little bottles whose labels Ivy could not read from her vantage point. At the very edge of her field of vision, Ivy glimpsed green curtains, and concluded there were hospital beds behind them. *Real hospitals don't strap their patients down to the operating tables.* She spied heart monitors, blood pumps, oxygen tanks, computer stations: every instrument, every piece of medical machinery blissfully asleep. To Ivy, the surgery contained as much soul as a decked-out model home where no family could ever truly be happy.

"We spent a lot of money on all this stuff but we don't really have anyone on staff who knows how to use it." There was embarrassment in the young man's voice, as if he was concerned that Ivy would judge him harshly for a poor financial expenditure. "By the time the guys get here—well, there's not much that can be done anyway." His explanation failed to clarify anything for his immobilized passenger.

"Let's take this show on the road," the man quipped as he thrust her forward. With this first push, the tip of Ivy's left foot caught on the floor and rolled back, stopping the wheelchair in its tracks and shooting a burst of pain through her leg. She found herself grateful for the sensation. *I want to feel my pain. It belongs to me.*

"I'm so sorry!" The man hopped into a crouch. He returned her foot to its designated holder, met her gaze and smiled brightly. "I'm Piper Tanaka," he announced with shining eyes. "I'd ask your name but…" He frowned and seemed to wrestle with a troubling thought for a couple seconds. *So there are things he doesn't say. I was beginning to think he articulated every little thought that flew into his mind.* "Anyway. Well. Let's get you to your next stop."

They passed through the heavy door and into the hallway and swerved to the right. The corridors were endless stretches of grey concrete, with grey walls and floors and ceilings and doors. The drabness was illuminated by long tracks of fluorescent lighting. The smell that met Ivy's nose was similar to the operating room, an unappealing mixture of industrial cleaner and mildew. The corridors branched out at numerous junctures, and Ivy struggled to remember the many twists and turns until she lost track and decided she didn't want to know how to return to the operating room, anyway.

With Piper at the helm, the pair flew past many doors, all of which were numbered (126, 124, 122) but none of which displayed any words explaining their functions. Some of the doors were alarmed, with illuminated keypads jutting out of the wall. Scowling goons were stationed outside many of these alarmed doors; behind one, Ivy could hear male voices raised in shouts. Their words were obscured by insulation and language barriers. The goons carried guns and katanas. Ivy wondered how many of the katanas had been crafted by Victor's strong, callused hands. For the most part, the goons were a sullen and silent lot, dressed in same-looking black suits, white shirts, and black silk ties. *So many missing fingers.* The corridors were silent deserts, save for the incessant hum of the air-conditioning system and the squeak of the wheelchair as it manoeuvred the maze.

"Hey Hugo, how's it going?" Piper inquired of a particularly burly suit leaning against a closed door. The bigger man raised his eyebrows and grunted as Ivy and Piper swept past.

A kernel of panic began to grow in Ivy's back. In her month of revelations, she had grown to believe that life wouldn't be worth living if Victor wasn't by her side. *I deserve an explanation.*

"Not ready to die," she croaked with much difficulty. She was pleased at least that the words had emerged. The rest of her body remained cocooned in the drugs.

The wheelchair skidded to a sudden halt. Piper was at once at her side. His brow was troubled. Again Ivy was reminded of a child playing at being an adult. "Die? Mariko never said anything about that. She only asked me to pick you up from the hospital and deliver you to her suite. Are you sure you're going to die today?" Ivy was aghast. *Is he blind, deaf, dumb, or crazy?* She marvelled at his oblivion and actually felt a little sorry for him, before recalling with a start that she'd heard the name Mariko before.

"Mariko?" She could only push out a whisper. Joji had uttered the name in her bedroom. Her head remained rolled to the side. Piper didn't seem to hear her.

"You're not a wounded animal. I can't imagine Mariko putting you down." Piper's eyes snapped up to hers. His confusion seemed genuine. "What's your name?"

"Ivy."

"Eileen?"

"Ivy." Stronger this time. She managed to raise her head a little more to meet his gaze.

"Well, Ivy, my feeling is that, if they were going to kill you, they would have done it already, so why not push death right out of your mind, okay?" He flashed his white, pearly teeth, obviously satisfied with his pep talk, and resumed his previous position behind the wheelchair. He seemed to be running now, and she wished he'd return to a leisurely pace.

CHAPTER 11

Their destination was door number 8. The two suits stationed outside the door scowled at the pair as Piper brought their journey to a close. Ivy wondered if Piper was ever able to pull anyone in Joji's organization into a conversation, or if he was doomed to wander the dank corridors brimming with words but without a friendly listener. *You're in the wrong business, buddy. How did you end up here?*

"Open up, boys. I'm expected." Piper's tone was playful. He clicked his heels. The taller of the guards cast a suspicious glance at Ivy's leather-bound fists before rapping lightly at the metal door.

"Show them in." A woman's voice wafted through the door. The voice was caramel and throaty. The shorter of the goons swung open the door, and Piper inched Ivy forward. They stopped a few paces inside the room before the door clicked shut behind them.

Ivy felt the heat on her skin before she noticed anything else. The harsh fluorescent lighting of the corridors was gone and replaced with warm, dim hues emanating from several Japanese floor lamps and a giant fish tank. With her head still rolled to one side, Ivy took a series of mental snapshots of fine furnishings and first impressions. She spied deep couches swathed in lush exotic fabrics. A towering armoire carved with a scene of a bustling fishing village. A long lacquered table surrounded by contemporary armchairs. A wall of televisions broadcasting news channels from around the world. Bottles of premium sake atop a rich mahogany bar. A glass case displaying five jewel-encrusted katanas. Ivy choked on European perfume and rich religious incense. For Ivy, the windowless room was a cross between an

Asian boudoir and a boardroom, rampant with suffocating femininity and corporate hostility.

Ivy still could not see the woman, but her searching eyes found Joji. He reclined in one of the armchairs. A shadow darkened his mangled features when Ivy fell into his line of sight.

"Joji, leave us." The unseen woman delivered her order with haughty authority, and Ivy was shocked when Joji actually pushed himself up and off the chair and slunk towards the door. As he passed Piper and Ivy, he struck out with his elbow and delivered a sharp jab to Piper's arm that nearly sent him off his feet. Piper gripped the handles of the wheelchair but said nothing. Before exiting, Joji paused at the door and called out over his shoulder. "Don't get too comfortable, Ivy. We have much to discuss." He slammed the door.

"You too, Piper. Into the hallway. But stay close. You'll be needed again soon." Piper relinquished his hold on the wheelchair and turned on his heels. The women were alone.

The woman emerged from a dark corner. From a distance, Ivy guessed that the woman was older than Joji and possessed his eyes, jaw, and mouth. Dressed in an elegant pinstripe suit with her hair swept up into a fashionable bun, the woman moved towards Ivy with the grace of a dancer. It was only when she neared that Ivy noted heavy makeup, tattooed eyebrows, fake eyelashes, collagen lips, enhanced breasts, and a thin nose that hinted recent plastic surgery. She had the look and air of a woman who had, until recently, been breathtakingly beautiful. In a couple more years, she would likely be a caricature of the woman she yearned to be. Her expression was inscrutable.

Mariko stopped at the end of the lacquered table, sunk into in a chair, and produced a cigarette from a slender jade case. "Are you able to speak yet?" Her exhale was prolonged and sensuous. Smoke swirled around her.

"A little." Ivy's voice was raspy and hollow. The power remained trapped in her chest.

"My brother insisted on these precautions. He believes you can't be controlled without them. Personally, I believe that you can be reasoned with, and so I expect that we won't have to keep you restrained for too long." She took another drag off her cigarette. Her long fingernails were painted black. Ivy found the strength returning to her neck and rolled her head above her shoulders. "I am Mariko. Joji is my brother. You are

Ivy. You fucked Victor. Now we're all acquainted." In that moment, Ivy realized that Joji's criminal organization was not quite what she had initially believed it to be. *Mariko is the boss.* She didn't like the familiar manner with which Mariko had tossed out Victor's name.

Mariko leaned forward and propped her painted face in her hands like a daydreaming schoolgirl. "Yes, I see what Victor saw in you. Youth and sex and innocence." Her cooed words were drenched in bitterness. "But it wasn't enough, was it, Ivy?" Here Mariko laughed greedily, sending shame to Ivy's cheeks. *Sitting here in front of this woman, I cannot imagine Victor negotiating me away. I must believe in our life.*

Ivy was blinded by sudden indignation. "There is nothing you can tell me about Victor." Ivy would have spit the words out if she could.

Mariko's eyes danced. "No, Ivy, there is nothing *you* can tell *me* about Victor." Her mocking tone was like syrup. "I've known him a lot longer than you have. Didn't he tell you about me? Didn't he tell you that he kept calling me from that godforsaken town?"

Ivy was again in the cottage, in the bright bedroom, glancing through the window and wondering where her lover had gone. *He left me to call Mariko?* She blinked a few times, and the bedroom and the emptiness disappeared. Her spine turned to steel. *No one speaks for Victor but Victor. I will wait. I will wait to hear his words.* Her eyes flashed, but she said nothing in reply.

Mariko waved her hand impatiently. "I don't want to talk about Victor. The fact is that I know what you can do. My brother was too angry to see your value, but I see it, and I intend to use it." She paused, evidently waiting for Ivy to engage in fervent denial. Ivy bristled. She felt the strength returning to her limbs, and the buzzing to her palms, but she kept still and quiet. Mariko ground her cigarette into an ornate marble ashtray and strutted over to one of the deep couches a few feet away from Ivy. She collapsed into the cushions with practiced grace. "You can fix people and hurt people. You fixed Victor, and you scarred my brother." Mariko swung her long legs up onto the couch. Her slender feet were ensconced in black patent leather stilettos. She sighed heavily. "What you did to my brother is going to cost a lot to fix, you know. Plastic surgery isn't cheap. So the way I see it, you owe me." She paused and looked Ivy square in the eye. "Give me your power."

Ivy blinked. The meaning of Mariko's words took a couple seconds to register. "Excuse me?"

Mariko was insistent. "Tell me how you do it."

"I-I can't," Ivy stammered. "It's like breathing. It's just something that happens. It's part of my body." *Is she for real?*

Mariko leapt up from the couch, strode up to the wheelchair, and pushed her face into Ivy's until their noses were only inches apart. Mariko's stare was threatening and imploring. Ivy was acutely aware of her own drug-enhanced vulnerability. Neither woman spoke. Ivy observed that Mariko was wearing gold contact lenses, and that the makeup on her face failed to conceal several pockmarks. Eventually, Mariko frowned and straightened. "You're being difficult. Selfish. You just don't want to share." Mariko's golden eyes went far away. "If I had your skill, I wouldn't need to hide my power behind that spineless little man. Always concealed. Always pretending that I'm weaker than I am. My power would surpass any leader in my family's history."

Despite her revulsion, Ivy couldn't contain her confusion. "How do you work that out? I'm a healer, not a…"

Mariko's laugh was tinny. "Monster? Murderer? Crime lord? You can say it. You won't offend me. It arouses me to hear you say it." She fell into the lush cushions once more. "I would be feared, because I would be able to do something they couldn't control. That is the greatest power: never having to use it." Ivy had heard that sentiment before. *In a different lifetime.*

"Well, if you're not going to pass your powers on to me, I have other work for you to do." Mariko was all business. "Your gift is my tool. I have men for you to heal." Ivy imagined Mariko's head on the body of a giant, long-limbed spider. She was caught in Mariko's web.

"I won't heal your men. You said yourself it can't be controlled."

This time, Mariko's laugh was like her brother's: gleeful and giddy. "Of course you will. You won't be able to help yourself. You're a bleeding heart." She practically purred. "I understand you healed Victor before you even knew him, and Victor is a very bad man."

Ivy felt Mariko baiting her into an outburst. She knew it would give Mariko much pleasure to watch her crumble over Victor. *He said he wouldn't fail me. I need to trust him. I will not be baited.*

Mariko's eyes betrayed her disappointment, and it was clear that she was tiring of her prisoner. She called out for Piper, who entered in a flash and took up the reins behind the wheelchair once more.

"Piper will keep an eye on you because frankly I suspect the other guards will damage the merchandise if given the chance." Mariko's eyes wandered down to Ivy's cleavage. Ivy felt like a cornered mouse about to be devoured by a hungry cat. "Piper is the only one who can be trusted with you." Mariko admired her slender ringed fingers, and then looked up with a start. "Oh, he's not gay. He's just eager to please me. Few are as obedient as Piper." Ivy felt Piper stir behind her. She wondered if Mariko and Piper were lovers, if Victor had ever shared her bed.

"And if I refuse to help you?" *They can't force me to heal their goons. I'm not her tool.*

"Death." Mariko tossed out the word as if it held no meaning. "But if you do as I say, you'll be looked after. After all, we want you healthy in order to fulfill your obligations." Mariko smiled and made an impatient shooing gesture with her hands, as if Piper and Ivy were pesky mosquitoes. Piper wheeled Ivy towards the door. "I should mention that I place a high value on obedience, and I enjoy discipline"—she delivered the word with a hiss— "above all else. Behave or I'll unleash my brother on you. Piper, take her to the VIP cell, and then return to me."

The cell was located at the far end of a corridor that required keypad entry to access. Almost all the doors in this particular hallway possessed narrow glass slits for which Ivy, still in her wheelchair, was too low to the ground to peek through. *Who are my neighbours?* The silence was eerie. She wished she could see Piper's expression and hazard a guess as to what thoughts were speeding through his mind.

It hadn't been more than twenty minutes since Piper had first wheeled Ivy into Mariko's suite, but in the interim it appeared that he'd morphed into a different person altogether. Contrary to his earlier buoyancy, Piper was virtually silent on the journey to the cell. He seemed acutely uncomfortable in his blue suit. Ivy wondered if Joji's arm jab had knocked the enthusiasm out of his sails, or if he had eavesdropped enough of the women's conversation to know that Ivy was not simply the beautiful, helpless cargo he'd pegged her for at first sight. *This is a simple man who craves simplicity. There is nothing simple here.*

The corridor was lined with a dozen armed guards, many of whom viewed Ivy with open hostility. One grabbed his crotch as she passed. Ivy kept her eyes glued to the windowless door at the end of the corridor, which happened to be their final destination. Door 60-A.

Ivy's disconnect from her body had been tortuous, but the drugs were waning and her muscles and organs and limbs and nerves were regaining their strength. She was delighted when her left leg cramped up, when her stomach cried out for sustenance, when the inner energy flow grew louder than the air-conditioning. She yearned to splash water on her face, stretch out her arms and legs, and strike out at the wall. Her mastery over her body had all but returned by the time Piper swiped an access card and wheeled her through the door.

"Only a few of us have these all-access cards," he confided as if to reassure her of her safety in her cell. "Me, Mariko, Joji, a couple others—so don't worry. No one's going to pounce on you in the night." *He didn't notice the hatred in Joji's eyes.* She marvelled at the young's man inability to grasp the inappropriateness of his compassion. *And yet I'm glad he's here and I hope he doesn't leave.*

Ivy's first impression of the room was of jarring whiteness. Concrete walls painted white. White ceiling. White tiled floor. A narrow white bench and a single folded white sheet. White toilet, sink, and bucket ("for bathing," Piper explained). White jumpsuit on a hook. A small white towel on the floor. Again there were no windows, only a single tube of fluorescent light and a vent through which the air-conditioning swept in with its icy breath. The sole item to break the sea of white was the black video camera near the ceiling. Its lens was fixed on the bench. If the amenities and furnishings of the VIP cell were any indication that Ivy was the recipient of preferential treatment, than she was loathe to discover how non-VIP "guests" were housed.

Unsteady and aching, Ivy rose from the wheelchair. Though her mind was willing, her knees and legs were gelatinous, and she staggered a few paces before falling forwards onto the bench. Her leather-bound fists broke her fall. Piper rushed forward and fumbled with the remaining bindings until her fingers were freed and she was able to stretch and rub her sore hands.

Piper sat at the edge of the bench. Indecision was stamped all over his youthful face. Finally, when it looked to Ivy that he was about to burst, he jumped up and began pacing the length of the small cell. "I don't mean to be rude, but I've been struggling with a question that I can't answer on my own and so I really must ask you." His words poured out in a torrent of jumbled syllables and consonants. "Why are you here?"

"Why am I here?" Ivy chuckled ironically. Once again she wondered why Mariko had seen fit to bring them together. "Why are you here?"

"I asked you first." He halted and gazed down at her with sincere eyes. Despite her general horror, Ivy was moved by Piper's earnestness. "Not many women pass through this place. And I've never been asked to leave my desk to do anything like this before, so I have to ask. Why are you here?"

Ivy shrugged. "Because I gave Joji cosmetic surgery and he didn't like it."

"You did that to his face." Piper's eyes shone disbelief. Ivy suspected she'd earned his respect. There was clearly no love lost between Piper and Joji. "How?"

"With no great difficulty," she replied and raised her hands, palms forward. "With my own two hands."

"I don't understand…" He scrunched his face up and Ivy was once again reminded of an anxious child.

"They really keep you in the dark, don't they?" *Maybe that's why you're here with me. Because they know you can't really tell me anything.* Fatigue bore down upon her. Ivy stretched her tired arms over her head and yawned.

"But how do you even know Joji?" Piper pressed on insistently. "You don't look like you travel in the same circles."

"Victor." Ivy felt the pervasive panic biting at her heels. *Where is Victor? What happens now?*

The name had barely passed Ivy's lips before Piper beamed with a sunny smile entirely incongruent with the stark white surroundings. "Victor Morgan?"

"You know him?" Ivy had difficulty controlling her excitement.

"I wanted to apprentice with Victor. He mastered every part of the sword-making process, and he's not even Japanese. I thought learning even one step would better connect me with my Japanese heritage." Piper scowled slightly as he remembered something unpleasant. "Not the most social guy in the world, though. He said I talked too much and shoved me through the door." Ivy heard Victor's gruff tenderness in Piper's words, and her crippled heart ached. *Stay focused, Merchuk. Piper's connected to the outside.*

Piper's eyes snapped to hers. "Him and you? But you're…" He smiled guiltily. "And he's so…" He grimaced. "Are you Victor's girlfriend?"

Ivy tossed the word around in her mind. 'Girlfriend' seemed such a trivial word choice when measured against the passion that had gripped Ivy when she'd clutched Victor's hand, pressed her palms against his back, and cast off the fear and anonymity that had defined her previous life. "We were one person," she managed finally. *But I don't know what Victor's thinking now.*

"So you can put in a good word for me, then?" Piper radiated an adolescent glow despite being at the end of his third decade. Ivy understood Victor's reluctance.

"I don't know if you noticed, Piper, but I'm a prisoner." Ivy motioned to the surveillance camera and leather bindings loose on the floor. "Mariko has plans for me. Do you know what they are?"

Piper shook his head. "I'm sure I'll find out soon enough." He checked his watch. "She'll wonder why I'm taking so long. I've got to go."

"Wait, Piper. I need to understand something."

"I don't know how much I'm allowed to tell you." Regret in his voice. *We're all prisoners here, even if some of us are allowed to wear expensive suits and smoke cigarettes.*

"What do you do here?"

Piper was relieved. "Me? Here? Oh, I'm the accountant."

"The accountant?" Ivy's eyes widened. "You're kidding."

"I'm the money guy. Spreadsheets. Bank accounts. Exciting stuff." Piper stood and spread his hands out apologetically. "I'm sorry, Ivy. I have to go. I'm sure I'll see you again soon." He scooped up the leather bindings, stuffed them into this jacket pocket, and pushed the wheelchair towards the door. *Don't leave me alone with myself. Keep talking.* Piper turned as if to prolong the conversation, but then his eyes fell upon Ivy seated dejectedly on her bench, and the words seemed to catch in his throat. She watched him hurriedly swipe his key card and jet from the room.

"Don't leave," Ivy whispered meekly to the empty room. *I don't know where my thoughts will take me.*

CHAPTER 12

Ivy was alone with her body, her energy flow, her fear, panic, grief. Alone with everything they couldn't withhold from her.

She stretched out on the bench and covered her face with her hands. She had dreaded these first moments of solitude, knowing full well that she would have no choice but to confront herself the moment that Piper took flight. *Not yet.* She decided to splash water over her face. The cold water revived her thirsty skin. Steam rose from her warm palms. She lapped at the tap with her tongue, became obsessed with replenishment, with cleansing, with washing away the traumas of the day. She filled the bucket with cold water, tore off her clothes, and rubbed frantically at her skin with the coarse washcloth. Her eyes and thoughts were equally wild. She sat cross-legged on the white concrete floor, dunked the washcloth in water and scrubbed her legs, chest, arms, until her skin was red and raw. *Not enough. It's not enough.* She gripped the bucket, dumped the icy water over her head, and threw the bucket against the door. And then she curled up in the puddle and wept.

She wept for Bill, who was dead because of her toxic presence in his happy home. Wept for Victor, who she loved so passionately, who owned her heart, and who had so suddenly become a stranger. Wept for her mother, who died believing that her precious Ivy, her miracle baby, would embrace life and do great things. Wept for her father, perhaps the only person to see her true self. Her sobs were heaving, angry, violent. Her salty tears mingled with the icy water. Above her, the fluorescent lights flickered. She felt nothing but grief.

Rattling at the door. Ivy bolted upright and scrambled to cover herself with her discarded clothes. A four-fingered hand appeared through a panel at the bottom of the door. The hand pushed through a protein bar and a container of apple juice before sliding the panel shut. She sat as still as a statue and implored her racing heart to pull back. Her eyes darted up to the surveillance camera, forgotten until that moment of clarity. *I have to hold on to what remains of myself. I have to keep the storms contained, or Joji and Mariko will win.* Ivy flashed to her sword, to the fiery Tomoe Gozen that Victor had delicately etched onto the tsuba. *Victor said he'd follow me into battle. I will try to be that woman.*

She rose and strolled to the locked cell door, scooped up the meagre food offerings, and tore open the protein bar wrapper with her teeth. Naked and red-eyed, her curly hair a wild halo around her head, she looked directly into the camera lens. "You cannot know my own strength," she announced defiantly. The camera gave no indication that it registered or understood her words.

As Ivy's exhaustion mounted, her resistance waned. She slipped into the white jumpsuit with no small degree of reluctance. Even though she didn't want to accept any of Mariko and Joji's offerings, Ivy couldn't bear the cold that now wracked her weary body. The jumpsuit was an American name brand, white velour—a perfect fit. She wondered if it had been specially purchased for her use, and decided that it must have been. The drugs had left a metallic taste in her mouth and she wished she had her toothbrush. She drained the apple juice container and cast wary glances at the surveillance camera—interminably present, immobile, invasive.

Ivy lay back on the bench and vowed to dodge sleep as long as was humanly possible. Joji could barge in at any moment to taunt her, rape her, bash in her skull. Ambush her under the cowardice of unconsciousness. *I don't know what kind of control Mariko has over him.* She wanted to see his mangled face as it charged towards her. The lights switched off and she was in complete darkness. Was it truly night? Was it only 24 hours since she'd last fallen asleep in Victor's arms? *He said he'd figure it out. This can't have been what he had in mind.*

Tears stung at Ivy's eyes and she clamped them shut. *Why can't I steer clear of sour thoughts?* Anger welled up inside of her, but this time the fury was self-directed. *What do I actually know and what do I only suspect?* She attempted a rational examination of the facts. Her doubt, she reasoned, sprang from several factors: Victor's unexplained absences and sad eyes. His desire to settle things with Joji. The pain of Joji and Mariko's insinuations. Joji who hated her. Mariko who probably hated her, too, or maybe hated Victor enough to goad Ivy into killing their dream. Psychological warfare as only a woman could wage it.

Her ensuing sighs were weary. *I am doomed to chase my tail.* She called the light to her palms and illuminated the blank white walls and suffocating isolation. *They can't take away my light.* There was a click in the air conditioning vent, and an unfamiliar floral scent met Ivy's nose, and darkness proved victorious.

Fragrant honeysuckle on the cool night breeze. Ivy flashed to her youth, to her mother seated in front of her bedroom mirror, anointing herself with honeysuckle perfume as Ivy watched from the doorway. A dab behind each ear. A long stroke along the collarbone. But it had been many years since those precious moments. The memory of honeysuckle had now invaded every corner of Bill's cottage. This new blend possessed an unfamiliar tinge of rot. It was not as Ivy remembered. She sought to escape its sickly sweet tentacles. The house was dark. Bill and Milo were inexplicably absent. She searched for Victor.

The clanking of swords led her outside. *Who is Victor fighting?* But when she located him on the porch steps, he was alone with his body turned away from hers and his face raised towards the night sky. The honeysuckle was now unbearable to her. Ivy wondered how she could have ever loved the fragrance. Her eyes fell upon Victor's sword. It had been discarded at his feet. Ivy was suddenly afraid.

"Victor?" She approached him timidly. His posture was slack. "What are you thinking?" She was scared to hear his words. He trembled slightly. Her heart burst with compassion and she rushed towards him and pressed her buzzing, pulsating palms against his back. Through his thin t-shirt, she felt ice. "Victor?" Her voice so soft. The honeysuckle left her lightheaded. "Hold me. Kiss me. I'm forgetting myself." He made no movement and so she closed her eyes, stepped around him, and pushed her face to his. Her lips met smooth skin. Her eyes snapped open. Victor's face was featureless. Only indentations and curves where his eyes, lips, and nose had once lived. Terror, horror. Over-arching sadness. Ivy stumbled backwards. Victor raised his hands to her shoulders and felt his way up to her neck. His hands were callused and cold. His right hand was missing a finger. Victor wrapped his nine fingers around her throat and squeezed until the world was dark and Ivy was falling, running…

…descending an endless spiral staircase. Mariko's voice was in front of her, behind her. "Give me your power. Make me as you are." The staircase narrowed with each step and closed in on Ivy until she was buried alive.

When Ivy awoke, the white room was once again bathed in fluorescent light. The wrapper for the protein bar and the empty apple juice container had disappeared, along with her yoga gear. A fresh towel was visible on the hook. A boiled egg, a muffin, and an orange juice container sat on the floor near the door. Ivy's head was heavy. Her limbs ached. The metallic taste in her mouth was stronger than ever. *They gassed me to sleep.* Ivy was startled by this realization. Mariko and Joji were exercising control over her most basic functions. She splashed water on her face and lay back on the bench, unsure as to what she was expected to do next.

Ivy retreated inside her energy. There was nothing else to occupy her time and thoughts. Ivy took this as further evidence of Mariko's cruelty. *I must not fall into complacency.* Ivy sought solace within meditation, within the whipping wind and white light. The unseen watchmen did not gas her into unconsciousness. She wondered what they made of her light and wind show, and if Piper was now a party to her unique skill set. She tried her best not to think about Victor, or Bill, but she was anchored by sadness regardless. Finally fatigued, she flung herself on the bench, and remained in that position for an eternity.

Eventually, Piper strolled through the door, much to Ivy's gratitude. He carried a brown paper shopping bag and was once again the embodiment of inappropriate jocularity. The goatee was gone.

"Mariko didn't like the goatee, Piper?" Ivy was surprised by the tinge of bitterness in her tired voice. After only a couple interactions, she'd become protective of poor Piper, as one is protective of a battered stuffed animal or a bullied playmate. *And yet I am the one in the prison cell, and he walks free.* She wondered if her compassion for Piper was rooted in objective observations and universal truth, or if this was symptomatic of the beginning of Stockholm Syndrome.

"She's not evil, Ivy." Again the earnestness. "She's had a tough life." Ivy recognized in Piper that chivalry, inherent in many men, to blindly protect everything that is feminine. *There's nothing quite as pathetic as misplaced self-sacrifice.* But Ivy knew she was a prisoner of war, and Mariko was her enemy, and she risked losing her sole ally if she continued to question the content of Mariko's character. *I've got to trust my instincts about Piper.* Ivy chose to err on the side of strategy and bit her tongue.

Piper fished through the brown paper bag. "I brought you a toothbrush and toothpaste and shampoo and some... under things." He blushed and laid all the items out on the bench. Unsurprisingly, everything he produced from the bag was bright white. He surveyed his wares and jumped slightly. "I almost forgot." He dug into his pocket and produced a single white pill, which he pressed into the palm of Ivy's right hand. "Mariko wants to you take this vitamin." He looked at her with expectant eyes, and she remained motionless, until she remembered her war strategy, placed the pill on her tongue, and downed it without the assistance of water. *I hope it's really a vitamin.* She stuck her tongue out to reveal her compliance and Piper smiled widely, evidently satisfied.

After this, they stood staring at each other somewhat awkwardly, as Piper had obviously concluded his sanctioned business and Ivy did not wish to be alone. Ivy decided in that moment to engage Piper in casual chitchat. *Maybe he'll spill something.* She sat down on the bench, crossed her legs, examined her fingernails, and spoke without meeting his eyes. *I can't seem too desperate for information or I'll scare him away.* "You said last night that you don't see a lot of women here..."

Apparently this was all Ivy needed to say to unleash the floodgates. "Oh, no, we definitely don't house women here, or even really see them in the hallways. Sometimes they bus in for events, but usually there's just Yayoi. You met her in the hospital, and Mariko, who... well, you know her, too, but otherwise the women who, um, work for the organization are in the city."

So we're not in the city. "So who does pass through here? Where is here?" Ivy tried her best to sound vaguely uninterested, as if she and Piper were conversing only to wile away the hours in some distant café and she did not place immeasurable importance upon the content of this conversation.

Within seconds, Ivy realized her mistake. She had not given Piper enough credit. He shifted nervously. His eyes darted up to the security camera. "I can't tell you that." His pupils were large. "Please don't ask me anything."

Ivy nodded, but was suddenly struck by a bolt of desperation.

"Is Victor Morgan here? Is Victor in one of the other cells?"

Would I feel him if he was near? I don't feel him now.

Piper's eyes fell to the floor. "I haven't seen Victor here. I don't know where he is." He appeared crestfallen. "Mariko said that you'll be working soon, so rest while you can. And don't forget to eat." His voice was mechanical.

Piper departed from the cell without so much as another glance towards Ivy, and she wondered if she had blown it, if his words could even be believed, and if he carried the last of her hope with him out the door.

CHAPTER 13

A firm hand on her shoulder yanked Ivy out of sleep. She fought the fog of fatigue and wrenched open her eyelids. The harsh fluorescent lighting stung at her pupils. Piper and a glum goon stared back at her.

Immediately Ivy bolted upright. *Something is changing.* The goon kept his hand on the hilt of his sheathed sword. Ivy was suddenly defensive. *They are the animals, and yet they treat me as if I'm the dangerous one.* She met the guard's gaze with a ferocious one of her own. She'd never before made such an expression. *If I am to die, let it be by one of Victor's swords.*

"Sorry to wake you before morning, Ivy." Piper produced a pair of spotless white sneakers from a brown shopping bag. Ivy hesitated. *Where are these shoes going to take me? Am I walking to my death?* Her alert eyes flew up to Piper's. Time slowed. Ivy wondered if Piper could hear her doubt.

"Enough stalling, bitch." The guard licked his lips. It was clear that a confrontation would give him much pleasure. "Put on the fucking shoes. You think you're so important that people are gonna wait for you?"

Ivy was unsurprised that the shoes were a perfect fit. Piper must have been charged with the responsibility of procuring her jumpsuit, too. The realization left her slightly scornful. *He is complicit in this. I am looking for friends where I have none.* Her scorn lasted no more than three seconds.

Ivy stood, and the goon moved to cuff her. Piper pushed forward and installed himself between them. "No cuffs," he objected. "She won't do anything."

The guard seethed. "You've lost your mind, desk boy." His tone was jeering, and yet Ivy suspected that even the goon was somewhat floored that the desk boy was taking a stand against a burly adversary.

"Take it up with Mariko if you want." Piper tossed out his words with an air of indifference, but Ivy detected a hint of perspiration on his brow. Piper was treading out of his comfort zone. A standoff of sorts ensued between the guard, his hand on the hilt of his katana, and Piper, a wide-eyed man-child in a shiny suit, unsmiling despite the grin on his youthful face. After ten seconds, the goon grunted disgustedly. "Whatever. It's your neck if the bitch goes crazy." Piper nodded as if it was all the same to him, but Ivy glimpsed the sparkle of victory in his eyes.

The trio stepped into the corridor and began their journey. Piper and Ivy marched shoulder to shoulder while the scowling goon trailed close behind. At first glance, the world beyond door 60-A seemed unchanged. The hallway remained a cold, concrete desert. But there were no goons in the hallway to glare at Ivy or make lewd gestures. Ivy sneaked a quick peek through the narrow window of a neighbouring cell. Its interior was drastically smaller than her cell. A half-dozen white benches jutted out of the wall like bookshelves. *Where are the occupants?* Ivy shuddered and wondered again if Victor was among them.

The corridors beyond the hallway of cells were similarly deserted. The air conditioner hummed and Ivy's new sneakers squeaked on the grey concrete floor, but there were no other sounds to break the monotony. Piper remained mum, and despite several inquiring glances in his direction, Ivy failed to catch his eyes and read his unspoken thoughts. She focused instead on her buzzing palms, and on the rush of energy coursing through her limbs. *If I am a dead woman walking, I won't go gently. I won't make it easy for them. I will fight.* Their journey seemed interminable. The maze beyond her cell was much larger than Ivy remembered. She wasn't sure how to feel in this moment, and as a result carried with her an uncomfortable burden of dread, scorn, anger, and fear that sat heavy in her stomach.

Suddenly Ivy was hit with an old memory. This was not the first time she'd hoisted a toxic emotional cocktail down a long, stark corridor. It had been more than fifteen years since Ivy had suffered excessive lunchtime cruelty at the hands of her classmates. *You're so flat, you're indented. You're an ugly geek in monkey clothes. You're the Queen of the Freaks.* Back then, she'd tried to keep her cheek turned away from their incessant taunts, but one recess, as Megan—who had become the most popular girl in school—hurled insult after insult in her direction (*Your mother is an ugly slut*), Ivy reached her limit. She'd dropped her book and shoved Megan so hard that her one-time friend fell off her feet and landed in a muddy puddle. Megan's look of shock had been followed closely by crocodile tears and a gawking crowd. Ivy had been directed to the principal's office. The deserted school corridor had seemed endless. Ivy could hear the kids roughhousing and shrieking on the playground. *I didn't ask to be a loser freak, and now I'm going to be punished for it.* The principal, aware of Ivy's chronic victimhood, had chastised her lightly and permitted her to spend her lunch hours in the library for the remainder of the school term. Ivy had savoured her exile.

And it was this sour memory that played through Ivy's tormented mind as she marched to her unknown destination. *I have always been the victim.* The thought submerged her in bitterness, and in that moment she hated all the bullies—from Megan to Mariko—that had dogged her and prevented her from basking in invisibility. Suddenly Ivy felt like a wild cat. She wanted to let the rage out into the universe. Instead, she kept her inner world concealed, and walked as if she wasn't fraying at the seams.

They arrived at their destination. Ivy recognized the heavy steel door that now loomed before her. The operating room. She dropped her brave facade and spun towards Piper. "What's going on? What are you going to do to me?" She reeled backwards until her back was pressed against the opposite wall. The goon growled and lurched towards her but Piper got to her first. He gripped her arm and pulled her to the door.

"I'm asking you to trust me." Piper whispered so that the goon could not hear. "You will not be harmed."

"I'm already being harmed," Ivy retorted in anger. "I'm here against my will." Immediately the blood rushed to Piper's cheeks, and Ivy realized that her accusations were misdirected. *He's got no power here. He's just trying to make me feel better.* Ivy sighed and Piper relinquished his hold on her arm and ushered her through the door.

Whereas during Ivy's previous visit the operating room had been little more than a showroom, now it burst with activity, voices, groans. Five of the twelve tables were occupied by half naked men. Ivy could not yet make out their faces, but the air was electric with their pain. The bird lady was in frenzied flight between the tables and the supply cabinets, carting bandages, towels, and bags of fluid from patient to patient. She wore the same Mickey Mouse t-shirt. No surgical mask or latex gloves. She alone tended the men. She looked directly at Ivy but her face registered no recognition. Almost against her better judgment, Ivy inched a few feet into the room. She nearly slipped and grasped at Piper to steady herself. The floor was an uninterrupted ocean of blood. Her new sneakers were no longer white.

A wounded man emitted a boar-like shriek from atop the table closest to the door. A geyser of blood sprang from his abdomen. The bird scrambled to stem the geyser with towels and clamps. Her efforts did little to hinder the flow, and Ivy wondered how much more blood the man could afford to lose. His face was bloodless. He was already a ghost.

The air conditioning was on full blast, but still the room was stifling. Ivy wretched at the rot, pain, vomit, and the realization that Mariko expected her to heal these men. And she knew that she would. *I will always choose life.* It was the definitive answer to what had once been a gnawing hypothetical.

Ivy's eyes adjusted to the dim lighting and she spotted Mariko across the room in front of one of the green curtains. Waiting impatiently. Her eyes fell on Ivy and she smiled. She sailed across the bloody puddles with ease, stopped four feet short of Ivy and Piper, and tapped her foot. The ball of her stiletto hit the blood puddle and made a slapping sound that reminded Ivy of summer rain.

Ivy could barely contain her rage. "What happened to these men?"

Mariko waved her hand in the air. "Enough talking, young one." She seemed to revel in her condescension. The spectacle of the butchered man writhing before her did not phase her. She produced a long cigarette from her jade case and lit up. A chunk of burning ash floated down to the blood puddle. "Earn your keep." Ivy stared. She was past sadness, past regret, past mourning. There was only anger. She shook her head, even though she knew she would not deny these men their access to her regenerative energy.

Mariko seemed to see past Ivy's act of defiance and snorted through her pinched nostrils. "Spare me the dramatics." Her tone was dismissive and amused. "What happens if he dies because of your unwillingness to cooperate? Will you have proved your point? Will you be able to live with the knowledge that you cost a"—she sniffed mockingly—"poor, wounded man his life?" Mariko giggled and blew a smoke ring. Over the course of her diatribe, the goon who had accompanied Ivy to the hospital had wandered over and now stood by the wounded man's dirty feet. His hand rested on his sword. *Healing under the threat of death. I should have taken the offers of money in Tumblestone.* Ivy managed a bitter laugh, much to Mariko's displeasure, and turned her attention to the bloody mess on the operating table.

"If you want me to do this, give me some space." Ivy surprised herself with the coldness of her tone, and was further surprised when Mariko stepped back a few paces.

The young man with the geyser wound was not Japanese. His dark features suggested Eastern European origins, and when Ivy asked him for his name, he sputtered in a guttural language she did not recognize. The man was shoeless and shirtless, clothed only in bloodied white linen pants that ended just above the knee. His arms were riddled with old needle marks, his wrists strapped to the table, as Ivy's had been a couple days previous. The number 9 had been branded onto his shoulder. He was drenched in sweat, and past the point of feeling his pain. His bloodshot eyes were glassy and glazed. His wounds spoke of unrestrained violence. Long slashes across his abdomen and forearms. A gash on his cheek. Chunks of flesh missing from his shoulder. His attacker had been relentless. In her previous life, the sight of such wounds would have left Ivy horrified and changed. She mourned the loss of her sensitivity.

"What happened to you?" Ivy grasped the man's wrist. His groans were sinking deeper and deeper into his chest. She felt the echo of his calls and knew he was losing his battle. Ivy placed her hands upon the man's torn chest and called out to the universe.

The healing of the geyser man was arduous. The man's internal organs had suffered untold traumas. His spleen had been sliced and diced like a tomato. The wounds were straight lines and clean cuts. Ivy did not know the names of all the organs that she mended—anatomy had only been of interest in her previous life when she thought it might hold the key to the secrets of her buzzing palms—but the sheer volume of healing energy required to pull the young man back from the edge of death told her that his wounds had not been sustained under normal street-fighting conditions. Even at the conclusion of the healing, the colour had not yet fully returned to the man's face, though his organs were resuscitated and his skin had grown over the geyser. Ivy was left drenched in sweat and gasping for air.

If Mariko was impressed by Ivy's wind and light show, it did not register on her painted face. Ivy gripped the edge of the table where the healed man now slept blissfully, and asked the bird lady for a glass of water. But before she even had a chance to drain the glass, Mariko pushed her to the next table. "There are other men." Suddenly Ivy saw herself through Mariko's eyes: as the latest high-tech acquisition, to be scrutinized during its trial run.

The four consecutive healings were much like the first. The men were Filipino, European, Chinese, Malaysian. These were not Joji and Mariko's run of the mill goons. They had strong hands, jagged shoulders, and sharp stomachs. All were muscular, all pale, all shaved, all branded with numbers as the first man had been. Needle marks covered their arms. Their organs were torn. Their limbs were slashed. One man had lost two fingers, and Ivy could do little for him but send the skin cells regenerating over the stumps. Each healing took approximately thirty minutes—the longest she'd ever performed—and left her shivering, sore, thirsty, and drenched in blood. The wounds demanded so much of Ivy's strength that at several intense junctures she nearly lost herself to the white light. This was the first time in Ivy's life that she had been called upon to perform consecutive healings and despite the terror of the situation, she was staggered by the depth of her reserves. *There is no limit to the energy passing through me.* And she wondered if there were more people coming, if Mariko and Joji intended to keep her working through the night.

Piper was always nearby with fear and awe stamped all over his youthful face. Ivy wasn't sure what he was waiting for, but his presence reassured her. As for the bird, she remained in the background, pumping the healed men full of drugs, and ready with a glass of water for Ivy between healings. Her expression was impassive.

After five healings, Ivy was disconnected from her intellect and fuelled by instinct alone. Mariko shoved her to the final table. The man had been wheeled in moments before, accompanied by a scowling Joji and a fresh pack of goons. "He's the most talented of the lot," Mariko barked, as if this cryptic statement would make a difference to Ivy. *They're all the same now. Just flesh and bones and pain.* Ivy placed her hands above the man's heart without even looking into his face and commanded the energy to bore down upon her, through her, and into the wounded man. But she hit a brick wall. She couldn't peer inside him. She couldn't see the indignities that had been waged against his muscles, nerves, organs, and tissue, couldn't reach beyond her own light and frenzied energy. She flailed, and the energy built up in her fingers, chest, heart, and throat, but still it had nowhere to go. She met a barrier of complete darkness. Finally her brain registered the fact that her fingers were pressed against ice. Her eyes snapped open, and the light and wind died down at once. She stared into the unseeing eyes of a corpse. He was Japanese. His irises were cloudy. His mouth was slightly open, as if his last words had died on his chapped lips.

"He's dead," she gasped as she reeled away from the table and collided with Piper. He gripped her shoulders and peered around her, horrified.

"Impossible," Mariko snapped and pushed past Ivy. She snatched up the dead man's wrist and stood perfectly still with her eyes closed. After several seconds of deep concentration, she dropped the wrist and spun to face Ivy. Her eyes were wide with indignation.

"Fix him." Mariko's directive dripped with impatience. She wiped her bloody fingers on her trouser leg.

Ivy pushed a sweat-drenched curl out of her eyes. Her knees buckled slightly. Piper held her upright. "I can't." Ivy's voice was small against the crush of fatigue. "I can't reverse death." Mariko continued to stare at her and Ivy didn't know what else she could say to shake off Mariko's disbelieving gaze. "I only know how to do what you saw me do. I'm not holding out on you." Her words sounded feeble and defensive. Weak. Ivy brought her icy fingers to her temples and pressed so hard she could see her beating heart in front of her open eyes. *I have nothing left to give them. They've taken everything and it's not good enough.*

Mariko threw back her head and screamed. It was a wail of desperation, of a train pulling back its brakes and smashing into a car parked across its tracks. She screamed for more than thirty seconds with her arms stiff at her sides and her fingers splayed out. The scream ricocheted around the operating room and left no one unscathed. Ivy cringed and slumped against Piper, who pulled her away from the epicentre. On a surgical table, a healed man shifted and moaned despite the heavy sedation. The scream ended in a choke and a flurry of motion. Mariko rushed at the table, grabbed a scalpel from a nearby instrument tray, and stabbed the dead man once, twice, three times through the heart. With each violent thrust, the corpse's heavy head bounced against the table with a thud that echoed throughout the operating room.

"Will it never end?" Mariko bellowed and fell silent. Her outburst hung in the air for a moment before evaporating. Her chest heaved and a thin line of saliva dribbled down her chin. Again her face was in Ivy's. "Next time it'll be you with a knife in your chest."

Ivy was a statue. She looked into Mariko's face and saw clown make-up, hysterics, and chaos. *I wouldn't follow her into battle.* Ivy pulled herself up to her full height. Instinct was now in full control. "End it, then. I'm ready." She stuck her chin out in defiance.

For ten seconds, Mariko's own chin quivered slightly. The quiver was barely perceptible, and Ivy was sure that she was the only witness to this involuntary facial movement. But then Mariko snorted and seemed to force out a dismissive laugh. "I'm not going to make it that easy for you."

Joji strolled over from where he'd been skulking across the room. He chuckled softly. "You said she was the key to our success. Doesn't look like a success to me." His tone was mocking. Mariko pivoted on her heel and slapped him across the face. Her force was impressive. Joji stumbled backwards and brought his four-fingered hand to his disfigured cheek. His eyes were incredulous.

"Enough out of you. All you do is cost me money." Mariko gazed down at the dead man. "We'll do this differently next time." Her voice was quiet. She wrenched the scalpel out of the man's chest. "Such a waste." It wasn't clear to whom she was speaking. A full minute of silence passed. Those around Mariko seemed to be holding their breaths. Ivy shifted her weight from leg to leg and wondered if she'd ever be allowed to rest her weary limbs, to wash, to sleep, and realized with a start that what she wanted more than anything at that very moment was to be allowed to return to cell 60-A.

Eventually, Mariko reached out for her brother. Her hand seemed limp, as if controlled by a disinterested puppet master. "Joji, it's been a long night. Let's take a drink together. Piper, take her away. We'll debrief tomorrow."

Whether it was an oversight or a reward for a job well done, Ivy couldn't be sure, but Piper alone escorted her back to her cell. Ivy marched without speaking, without replaying the events of the evening in her mind, without stewing in sadness or pain or trying to guess what Piper was thinking. Her basic needs became her single focus. *Need to wash. Need to sleep.* The return journey was a blur of grey surfaces and harsh lighting. She glanced down at her clothes. Her white jumpsuit had proved a perfect canvas for blood spatter. When they arrived at the door to her cell, Piper moved to swipe the key card but instinct drove her to grab at his wrist.

"Please. I need a shower," she said hoarsely. "I can't shower with a bucket."

Piper stared at her, hardly blinking, as if her words did not compute. Ivy noticed for the first time the dark circles under Piper's eyes. His shirt was unbuttoned and his tie loosened. He lowered his hand and nodded.

"Of course." Piper bit his lip as he seemed to consider a course of action. "You'll need to be quick." On impulse, Ivy flung her arms around his neck. Piper froze. Eventually, he raised his arms and held her awkwardly. She pulled away, looked into his face, and smiled. It was such a relief to smile. *There's decency here.* Piper's cheeks were crimson. "We don't have far to go but, as I say, you've got to hurry."

They didn't leave the hallway. Piper led Ivy to a door five steps from her own cell. Through the narrow window, Ivy spied concrete. Piper hesitated for a few seconds, as if his brain was so tired that every action required an extra push. Finally, he swiped his key card and the door swung open. "It's pretty self-explanatory in there. I'm going to seek out a towel for you. I'll be two minutes. Please hurry."

Ivy stepped into a concrete box no bigger than her cell. The door clicked shut behind her. She peeled off her shoes and clothes and surveyed the room. The concrete box was illuminated by a single fluorescent tube. Four rusty shower heads hung from the ceiling. A single drain broke the smooth surface of the floor. There were no hooks on the walls, no mirrors, no soap dispensers, no towel racks, no benches, no features encouraging comfort or rejuvenation. Only the bare bones of cold efficiency. Even in this shower room, the air conditioning system was on full blast. Ivy placed her bundle of bloody clothes on the floor against the door and cranked a rusty knob. The four shower heads sprang to life.

The water was hard and arctic, but Ivy didn't care. She watched as the blood that had dried on her neck, face, and hands mingled with the icy rain and raced towards the drain. She raked her fingers through her hair and pulled them away to discover more blood. Blood everywhere. Other people's blood. At once the events of the surreal evening bore down upon her. Through the water she again glimpsed the black shadow of death that had consumed the dead man. She hadn't saved him. Was she a murderer? Mariko and Joji were obviously murderers. But Ivy? Because of Ivy, those other men had lived through untold violence. Their appearances and wounds suggested hardship and sorrow. What was she saving them from? And for?

Ivy looked down at her feet and watched as the last of the blood, now pink from dilution, swept over her toes and disappeared down the drain. Piper's face appeared at the narrow window. Ivy sighed heavily, switched off the shower heads, and reached for the towel that Piper pushed around the door. He kept his eyes averted. Again he was allowing her a taste of dignity. Ivy wondered if the men she'd healed were ever offered such a privilege. She flashed to Mariko, wielding a scalpel and unleashing her rage on the corpse, and shuddered. She knew she was now part of something truly rotten. *Even if I'm an unwilling participant, I'm playing a role. I need to know the big picture.*

Ivy towelled off and prepared to slip back into her bloodied jumpsuit and shoes. She was clean now, but still she felt drenched in blood. In minutes, she'd be asleep. She hoped that her sleep was dreamless, but that if she did dream, that she would lose herself in Victor's tattooed arms and forget the blood and blinding white of Joji and Mariko's violent world.

CHAPTER 14

Ivy awoke dressed in a clean white jumpsuit. She spotted a boiled egg, small loaf of bread, and carton of milk in front of the door and, with much effort, pulled herself off the bench and staggered over to the food. As she ate, she struggled to focus on the fact that she couldn't remember the last time she'd eaten, and not that she had been undressed and dressed while unconscious. There was no way to know the extent of the violation. *Stay in the moment. I'm only in control of what I can control.* She grimaced at this pathetic re-writing of her training mantra, and took a big swig of milk. Wondered what time it was, what day of the week it was. Yearned for the sun on her face, damp mulch under her fingernails. Suddenly she snorted, disgusted with herself. *The second I tell myself to stay in the moment, my thoughts pull me off course. I'm my own worst enemy.* Sadly, she remembered that she hadn't dreamt about Victor. She hadn't dreamt about anything.

Ivy sat on the floor with her back against the door and glared up at the security camera. She wondered if it was always the same goons keeping track of her every movement, if they were the ones who'd poured her into the jumpsuit, if they'd seen her in action in the operating room. Again she thought of the healed men, and tasted guilt. *They're treated no better than cattle.* Organs and limbs violated by a deadly foe. Without her, there would have been six corpses, not one. And yet she could not be pleased with herself. She had not performed a good deed. The branding. The needle marks. The shaved heads. The strangled words in foreign languages. The corpse's head bouncing against the operating table. Ivy could not move past the fear that she was prolonging the slaughter. She closed her eyes and wondered what it would take for her to remain unruffled like the little bird lady in the Mickey Mouse shirt.

A new sensation. Nausea. Ivy rubbed her abdomen, suspecting that this was simply a physical manifestation of her frustration and that the feeling would soon pass, but this was more than a feeling. The milk crept back up her throat. She barely made it to the toilet bowl in time. She hugged the bowl and was surprised by the cold sweat and trembling. Two minutes passed and again she was sick. There was nothing left of the breakfast in her body. Shaking and faint, she rose, rinsed out her mouth, and splashed water on her face. She didn't have to press her hand against her forehead to know she was burning up. She collapsed onto the bench and pulled the sheet tight around her. *This is all happening so fast.* The flimsy sheet was no match for the chill. Immediately she was floating in a semi-conscious fog.

Ivy didn't encounter a soul for the rest of the day. She knew precisely when the four-fingered hand pushed the second and then the third batches of food and drink through the sliding panel, but the food remained untouched. She did not train. Piper did not visit. She did not long for Victor, or the cottage, or the sun on her face. She did not obsess over the events of the previous night. Instead, she lay on the bench and shivered, drifted in and out of consciousness, and battled wave after wave of nausea. After countless hours, the light switched off, the air conditioner released its honeysuckle poison, and Ivy was finally asleep.

When Piper arrived the next morning, Ivy was once again at the toilet bowl, struggling to keep the nausea at bay. Piper was chipper and dressed immaculately in a herringbone suit and alligator boots. He bounded into the cell already well into their conversation. "It's amazing how paperwork just piles up and then, before you know it, you have a week's worth of work to plough through and only one day to do it. So I'm sorry I didn't come and visit you yesterday." Soon his brain seemed to register the fact that Ivy was not paying him much attention. In an instant Piper was crouching beside her and rubbing her shoulders. His touch was awkward, as if he didn't quite know what he was doing but felt he had to offer comfort regardless. "Are you sick?" Ivy laughed hoarsely and hoisted herself up onto the bench.

"I had a rough day," Ivy said as she stretched her arms toward the ceiling. Her limbs and abdomen were sore, but the fever had passed with the night. "I think my body is playing catch-up. I've never performed five healings in a row. It must have taken its toll on my system."

As she spoke, Ivy paid special attention to Piper's face. Over the course of their brief acquaintance, Piper had never once alluded to her unique skill set. Before she had only suspected that he knew what she could do, but now there was no doubt. He'd had a front row seat. *Even here, even in this crazy world, I must have made an impression.*

Piper did not disappoint. "I keep replaying it in my mind: the way the wind swept around you and the light poured from your body and the way the wounds just healed over. It was magical." He spoke with much reverence, and was increasingly breathless with each word. "But how did it happen? How does it work? Is it something you learned? Is it from your family?"

Ivy called the light to her hands. "It's just a part of who I am." The orbs danced on her palms. Piper's eyes widened, transfixed. For a moment, she took some pleasure in his child-like amazement, but then felt bitterness. "And it's the reason I'm a prisoner." Suddenly she snuffed out the lights, and Piper recoiled as if he had been slapped.

"Well, you were amazing to watch." He dug into his pocket and produced a pill. "Another vitamin from Mariko. She really wants to make sure you're healthy. Your work means a lot to her. You'll be working again soon."

Ivy reached for the pill and grabbed Piper's wrist. "Who were those men, Piper?" She spoke in whispers. Her questions were not meant for the security camera. Piper bristled and shifted his weight from leg to leg. "What's going on here? What am I a part of now?"

Piper's hushed reply was unexpected. "Oh Ivy, you'll find out soon enough, and then you'll wish you could go back to knowing nothing. I wish I could forget so much of what I've seen here. The things I see when I close my eyes keep me up at night." Gently, Piper pulled his wrist from her fingers, turned on his alligator heel, and left Ivy alone with her nausea and anxiety.

Long days of isolation followed. The sickness subsided but the boredom began to take its toll. Ivy lay on the bench, a lethargic lump with no appetite or drive to rise. Training provided no solace. *I'm here because I'm a freak.* Her thoughts swirled around Victor, around Bill, and all the unknowns of her past life. The unanswered questions kept her pinned to the bench. *Did Bill survive? What is Victor's role in this? Did he really call Mariko?* And still, despite the possibility of betrayal, she yearned for Victor. Her despairing heart left her restless in her skin. She welcomed the telltale click in the ventilation system that signalled a reprieve from her depression. By the third day of solitary confinement, the despair, guilt, and frustration were so repetitive that Ivy surprised herself when her mind touched on the subject of escape.

Escape. The word was invigorating. In an instant Ivy was upright and pacing the cell.

To date, Ivy had not considered escape a viable option. There were too many barriers between herself and freedom. Too many guards and guns and swords and cameras. Guiltily, Ivy realized that there was a small part of her that had expected Victor to swoop in and rescue her. *Victor isn't coming for you, sweetheart.* She cringed, shook her head, thought of the security camera, and fancied that at that moment she must look a little mad. At this thought she barked out a laugh and continued walking the length of the room, with palms buzzing.

Ivy halted in her tracks and examined her palms. Her attack on Joji had sent him scurrying. That had been the only time she'd wounded someone with her healing hands, and she doubted she could call forth that dark, primal energy again. *Victor was dying.* She didn't know if she wanted to weaponize her hands. *It's not who I am.* She dropped her hands, slumped down on the bench, and sighed heavily.

What am I good at? Soon Ivy was bemoaning her apparent lack of any skills that would be useful in an escape. *I'm good at being a victim.* She considered throwing her head back and screaming as Mariko had done in the operating room. *Will it never end?* And when she thought of Mariko, she thought of Piper, of his hands moving her away from Mariko's tantrum, and she knew that her strange friendship with the chatty desk boy was the key to any successful dash for freedom.

As if on cue, Piper stepped through the door. "You haven't been eating," he said sternly without saying hello. "You're not keeping your strength up." Energized by his sudden appearance, Ivy opened her mouth to say something light-hearted, but then she noted the stress on

Piper's face, and the complete lack of joviality, and she rose from the bench and faced him.

"What's wrong, Piper?" Panic spread across Ivy's shoulders.

Piper produced a pair of handcuffs from his jacket pocket. "We're going on a long walk." Piper's clipped delivery betrayed his anxiety. "I've been asked to handcuff myself to you." He snapped one end of the handcuffs onto his left wrist, and the other onto Ivy, and then turned towards the door.

"Piper," Ivy began. Her feet were rooted in place.

Quick as lightning, Piper's lips were close to her ear. "I wish I didn't have to take you where we're going." His words were a tumble of whispers. "I hate it there. I'm dragging you into a nightmare. But we'll be inseparable"—he raised his wrist, and Ivy's by extension—"so you'll be alright." He stepped back. There was something jarring in Piper's discomfort, and nothing else Ivy could do but pull on her white sneakers and follow him out the door.

They raced down the empty corridors. Piper was distracted, silent, brooding, and for the first time in his presence, Ivy was scared of him. That they were cuffed to each other gave her some comfort. They would not be easily separated. But he'd seen so much, and had managed to get used to so much, and where he was taking her had shaken even him, this simple little office boy who only saw the good in those around him. Piper's fear loomed large before her.

They sailed past the operating room and into a hallway that required Piper to pause and swipe his key card for entry. There was only one other door off this new corridor, located at the far end of a long stretch of grey concrete. Between Ivy and Piper and this door sat a thick-necked goon on a stool. As they approached, the goon leapt to his feet and reached for his sword.

"Don't give me any grief." Piper was irritable. Another deviation from the Piper that Ivy thought she knew. "I know you were told that we'd be coming through."

"Doesn't mean I have to like it." The goon smirked, and ogled Ivy's breasts. Quickly she raised her free arm to block her chest and flashed to the faceless ghosts that invaded her room in the night and handled her like a rag doll.

Piper strode forward and pushed his face right into the goon's.

"Let us pass or I'll make sure you'll suffer for the delay." Suddenly Ivy was less afraid.

The goon snorted. "Easy, little man. As if I want to waste my time on you." Still, he stepped aside and jabbed a stubby finger against a button on the wall. The door slid open and Ivy's pulse quickened as Piper pulled her past the goon and into the illuminated interior of an elevator.

The elevator was old. A dirty carpet underfoot. A single bulb overhead. The walls were spattered with what Ivy assumed was dried blood. The panel indicated three levels: B2 (where they stepped onto the elevator), B1, and M. Piper hit the M button and the elevator began a shaky ascent.

With an apologetic smile, Piper produced a long, white scarf from his pocket. "I've got to blindfold you. I'm sorry." Ivy did not resist. A blindfold was insignificant when compared with all the other indignities she'd already suffered. By the time the elevator arrived at M level, Ivy was completely reliant on her desk boy.

Piper led Ivy from the elevator into a damp room and halted in his tracks. Ivy held tight to his arm. Her palms buzzed when her ears picked up the sound of rain pounding against a low metal roof overhead. A window was open and the chaos and fury of the storm felt so near. A cold rush of maritime air met Ivy's skin and she struggled to calculate how long she'd been removed from Mother Nature's reach.

They were not alone. "You're late." The voice of the unseen man was hoarse. A chair scraped against a wooden floor. The stranger lumbered heavily towards him. "Fifteen minutes late." Ivy noted his irritation with a burst of indignation of her own.

"We're here now." Again Piper's voice held an edge. The unseen man grunted and Piper led Ivy through another door, into the storm, and piled her into the backseat of a car.

The anonymous driver drove slowly over what felt and sounded like gravel. Ivy sat close to Piper in the backseat. Raindrops drummed the roof of the car like thousands of muted gunshots. The windows were down slightly and, through the rain and thunder, Ivy's straining ears caught the cries of seagulls. A spray of rain landed on her face, and she thrilled at this replenishment. Beside her, Piper radiated anxiety. His thoughts were evidently on their destination.

Ivy shifted nervously on the leather seat and tried to focus on the new insights she'd gained into the circumstances of her captivity. *I'm definitely underground. I'm probably on the waterfront. Elevator access. There's one guard at the bottom, and one at the top.* Despite the obvious gaps, this was more information than she'd previously possessed, and she was exhilarated.

The surface under the car smoothed out and the rain ceased. They were indoors. The car rolled to a stop. The journey had lasted no longer than ten minutes. Through the open window Ivy heard a cacophony of indistinct male voices that seemed to echo through a large space. There were rhythmic thuds, and the sound of heavy machinery beeping and heaving. As Piper awkwardly attempted to pull her from of the car, a wave of panic bore down upon her and she dug her feet into the floor.

"Piper, where are we? What's going to happen? Why are you so afraid?" Her desperation burned bright behind her closed eyelids.

Ivy heard the driver walking around the car towards them. "Not now, Ivy." Piper whispered through clenched teeth. "Trust me." It was hardly enough but then Ivy realized that fear was making Piper more protective of her. He would not throw her to the wolves. She rose from the car, felt concrete under her sneakers and took a deep breath. Her lungs filled with cold, stale air. *What have you got in store for me now, Mariko?*

Cigarette smoke reached her nose. "What now, boss?" Blatant mocking in the driver's voice.

"You wait for us." Piper was curt. "No hospital runs tonight. We're trying something new."

CHAPTER 15

"Another hallway?" Ivy was almost indignant. They were alone. They'd passed through several doors before the voices and machinery were behind them and Piper had stopped and removed the blindfold. The big reveal had revealed only more of what she'd left underground. Grey concrete floors and walls. Fluorescent light and recycled air. Ivy guessed their final destination lay on the other side of the large steel door at the far end of the corridor. "I'd be disappointed if I wasn't so terrified."

"I'll be with you every second." Piper's eyes were distant. Again he seemed lumbered down with dread, and again Ivy wondered what kept him in Joji and Mariko's hellish world.

"You're stalling." Ivy's nerves were as taut as violin strings. She needed a resolution.

"We'll be there in two minutes." Piper's eyes were on his feet.

"Tell me where we're going."

Piper closed his eyes and brought his free hand to his forehead. "Into my nightmare."

"I know you want to protect me, but you're scaring me to death." Ivy slumped against the wall, frustrated. "I'm so tired of this."

For at least a minute, neither spoke. Ivy felt the dampness invade her bones and wondered if Piper would be reprimanded for the delay. Perhaps he was cracking under the pressure of his work. She glanced in his direction. He seemed to be waging a vicious war behind his forehead. *Don't go crazy on me, Piper. I can't escape without your help.*

"I was the banker for all of Joji's games," Piper blurted out after an eternity. The uncharacteristic bitterness in his tone caught Ivy off guard. "I worked for a tax firm during the day but at night I worked for Joji. It was just another freelance job, and I liked it because I could observe numbers at play. I've never been good with people but numbers, they're like music to me." He smiled slightly and cocked his head as if he could hear the music. Ivy thought of her books. "It got to the point where I couldn't watch from the sidelines anymore. I started gambling. With gambling, there are so many probabilities, so many ways it could all play out. It was intoxicating." Piper began to laugh bitterly and his wide, crazy eyes snapped up to Ivy's. "In the beginning, I won all the time, but then I started to lose, and I kept losing. I was in a hole. My debt was more than I could ever pay off. And my shame..." His voice was rich with self-loathing. "That's when I met Mariko and she said she'd wipe out my debt if I came to work for her full-time."

Ivy knew she was the first person on Earth to hear Piper's story. "That seems to be the way they recruit people," she began when it appeared that Piper expected her to say something. "Victor told me..."

Piper waved his free hand in protest. "If I hadn't owed all that money, I would never have been a part of this. Never." He practically spat out his words. *He's apologizing.* "But I'm part of it now and I can't leave. I'm tainted, and I wish I wasn't. I want you to understand that, you more than anyone, before you see the cutting room."

Piper hung his head and began a mournful march towards the steel door. Ivy, chained to his wrist, followed suit with her lips clamped shut. She knew whatever she might say—that she understood his self-hatred, that none of this nightmare was his fault, that the bait-and-switch was classic Mariko—would fall on deaf ears, locked as Piper was into his skewed self-perception.

But there was another reason for Ivy's silence. With each heavy step towards the end of the corridor, a white-hot dread was building up in her chest. She was desperate to see behind the closed door. And desperate to run screaming in the opposite direction. *What happens in a cutting room?* The question sent shivers racing up and down Ivy's arms, legs, spine. Piper gave her one last anxious look, swiped his key card, and, as gently as possible, led her into the cutting room.

The air was thick with cigar smoke. Ivy could make out little else but lights high overhead and a stack of crates a few feet in front of her face. The door clicked shut behind them as they peeked over the crates and Joji and Mariko's surreal world snapped into focus.

An arena. Perhaps at one time it had been a factory or a warehouse—there were rusted pulleys dangling from the high ceiling—but now it was a crude arena illuminated by bright spotlights. At the centre of the floor was a large rectangular platform surrounded by a ten-foot high chain link fence. A cage. Cameras pointed into the cage from its kitty corners, their images broadcast onto giant screens suspended above the spectators. At the moment, the cage was empty, and so the screens broadcast the words "The Cutting Room," which had been painted in thick red letters onto the white surface of the cage floor.

Ivy's heart caught in her throat when her eyes fell upon two smaller cages. Each cage housed twelve half-naked young men. *Holding pens.* White linen pants, shaved heads, shoulders branded with numbers. The men—some were little more than teenagers—sat on benches with their faces forward. Jittery. Wild-eyed. One teen muttered to himself with his lips in constant motion. Many of the bodies displayed patchworks of stitches at various stages of healing. *Five of those men aren't strangers to me.*

Looming high above the assortment of cages were bleachers populated by hundreds of suit-wearing, cigar-chomping men. Peering in closer, Ivy noted racial divides—Chinese, Japanese, Nordic—and blatant displays of decadence and wealth. Smiling women in body-hugging gowns sauntered up and down the aisles, distributing cigars, caviar, and flutes of champagne. Officious types in cheap suits scurried from row to row, conversing with the spectators, scribbling in notebooks and collecting money. The spectators consulted their programs, pinched and fondled the smiling women, laughed loudly, and checked their watches. It could have been fight night in Las Vegas had it not been for the abundance of sword-toting goons patrolling the perimeter of the bleachers and snarling at the young men in the cages.

Joji lounged on a lush velvet couch that had been hauled onto a raised dais. A place of honour. He wore huge sunglasses. A large gong sat on the ground beside him. Ivy searched the crowd for Mariko and finally spotted her in the shadows on the far side of the arena. She was dressed in a leopard print suit and leaned against the wall, surrounded by an air of impatient, simmering power. With a start, Ivy realized that Mariko's eyes were locked on her. Piper waved in her direction, and Mariko raised her painted eyebrows before turning her attention to the ring.

The public address system crackled and a hush fell over the jubilant crowd. "Welcome to the Cutting Room." Joji stood tall and proud on the dais with a wireless microphone in his four-fingered hand. "I hope you've all placed your bets. You're in for a wild night of the bloodiest swordplay you'll find anywhere on the planet." The crowd roared with vicious enthusiasm.

Ivy felt her knees give way. At that moment all the pieces of Mariko's sick puzzle fell into place. *Those boys butcher each other for sport.* Her original suspicions had been justified. She'd healed Mariko's men only to send them out for slaughter all over again. There was no satisfaction in being correct.

"This is insane, Piper." Two men had been plucked from the holding pens by a pack of well-armed goons and were being pushed towards the cage. Each fighter was handed a simple unsheathed sword before being shoved up a gangplank and through the cage door. The fighters waited in opposite corners of the rectangle with their swords grasped in their hands. The slighter of the two seemed unsteady on his feet. A beefy goon stood between the fighters. Ivy's eyes flew up to the video feed. A close-up of the larger fighter filled the giant screens. It was her first patient. Number 9. His glassy eyes were filled with fury. He spat, and twitched, and waved the sword above his head. The pink scar on his abdomen shone under the hot lights. Ivy knew there was anguish beneath the drugs and delirium.

"This first battle is going to be epic, folks." Ivy bristled at the smarminess of Joji's amplified words. "From the home team is Sergei from Chechnya. Number 9 on your score cards. Fifteen wins, two losses. You might remember that Sergei laughs like a hyena when he slices into his opponents. He might not be laughing after newcomer Wen Li from Jiang Chen's team is finished with him." Here Joji bowed deeply to a fat Chinese man in a flashy blue suit sitting in the bleachers. Jiang Chen raised his champagne glass in Joji's direction and took a big swig. His bulbous, diamond-encrusted pinkie ring caught the spotlight.

The face of the Chinese fighter filled the screen. Like Sergei, he was young and thin and glassy-eyed. Unlike Sergei, Wen Li's fear was stamped all over his pale face. Ivy felt tears on her cheeks. *There's no way this is going to end without bloodshed.*

The goon in the ring pulled a microphone out of his back pocket. "You animals know the rules," he barked out with a dramatic flourish. He clearly loved the spotlight. "There'll be three, three-minute rounds. The first one to pierce his opponent through the belt zone wins the match." With one last snarl, the goon strode out of the ring. The cage door slammed shut behind him. The expectant crowd fell silent.

Joji struck the gong. "Fighters, begin!" Ivy felt the vibrations of the gong in her gut as the fighters began to circle each other. Sergei and Wen Li locked eyes. All their aggression, all their anger, all their fear and hatred was focused on their opponent. Their ferocity grew with each slow step.

"These men are slaves," Ivy seethed through clenched teeth. "They're forced to fight so that these rich men can get even richer off their blood. It's sick. It's…" She grasped for words that would accurately illustrate her horror, and found none. Piper remained mum. Now she understood his pre-fight explanation. She was preaching to the choir.

Sergei was the first to make a decisive move. He slammed his sword down over Wen Li like a hammer. Wen Li blocked Sergei with a resounding clank and a flash of sparks and the match was in full swing. The fighters parried the length of the rectangle, their limbs and swords in continuous motion. Sergei swung and thrust his sword at Wen Li, who succeeded at meeting Sergei's assault with blocks of his own. Their movements were fast and frantic, but lacked Victor's razor-sharp refinement. Ivy watched their faces on the giant monitors. Sergei's expression was mocking. He threw words at Wen Li that were not picked up by any microphone. Sweat ran down their faces and backs. Wen Li's eyes were desperate. He did not initiate any thrusts or swings. Sergei was in complete control of the match.

"Less than thirty seconds on the clock." Joji's hushed voice filled the arena. "Will this match end in the first round?"

Wen Li's back was now pressed against the cage. He was shaking uncontrollably. His sword was at his side with its tip on the floor. His eyes shone bright with terror. A cowering animal with no hope for escape. The newcomer had given up. On the far side of the cage, Sergei bounced from foot to foot and smiled maniacally in the face of Wen Li's horror. And suddenly, Sergei threw his head back and laughed with his entire body. A bone-chilling cackle. Wen Li responded with a bellowed string of indecipherable Chinese words as Sergei charged towards him and ran his sword several inches into his abdomen.

Wen Li dropped his sword and crumpled into a heap. Blood poured from the gaping wound. Sergei loomed over him with his sword in his hand. Sergei's mocking was replaced first with confusion, then vacancy. The spectators erupted into cheers and applause at the very moment Wen Li began to wail.

"Sergei does it again!" Joji proclaimed triumphantly. Bass-heavy electronic music filled the arena. The spectators would no longer have to bear the disturbing sounds of Wen Li's suffering. "Match to Sergei in the first round!"

Five goons entered the ring. One scooped up the swords. Another grabbed Sergei by the shoulders and shoved him back into the holding pen. Two goons threw towels over Wen Li and hauled him out of the ring and through a service door at the far side of the arena. The last goon mopped up the blood.

"Five minutes until the next fight, gentlemen. Filipino versus Ukrainian. You won't want to miss it." Joji switched off the microphone, drained a glass of champagne, and unfurled a self-satisfied smirk.

By now, Ivy was trembling with fury. *If I can't stop the fighting, at least I can ease the pain.* She spun towards Piper, who examined his shoes. "Piper, where do we go to heal Wen Li?"

Finally, Piper met Ivy's gaze. His eyes were filled with tears. He shook his head. Ivy realized why she had been brought here, why there were faces in the holding pens that she did not recognize. Mariko was only interested in saving the fighters that she owned, and Mariko did not own Wen Li.

Ivy felt a sharp poke in her shoulder. "Into the hallway." Mariko had slunk up behind them during the match. Her eyes were dancing. Piper and Ivy followed her out of the shadows and back into the harsh fluorescence of the corridor. Ivy felt Piper scrambling to steady himself.

"So Ivy, what do you think of our humble little league?" Mariko batted her fake eyelashes. It was clear to Ivy that Mariko had been looking forward to Ivy's disgust.

Ivy was ready for a showdown. "You are one sick bitch."

"Thank you so much. However, for once I have to give the credit to

Joji." She took a long drag from her cigarette and exhaled slowly. The smoke hung in the air between them. "Extreme sword-fighting was his idea. This league is one of a kind. We're very profitable, as Piper can attest." Piper cringed.

"Those men are slaves." Ivy's cheeks burned hot from indignation.

Mariko smiled coyly. "Slave is such a harsh term, don't you think? We feed them and house them. Most of them were dirt-poor before we found them: farmers, factory workers, scum bags. Now they are ruthless warriors. I'd say that's a step up in the world."

"Can they leave if they want to?"

"Leave? Heavens, no. When they start to weaken, we either trade them to another team or they under perform in the ring and…well, nature takes its course." *She might as well be talking about stocks or real estate.*

"You're a murderer. Men die because of you." Ivy knew that her accusations were unlikely to rattle her cat-like captor. All the same, it gave her some satisfaction to give voice to her horror.

"Well, it's not the preferred outcome. But that's why you're here: to minimize the losses."

"To protect your investments. And how do you explain…"

Mariko tossed her cigarette onto the concrete floor and ground it with the ball of her stiletto-clad foot. "I don't owe you any explanations. Piper, I expected better results from your supervision." She checked her watch. Diamond-encrusted. *Paid for with blood money.* "Should any of our men be injured, they'll be escorted into this corridor and you'll do your thing. Hopefully we won't lose any this time."

Ivy opened her mouth to expound upon her disgust, but Piper grabbed her arm and shook his head. She saw the conflict in his eyes and decided to bite her tongue. Mariko noted this exchange with some amusement. "Very good, Piper," she purred over her shoulder as she headed back into the arena. "Maybe you'll end up growing a pair after all."

One by one, the injured men were paraded into the hallway. Those that were conscious arrived still in fight mode with their pulses careening out of control, their pupils dilated, and their bodies rigid and defensive. Sergei had been lucky to win his match unscathed. He was to be the only one. The winners who passed through Ivy's makeshift hospital bore ghastly gashes and stab wounds. As for the losers, they teetered on the edge of death, and from the centre of her wind and light storm, Ivy struggled to pull them back from the darkness.

Ivy knelt in front of a slight Filipino man slumped over in a wheelchair. His slashed forearms bled profusely all over Ivy, the concrete floor, himself. The losing blow had been dealt to his abdomen. His clammy skin was covered with fading scars, torn stitches, and needle marks. His eyes were clenched shut. He mumbled and groaned in his mother tongue. He couldn't be more than sixteen-years-old. "I'm here to help you," Ivy cooed gently. The boy's eyes snapped open to reveal unadulterated horror. Ivy recoiled and quickly called the healing energy to her hands.

Boisterous cheers and Joji's sleazy announcements poured in from the arena. "That sure was a bloody fight, folks. No one cuts like the Malaysians." Ivy came to loathe the repetitive bass line of the electronic music, which signalled the end of a match and the appearance of another bloodied man in the corridor. She tried not to think about the battered men who were not receiving her special care.

Of the eleven wounded young men who received healings that night, four were return customers. Ivy could barely look into the faces of these men and was grateful when they fell unconscious. *Once again I'm patching them up and sending them back to Hell.* But she could not refuse them care, nor was she sorry when the bird lady arrived to pump them full of sedatives and wheel them away. Their departure meant Ivy didn't have to see her guilt in their pained faces.

Ivy remained chained to Piper throughout the healings, which presented complications beyond limited mobility. After the first healing, Ivy caught Piper rubbing his wrist.

"You're burnt," she gasped. Piper's skin was peeling off where the metal cut into his wrist.

"I'm sure it's nothing you can't fix," Piper replied lightly. He glanced towards the bird lady, who at that moment was jabbing a needle into the arm of the healed man, and lowered his voice. "I'm not allowed to remove the handcuffs until we're back underground. There are too many visitors in the arena. I'm sorry." Ivy sighed. *Between the swords, the guns, and the testosterone, I'd have no chance of escape anyway.* He leaned in closer and produced a wide smile that seemed obscene given the copious amounts of spilled blood under his shoes. "I'm feeling something else. Like the sun is shining on me. It's the most amazing sensation. Thank you." Ivy could only shrug. The sensation was Piper's alone.

Finally, the men stopped arriving. The crowds stopped cheering. Hours had passed since Ivy's first glimpse of the Cutting Room, and she was thirsty, cold, and spent. *Finally, I feel nothing.* Piper patted her arm consolingly and pulled the wrinkled blindfold from his pocket. He seemed fatigued but calmer than he'd been before and during his confession. She wondered if exposure to her healing energy had managed to soothe Piper's emotional wounds, or if Mariko's work was permanent. This time, he too was spattered with blood.

Back in the car, the windows were still rolled down. The rain had ceased. The scent of ozone was heavy on the cool breeze. Ivy sensed sunlight through the blindfold and revelled in the morning cries of the seabirds. *The world moves on without me.*

CHAPTER 16

Despite the ongoing horror of her existence, Ivy began to adhere to a routine. She woke, stretched, ate, played with her energy, and waited for Piper. Piper did not always visit, but when he did, he invariably brought her a vitamin and a conversation. His visits were never longer than ten minutes, but Ivy dug in her heels and managed to savour every second. Their chats were Ivy's only interaction with the world beyond her cell. Her favourite subject was Piper himself.

Ivy learned that Piper's mother was Scottish and his father was Japanese, and that he felt unwanted by both cultures. Too uncomfortably Asian for the Scots, too diluted for full-blooded Japanese. He'd grown up in a fishing village on the Sunshine Coast and high-tailed it to Vancouver as soon as he was old enough to drive. His parents had been killed in a car accident shortly after he'd started working for Mariko and Joji. He had no siblings, but he doted on a canary named Esther and a black cat named Stanley. He spent eighteen hours underground every day. He dreamed of going to Japan and riding the bullet train to Kyoto, where his father's people had once sold prayer beads at the gates to the Golden Temple.

Ivy was hungry for stimulation, and Piper's descriptions were so dense with colour that she could actually see the bare walls of his small apartment, the fridge that held little else but energy drinks and Chinese take-out boxes, the ski equipment he'd purchased on a whim but had never used. The conversations would inevitably grind to a halt at the moment Piper remembered to check his watch. "I have to report to Mariko," he'd say while fumbling in his pocket for his key card. "Well, um, have a good day. I'll see you soon." And then Ivy would be left alone to count the seconds until the drugs pulled her into her dreams and she could begin her routine all over again.

Ivy longed for books. "I alternate between absolute terror and absolute boredom," she confided to Piper. "I'm not sure which one is worse." Piper nodded sympathetically and asked what book he could bring her. She imagined herself at the library, running her fingers along thousands of book spines. Her imagined fingers stopped at Shakespeare. Piper said he'd look into it, and Ivy's heart leapt at the possibility. He returned the following day with a sheepish expression on his face. "Mariko said no books." He avoided her eyes. "She said you're not here to be entertained." Ivy sighed, but did not press the issue. Instead she spent her waking hours calling the light to her hands, staring at the ceiling, and waiting for the other shoe to drop.

In the week after her jarring introduction to the Cutting Room, Ivy and Piper returned to the corridor three times. Rarely would the cuffed pair enter the arena. They loitered outside the door and waited for the injured fighters to appear. Ivy did not grow immune to the horrific wounds, or the techno music, or the vacant eyes of the bloodied fighters. Her self-loathing increased with each visit.

On the first of the visits, a talkative Mariko popped into the hallway. "Oh, Ivy, you'll never again wear anything like this," she purred as she stroked her mink coat. At that moment, Ivy's hands were pressed against the torn chest of a Ukrainian teenager. A spurt of hot blood shot out of the wound and into Ivy's eye. "Don't I look a dream, Piper?" Mariko twirled and Piper mumbled in the affirmative as he dug into his pocket for a handkerchief and mopped the blood off of Ivy's face.

The following night, Mariko strode in behind a wounded Japanese youth. "You make sure he lives," she barked as she poked her manicured finger into Ivy's shocked face. "He's the best we have. I'm not about to lose another stallion." Mariko glared at Ivy for the duration of the healing, and disappeared back into the arena once the boy had been sedated and whisked away.

Mariko did not appear in the hallway during Ivy's third visit. "Mariko has a migraine," Piper explained as the car careened over the gravel towards the arena. "It's just the two of us tonight." Ivy felt a massive weight float off her shoulders. Until that moment, she'd had little idea how much she dreaded her brief encounters with Mariko. It was the first night that Ivy was able to heal the torn limbs and shredded organs with a demeanour bordering on calm. For a few hours, she imagined that she was a nurse on a battlefield. She had a role to play. She was saving lives.

The serenity lasted until the final healing. Ivy knelt in front of a wheelchair and peered into the heart of a Filipino teen. His opponent had pierced one of the chambers of his heart with the tip of his sword. The violated heart was drowning in pooling blood. Soon it would be silent. Ivy felt the boy veering towards the darkness and was fighting to pull him back when Joji and another man strolled into the hallway.

Ivy was immediately rattled. Beside her, Piper stiffened. The men stopped several paces from where Ivy worked on the injured teen. Ivy sneaked a peek at Joji's companion. It was the same rotund Chinese man she'd spotted in the crowd during her first sojourn into the Cutting Room. Another slave owner. The man reeked of cognac and cigar smoke. His eyes were locked on Ivy's hands. Joji spoke with much animation. Ivy could not hear his words through the wind and the rush of energy. She commanded herself to focus on her patient. Within minutes, the boy was saved. He would fight another day. She took little pleasure in this victory.

When Ivy was finished, Piper pulled her to her feet and thrust a bottle of water into her cold hands. The fat man knelt in front of the sleeping youth, poked him in the chest, and looked from the boy to Ivy to Joji with disbelieving eyes. The man began to laugh. Joji joined him. The fat man stood and began speaking cheerfully in a guttural Asian language that Ivy did not understand. Joji replied in the same language, nodded, and motioned back towards the Cutting Room. Joji shot a huge smirk in Ivy's direction before both men slithered back into the arena.

"This is terrible," Piper stammered. He'd gone completely white.

"What is it?" Ivy took a big swig of water.

"Joji is trying to sell you to Jiang Chen, but it's even worse than that." Ivy felt the hallway spin around her. "Joji is going to pay Jiang Chen to…" His terrified eyes snapped up to hers. "He's asked Jiang Chen to make it look to Mariko like he's buying you, but once he owns you, he's going to kill you. As a favour to Joji. Not good. Not good at all. Mariko needs to hear about this." Here he produced a small smile.

"Joji probably forgot that I'm fluent in Mandarin. I took a night course a while back. I thought it would be good for business." Piper implored Ivy not to worry, but it was too late. At least in Joji and Mariko's world, Piper provided some protection. But if Joji turned her over to Jiang Chen, she would be Piper-less and probably dead—unless Jiang Chen double-crossed Joji and exploited Ivy's abilities to his own ends. Horrible as it was, her current situation was the lesser of two Hells.

Piper did not visit the next morning. Ivy spent the entire day fending off waves of nausea and a panic attack. But when Piper strolled into her cell the following afternoon wearing a bright blue suit and a jovial smile, Ivy's panic instantly evaporated. "I took care of it," was all Piper said before launching into an elaborate description of the paperwork he'd conquered that morning. Ivy knew that this event marked a new stage in the war between Piper and Joji. She was safe, at least for the moment. At the same time, she felt more vulnerable than ever before. Next time, Joji would be careful to keep his plans concealed from Piper. She forced out a smile and tried to keep up with Piper's mundane anecdote. She was absolutely certain there would be a next time.

CHAPTER 17

Ivy was alone in what had once been *his* loft. It was unrecognizable. Abandoned, gutted, burnt to the ground. A desolate industrial trash pile remained in its place. Ivy surveyed the remnants of their shared life. The carcass of a motorcycle. A splintered bed frame. A shattered porcelain tub. Ashes where there had been hundreds of books. She hadn't expected to find him among the ruins. He was gone. He was dust. She'd forgotten his name.

Ivy strolled dispassionately through the wasteland. *I should be sad. I should be angry. But I feel nothing.* Ivy walked faster. She no longer looked before she stepped. She forgot her own name. She forgot what she looked like. She forgot her mother's face. She was just a girl with no past. An automaton. She began to weep. She brought her fingers to her face and pulled them away to discover tears of blood. *There is nothing left of me.*

The girl was running now, over the trash, the ashes, the broken bottles, the bricks and mortar and upturned chairs. She wanted out. She didn't know why she'd come. The rubble stretched all the way to the horizon. There was no end in sight. Her palms began to burn hot as fire and this frightened her, because she didn't know why they did that. She ran even faster.

Suddenly the girl with no name was flat on her face. She was furious now, heaving with a hatred for someone she could not recall, and it was as an afterthought that she glanced at the object that had tripped her. She took a second, longer look. It was a sapling with dew on its vivid green leaves. A Japanese maple in its earliest stages. *Amazing that it could grow here, where there's no sunlight, no warmth.* And the girl was humbled, and cried tears of gratitude that she'd lived to witness this little tree surviving and thriving amongst the ruins and the trash.

In an instant Ivy remembered her name, and her face, and her mother, and glimpsed a lone figure on the horizon. She rose and walked towards him.

The vomit was rising up Ivy's throat before she even opened her eyes. She stumbled out of bed and reached the sink with seconds to spare. Her stomach contents were minimal. Her appetite had been absent for days. She lay with her back against the cold concrete floor and pressed a hand to her forehead. Burning hot. She wondered if this was to be a regular occurrence following a night of healings, or if she'd managed to pick up a particularly resilient flu bug from one of the fighters.

From the very back of her consciousness, Ivy heard a din of voices. At first, the voices were faint and indecipherable. She strained to hear them, but their words were unformed. In seconds they were louder than the air conditioning, than the nausea, than her internal energy flow. Her instincts were singing out to her, and their words were crystal clear. *I'm pregnant.*

It made sense. The math of it made sense. Ivy didn't need to pee on a stick to know that it was true. Since she'd awakened into her underground Hell, she hadn't given a second thought to what was happening to her body, or to what wasn't happening that was supposed to happen like clockwork. She struggled to focus on a single thought, and was instead deafened by a chorus of anxious voices.

Pregnant. I can't be pregnant.
Victor and I are having a baby.
We weren't careful. We didn't care. We were in love.
I can't have a baby here.

Ivy's racing thoughts were frantic. Muddled. But what was obvious to Ivy, even from the centre of the tornado, was that this revelation must be concealed from the security camera. And so she remained on the floor with a calm brow and a relaxed jaw, as if the harsh truths of her surreal life had not just bowled her over.

Shock was the loudest emotion. But shock would be loud under normal circumstances. Fear that Mariko would kill the pregnancy competed for equal time. The fear boiled down into panic. This was real. This wasn't going away.

Yes, it was likely that Mariko would abort the baby. *Pregnancy would interfere with my productivity.* But what if Ivy was allowed to carry the baby to term? Ivy felt the hair on the back of her neck stand up and scream when she imagined her unborn baby ripped from her clutches. Imagined seeing her once and never again. *Mariko would expect her to be a healer, too. She'd whisk my daughter away and raise her with no memory of me.*

As Ivy's brain formed the 'her' pronoun, she felt a slight spark of happiness. She was growing a person. She permitted herself the tiniest smile. *Our baby. Our life.* She was likely seven or eight weeks into her pregnancy. The fetus was no larger than a kidney bean. The cells were multiplying by the second. She yearned to press her hands against her abdomen and flood it with love and light, but she dared not do this. No gesture would be more tell-tale. *Mom would be so happy.* At this thought, tears rushed to her eyes. She allowed a few to fall before brushing them away.

Ivy wanted this baby. She was without Victor now, but she had been with him once, and the baby had been conceived during the happiest time of their shared life. And she wanted to enjoy her pregnancy, to make a home for her baby away from the unnatural light and recycled air and daily violence, to raise her child to be fearless and free. Ivy pushed herself off the ground and glanced at the security camera. She half expected a pack of goons to burst through the door at that moment and drag her to the operating room. It would not be long until she began to show. Life would not stand still.

Only minutes had passed since Ivy had stumbled into consciousness, but everything had changed. Escape was no longer a fantasy. *It's not just about me anymore.* Ivy was scrounging for courage and wondering how to seize control of her destiny when the door swung open and Joji entered the cell.

Terror flooded Ivy's body. Joji stopped two feet inside the cell and smirked. *How could he possibly know?* Ivy fought to rein in her panic and chanced a glimpse into Joji's mangled face as the door clicked shut behind him. His eyes were mocking and hateful, as they always were in her presence. There was nothing new there. What was new was that he was present in her cell. On instinct, she crossed her arms in front of her womb and waited for him to speak. *He's not here about the pregnancy.*

Ivy didn't have long to wait. "Wow. Comfortable room. You really lucked out." Joji produced and lit a cigarette. He remained within arm's reach of the door. She realized he was wary of her. *If I hurt him again, I'm dead.*

"I don't quite see it that way," she said. It was hard to guess what would set Joji off. His body language was indecipherable. He seemed perfectly at ease in his expensive pinstripe suit and shiny loafers. He handled the cigarette in his four-fingered hand with confidence.

"If I had my way, you'd be drugged and thrown in with the fighters." Joji effortlessly exhaled a series of well-formed smoke rings. "Those animals would tear you apart."

You don't have your way. Piper made sure of it. Ivy hoped her eyes were devoid of defiance.

Joji scowled. "We haven't had the opportunity to speak since you arrived."

"You've kept me busy."

"Mariko has kept you busy." Joji eyes darkened when he uttered his sister's name. Ivy flashed to Mariko's open palm flying towards his shocked face. "It makes me sick when I think of you working for us. You should be dead."

He's come to murder me. Ivy's palms burned searing hot. If she were to defend herself against an attack, she'd be killed anyway. *I can't provoke him. I need to find the words to calm him.*

"I'm doing my best to make it up to you." Ivy was at a loss. Her instincts spoke on her behalf. "We didn't lose anyone last night. I was hoping you'd be happy." *Please, go away. Please, please leave me alone.*

For once, Ivy's instincts failed her. A red flush crept up Joji's neck. "Don't talk to me about happiness." Joji spat out his words with such venom that a tremor of fear passed through her body. She felt a dark energy rumbling within her. Above them, the fluorescent light flickered. Joji noticed this and winced. "You made me a freak. You have any idea what that means in this world? To look like this and try to command respect? It's bad enough that I have to deal with that arrogant hag. And who are you? A witch who was fucking a loser? You think you deserve to escape with your life?"

Joji was in a trance now. "I watch you all the time. When you're sleeping. Eating. Exercising. Life is good. Mariko's even keeping you away from my men." *How can he seriously believe that to be true?* "No way I'm going to let this continue. Mariko is convinced that you have something to offer us, but every day I'm working on her. You will be put down. It's just a matter of time."

"Why are you telling me this?" Ivy felt tears welling behind her eyes. She knew that her tears would thrill him, but the anxiety was becoming too much. *It's either cry or flail out at him with my energy.* Her body needed release.

Joji stamped his cigarette out on the wall and tossed the butt onto the floor. "I want you scared," he growled. "I want to be in your nightmares. I want you to dream of your death. It can come at any moment. And when it comes, it'll be slow, and brutal, and I'm going to push you right to the edge and bring you back so I can do it all over again."

The threats weren't empty. Ivy believed every single word. Joji had raped and murdered Victor's mother. Had casually ordered Bill's execution. Had built a business based on slavery, torture and blood sport. In Ivy's case, it was personal. Joji was going to kill her slowly, and he was going to savour every moment. Only Mariko stood in his way.

Joji continued to stare her down. He was clearly waiting for her to speak, and she wasn't delivering. "Okay, Joji." It was all Ivy could say. "I get it now. I'm living on borrowed time. If I could change things, I would. I wish you'd forgive me." She hoped her voice was suitably apologetic.

Joji grunted and moved towards the door. "If only you hadn't saved that loser's life," he said with mock regret as he swiped his key card and the door swung open. "You wouldn't be in this mess now. Tough break."

Ivy slumped on the bench with her eyes fixed on the door. Hours had passed since her confrontation with Joji. He hadn't laid one finger on her, but Ivy felt battered and bruised regardless. She forced herself to eat whatever food was pushed through the panel, and was relieved when she managed to keep everything down. *It'll be a miracle if I can bring a baby to term.* Otherwise, she stared at the door and imagined

Piper strolling in with a vitamin in his pocket and a ridiculous grin on his face. She was desperate to share the burden.

As Ivy waited for Piper, she waded cautiously through her shock. Her thoughts touched on Victor, but she turned away from him in anguish. She had reached a new stage of mourning. She knew that he was gone. He was no longer real. What mattered now was escaping with her life. She could see no other path but through Piper. There was no guarantee that he would visit that day, or the next. But waiting gave her purpose.

Fleetingly, Ivy wished that she could escape into a book. *What I wouldn't give for a pregnancy book.* At this thought, she snorted contemptuously. *A gun would be of more use to me now. I could shoot my way out of here.* She cringed and wondered if the microscopic cells multiplying in her womb would be tainted by her toxic thoughts.

A bone-chilling scream spilled into the cell from the hallway. Ivy gasped and pushed herself to the edge of the bench. Ears alert. Typically her cell was a dismal universe unto itself. But now it was invaded by a roar of male voices. Their words were obscured by the concrete and insulation. A single voice shouted in response. Ivy's heart raced. She couldn't understand the man's words but she recognized the desperation. There was a loud bang. The gunshot shook the walls. Ivy felt the vibrations in her feet.

It was over as quickly as it had begun. Once again there was no other sound but the hum of the air conditioner. As if it never happened. As if some prisoner had not just lost his life on the other side of the concrete. Ivy sat frozen with her palms flat against the bench.

Death in the hallways. Death in the ring. Death under my hands. I need light. I need to raise my baby in light. There is no life in the shadows. Ivy rocked from side to side and in that instant was immersed in all the pain she'd ever touched. The pain of losing her mother, Bill, Victor. The pain in Wen Li's eyes when they flashed across the giant screen. The pain behind Piper's bright smile. The pain of losing her freedom, her dignity, and possibly her pregnancy. The pain of every single injured soul she'd ever healed. The pain was too much, had nowhere else to go, and so she wept.

Smoke cut through the tears. Ivy's hands were scorching hot and she discovered two small fires burning beneath them on the bench. *Will this give it away? Will they swoop in and rob me of what's left?* She leapt up and scrambled to fill the bucket with water. Couldn't move fast enough. Couldn't pull in enough air to fill her lungs. She dumped the water over the bench. The fires refused to die down. She looked down at her hands and watched flames jump from her palms. *I'll burn in this hole.* She was as hot as the sun. Suddenly Ivy realized that there was wind against her face and all around her. She was in the eye of a small tornado. Ivy pushed against the wind, refilled the bucket, and dumped the water over her head. The cold water sizzled against her skin. Steam rose. She struggled to focus on the light and her breathing. *I am in control of this.*

Finally, the wind died away. Ivy managed to extinguish the fires, which left two large scorch marks on the bench. Her hands were cold as ice. When Piper entered, Ivy was surveying the scene, numb and lost. Water dripped from her hair, cheeks, the tip of her nose. Her jumpsuit was soaked through to the bone. She grasped the bucket in her shaking hands and stared at Piper. She scrambled to collect her wits. *This is the moment.*

"Hi," Ivy said.

For a moment, Piper was struck dumb. After a pause, he rushed forward and attempted to pull the bucket from Ivy's hands. At first, Ivy did not yield. Instead, she leaned against his shoulder so that her unseen watchers would think she was resting her head. "I need to talk to you where we won't be monitored," she whispered urgently. "Please. It's an emergency." Then she stood back and poured everything she had into his eyes. *Please understand.* She hadn't known how Piper would react to her request. He stared blankly at her, then at the bucket. Seconds passed. He placed the bucket on the floor.

"We'll have to get you a new bench," he said distantly. "It might take a while."

Ivy nodded, brushed the water off her face and watched as Piper hurried out the door. She resumed her waiting.

CHAPTER 18

"You might be surprised to know that there are no cameras in here," Piper explained amiably. Ivy didn't know how long she'd been unconscious before Piper had pulled her out of sleep and into the shower room. Moments before the drugs had knocked her out, she'd wondered if she'd made a terrible mistake.

Ivy had never seen Piper so nervous. He seemed intent on speaking until he exhausted himself. "I've never really asked but I guess there's no camera because there's always a guard in here when the men are showering. If we had a women's shower, though, it might be different. Anyway, the fighters are all heavily sedated after this afternoon's incident and the guards are taking the opportunity to get shit-faced so we should have some time to..."

"I'm pregnant."

It took Piper a couple seconds to process Ivy's words. When he did, the blood drained out of his face. "Oh, my God. Are you sure?"

"Pretty sure. With Victor's baby."

"Oh, my God." Piper rubbed his temples. His slender fingers were trembling.

"You're the only one who can help me, Piper," Ivy said, struggling to maintain an even keel. "I need to escape."

Piper began to pace the length of the shower room. He waved his arms around his head as if the motion would clarify the situation. Ivy bit her tongue and waited. Finally, Piper halted in his tracks and dropped his arms, defeated. "Ivy, it's impossible."

"It *is* possible because you're a decent guy." Ivy's quiet voice was electric with urgency. "You've known for a long time that what they're doing to those poor men is unconscionable."

"I'm in too deep, Ivy." There was sadness on his brow. "I told you that. There's nothing I can do to stop it."

"You're wrong," Ivy said decisively. "You're not helpless. You have power. You are in a position to save my life."

Piper looked like he was going to throw up.

"Piper, you're stronger than you think you are."

Piper resumed his pacing and waving. "I have no real power. I don't carry a katana. I wouldn't even know what to do with a sword if I held one in my hand."

"This is a life or death situation." Ivy was finding it difficult to remain calm. She hadn't wanted to get too emotional, but with each of Piper's objections, she was growing increasingly alarmed. "I can't hide this for long. You know as well as I do that Mariko will kill my pregnancy."

Piper stopped and stared at her, absolutely horrified. "You don't know that for sure."

"What do you want me to do, Piper? Go and ask her? 'Hey, Mariko, suppose I get pregnant. How would you react?'" Ivy's words dripped with venom.

"Oh, my God."

"Joji came to me yesterday and told me I'm as good as dead."

"What can I do? I'm sorry, Ivy. I'm so sorry. I'm no one. I can't help you." Piper was on the verge of tears.

Frustration pushed Ivy over the edge. "Then you're a monster like the rest of them," she spat, blinded by despair. She was no longer in control of her words. "You're worse because you think you're different than them, but you're not. You could make a difference. You could save two lives, but you're choosing not to. My death will be your fault."

Piper's wide eyes reflected his utter devastation. His cheeks were deathly pale. Ivy didn't care if she'd wounded him. In that moment, all she saw was his culpability in her death and the death of her unborn child. *He's been here too long. He's been poisoned. I didn't see it before because I didn't want to.* Ivy began to sob. There was no hope. Piper stood frozen in place. Ivy fell to her knees. Her burden was too heavy.

"Don't cry." Piper crouched down in front of her and squeezed her hand. Tears streamed down his face. "I'll find a way. I'm not a monster.

I'm your friend. Just be patient and please, please stop crying." And then he unleashed a small smile. "You're pregnant," he said. His smile spread into a grin. Ivy couldn't help but smile, too. It was an absurd moment to smile, and they both seemed to know it. "That's pretty amazing. You're going to be a great mom."

Ivy began to laugh and ended up choking on a residual sob. "Oh, Piper," she sighed and pulled him into an embrace. She was suddenly very tired. "I want to believe that I'll get the chance. Please help me."

A day and a night passed before Ivy saw Piper again. Her heart deflated when he finally strolled into her cell. Piper was accompanied by a burly goon. His eyes were on his alligator boots. He sported a purplish bruise on his cheek.

"We're going for a walk," Piper mumbled. Ivy pulled on her shoes and desperately tried to catch his gaze and read his face. He stared at the scorch marks on the bench and avoided her darting eyes completely.

"Into the hallway." The goon grabbed Ivy by the arm and shoved her towards the door. Piper did not intervene. "Mariko don't got all day." Ivy's palms burned searing hot. *One false move and it's all over.*

Ivy shook off the goon's grip and strode bravely into the corridor. She would deny everything. Reveal nothing. The voice in her head was defiant and resolute, but panic remained heavy on her back. *Piper is bruised and won't look at me, and I doubt very much that Mariko wants to have a happy chat over tea. No, this is not good.*

The goon did not follow the silent pair into Mariko's suite. After weeks *(How long has it been now?)* of stark white walls and clinical fluorescence, Ivy needed a few seconds to adjust to the dim light and shadows. Nothing had changed since Ivy's first visit. Same fish tank, same swords and sake bottles, same heat, same suffocating perfume. Joji was not present. Mariko reclined on the sofa.

"Come and sit with me, Ivy." Mariko's voice was lolling and musical. She patted the spot beside her. Her large rings sparkled in the soft light. Again Ivy was reminded of a seductive spider. Ivy took a deep breath, walked across the room, and slowly lowered herself onto the sofa. *You're sitting on a couch with your murderous captor and your unborn child.* Piper remained standing near the door with his head downcast.

"I understand my brother came to see you a couple days back? By understand, I mean that I watched the meeting unfold in real time." Ivy noted a twinkle in Mariko's eyes.

"You probably already know what he said, too."

"Yes. Nothing escapes my notice. I'm the Queen of the Castle." Here she laughed. Deep and throaty. "I also know that you and dear Piper enjoyed a secret rendezvous a couple nights back."

Not so secret.

"I needed to vent, and I wanted to do it away from the camera," Ivy said slowly. She had no idea how much Mariko knew, or where this troubling discussion was headed. "Your brother scared me and I needed a friend."

"You're transparent, Ivy." Mariko was giddy. "There are no secrets here. Piper can't protect you from my brother. Piper can't help you escape." *My God, does she know?* "Can't you see how weak he is? How loyal he is to me?" Ivy glanced towards Piper and wondered if the bruise had arrived via Mariko's open palm. He was motionless.

Ivy tried a different tact. "Your brother wants me dead."

"Yes, an inconvenience, to be sure." Mariko yawned and stretched like a cat. "I'm really trying to figure out how to keep you working and also satisfy my brother. He doesn't understand the business of things, and normally I wouldn't acquiesce to his ridiculous demands but he's particularly obsessed with killing you. He's relentless. He can make my life really difficult."

"Please," cried Ivy, realizing in that instant that perhaps what Mariko craved most of all was to be begged. "There's got to be more that I can do. I'll do other work. I'll make myself irreplaceable. I'll do whatever you ask. But please, please don't let him kill me." Ivy managed to push out a couple tears. The tears were not completely faked. She was genuinely scared.

"There, there, now." Mariko leaned forward and slowly brushed a tear off Ivy's cheek. Ivy bristled at the lingering touch but said nothing. Mariko was clearly intoxicated by Ivy's humiliation. "I've been thinking about renting you out to the other teams. Of course, that would forfeit my advantage, and profits would plummet if word spread too far about you, because who wants to waste money on a life-and-death fight when you're removing the threat of death? But I'm sure the other teams would pay a premium for a discreet service. We'll have to offer it to Jiang Chen, now that Joji's blabbed to him." Mariko rolled her eyes.

"Anything," croaked Ivy. *I'll say anything to stay alive.*

Mariko appraised Ivy's face for another moment before sinking back into the luxurious cushions. "Very well," she said and examined her long black fingernails. "I'll think about it. In the meantime, stop polluting Piper, and stop with the dramatics. I witnessed your little temper tantrum with the fire and the wind. Really, Ivy. You should be ashamed of yourself. You're a grown woman."

Piper and the goon escorted Ivy back to cell 60-A. Ivy couldn't see past all the questions swirling around her. *Will Mariko cave and give Joji what he wants? How long do I have before my pregnancy is undeniable?* Obviously Mariko did not yet know about the pregnancy. She'd made assumptions as to what Piper and Ivy had discussed away from the camera. But Piper was frightened. Ashamed. Avoiding her eyes. *What hope do I have if I've lost Piper as my ally?*

The goon left them at the door. Piper accompanied Ivy into her cell.

"Have you forgotten?" Ivy's whispers scratched her throat. She knew that Joji and Mariko were watching.

Piper was stone cold. "I haven't forgotten what you said to me in the shower room, Ivy." He did not whisper. "But you need to be patient."

Patient. Sitting terrified and alone in a narrow cell for days at a time. Unable to stop the unseen ghosts from drugging her, undressing her, monitoring her every breath. Frozen in the shadows while desperate men sliced at each other in the name of backstreet capitalism. Healing torn bodies so they could be ripped to shreds all over again. Over and over again. She'd kept her head. She hadn't attacked anyone with her energy. She'd done everything that had been demanded of her. Ivy had been patient.

But circumstances were shifting. "I'm running out of time, Piper." Tears gathered on her eyelashes. "You're abandoning me."

Ivy wanted her words to shake Piper out of complacency. They did not. "I'm sorry you feel that way." His response was hollow. He fiddled with his tie. Ivy collapsed onto the bench and dropped her head into her hands. *Once Mariko learns I'm pregnant, she'll kill my baby.* Piper was failing to grasp what was at stake. Ivy no longer recognized him.

"Look at me, Ivy." There was something odd about Piper's voice. Suddenly he was out of breath, as if he'd been running. Slowly, Ivy raised her tear-streaked face. Piper had loosened his tie. He was in the process of unfastening the top buttons of his collared shirt. "I'm sorry I can't find the words to make you feel better. You need to keep it together. You're doing good work here." But his eyes were screaming something different.

At first, Ivy did not understand the urgency in Piper's expression. She gaped at him, again fearing that she'd misjudged him, until her brain began to translate his body language.

"You need to find comfort in the work you do for this organization." As Piper spoke, he pulled back his shirt collar and, with a casual flick of the wrist, revealed a chain around his neck. Ivy inhaled sharply. A Saint Michael medallion. And from the sudden flush in Piper's cheeks, Ivy knew it was the very medallion she saw when she closed her eyes. Piper held the pendant between his fingers with his back to the camera. Joji and Mariko would think he was scratching his throat.

"You need to get used to this life because you're not going anywhere." Piper was speaking to her with his eyes. *Victor is near.* It was as if Victor's lips were inches from her ear, imploring her to keep the faith. He hadn't betrayed her. He never would. Ivy heard all of this. She nodded and struggled to conceal her frantic internal monologue. She hoped her own eyes reflected gratitude. Piper was risking his neck to save hers.

Piper quickly stuffed the medallion back under his shirt and buttoned up. "No more dramatics," he trumpeted for the camera, and promptly left Ivy alone with her racing heart and a hundred thousand questions. But at least, at last, there was hope.

CHAPTER 19

Saint Michael the Archangel was God's hit man. At the time of the great battle between good and evil, it was Saint Michael who kicked Lucifer out of Heaven. On Victor's medallion, Saint Michael was pictured driving his sword through a demon. The Bible promised that Saint Michael would return on Judgment Day to lead the army of God. In the meantime, Saint Michael was the patron saint of police officers, marines, soldiers, and anyone brave enough to walk into a firestorm, crush the bad guys, and pluck out survivors. For Ivy, it was no wonder that Victor still wore the Saint Michael medallion even though it had been years since he'd left the force and lost his faith.

In the hours after she glimpsed the medallion around Piper's neck, Ivy relived the thrilling moment again and again. She lay on her back as if in a trance. She wished Piper had left Victor's necklace with her. Impossible, she knew. But still, it had come from Victor. She wanted to run the chain through her fingers, savour the coolness of the medal, the rough edges and smooth contours of the engraving. And there was a part of her that fancied that she'd hold the medallion and finally learn Victor's side of the story. She had so many questions for Victor: about his mysterious absences before her abduction, about his relationship with Mariko, about Bill. But she could wait. Her hope no longer rested with his answers.

Ivy allowed her mind to dive into memories she'd long avoided. She was in bed with Victor. Their limbs were entangled. Her head rested on his bare chest. She stroked the medallion while he ran his fingers through her wild hair.

"What do you see for us?"

"It's been years since I thought about the future, Merchuk." Victor's smile was mellow.

"You and me both, handsome." The future had always belonged to other people. People who were coupled, went on vacation, bought kayaks, dared to be happy. "I want to hear about tomorrow, and the day after that, and on and on. Where are we going?"

Victor seemed to consider her query. "We're on the ultimate adventure. I see us enjoying the ride." Victor paused and Ivy's heart ached, because she knew that he felt a stab of insecurity. "Are you worried?"

She pressed the medallion to his chest and brought her lips to his. "Not a chance. How could I worry? I've never had a future before."

For the first time in weeks, Ivy looked to the future and wasn't completely terrified by what she saw.

And Piper. There was no way to thank Piper for stretching out of his comfort zone. For a moment, Ivy felt a pang of guilt. She'd bullied Piper into taking a stand. But then she smiled inwardly so that Mariko and Joji could not glimpse her happiness via the security camera. *No, Piper made a choice he can live with.* She wished she could pull him into the shower room for another revealing tête-à-tête. There were so many details she craved immediately: how had Piper found Victor? What had they said to each other? What was Victor's plan? How long would she have to wait? Was revenge on Victor's mind? *Does he know about our baby?* Ivy felt dizzy. For the moment, she contented herself with the memory of the Saint Michael medallion around Piper's neck, and when the lights went out and the drugs waded in, she succumbed to unconsciousness with a smile on her face.

When Ivy awoke, she was suspended in the air several feet above the bench. Her hands hung limply by her side. She was cradled by an unseen giant. She gasped, and panicked, and landed on her back with a thud.

"Good Lord," Ivy muttered as she rubbed her smarting elbow. "That's new." *Is this what happens when a freak gets pregnant?* But her bitterness was little more than a reflex. She wasn't particularly disturbed by the levitation. *I'd rather float than deal with morning sickness.* Quickly, she wolfed down her banana and protein bar and tried to meditate.

Piper bounced in shortly after her second set of rations had been pushed through the door. The bruise on his cheek was now a ghastly shade of yellow.

"Another vitamin for you," Piper chirped and pressed the pill into her hand. She downed it with a big swig of milk. *Mariko doesn't know that her vitamins are helping my baby.* "How are you feeling today? Still depressed?"

"Not in the slightest," Ivy said enthusiastically before chastising herself. *Take it down a notch, Merchuk. They're watching.* She took a deep breath before continuing. "You gave me a lot to think about, Piper. I feel much better today."

Piper smiled and clicked his alligator heels. "Good to hear." His voice was bright. "We're heading back to the Cutting Room tonight." For a moment, Ivy felt a wave of nausea. *Back into Hell.* Piper continued staring at her with a near-idiotic grin on his face. He opened his mouth to say something, reconsidered, then giggled. Ivy began to play with the cuff of her sleeve. *What does this conversation look like to Joji and Mariko?*

"I know you're nervous about going back, but it'll be okay," Piper said softly. "Rest up. Have a nap. You're going to be busy tonight." He gave her shoulder a gentle squeeze. She looked up, startled. *Tonight.* He winked and left her alone with her noisy thoughts.

Ivy had no way of knowing how long she'd been unconscious before Piper pulled her out of sleep. Her dreams had been formless and shapeless. Colours and light and her mother's voice singing the same breathless refrain over and over again. *This is the moment.* Piper wasted no time snapping on the handcuffs and leading her through the maze, up the elevator, and into the damp darkness. Unlike her previous journeys to the Cutting Room, Ivy was exhilarated to the point of distraction, and repeatedly stumbled and bumped into her beleaguered tour guide as a result. Piper said little and cleared his throat every few seconds. His suit was heavy with several packs' worth of cigarette smoke.

Outside, the skies were quiet. The frosty air bit at Ivy's nose. Ivy felt the crunch of the gravel under the car and wondered if Victor was monitoring them, or if he was already inside, or if she'd misinterpreted Piper altogether and this wasn't the moment. In a split second, Ivy was despondent, first with the fear that Victor would not come, and then with the terror that she would be forced to watch him die. *What if he rushed here and he doesn't have a plan? What if he's been captured or killed? What if it's over before we even had a chance?*

"It's Halloween," Piper blurted suddenly. Immediately Ivy's head snapped towards him, even though she could not see his face through her blindfold.

"Who gives a shit?" The driver growled from the front seat. "Every day around here is a freak show." They continued on in silence, but Ivy felt strangely relieved. She squeezed Piper's hand.

CHAPTER 20

Piper removed the blindfold and Ivy's heart sank. The corridor was empty. They stood directly outside the door to the Cutting Room. The usual bass-heavy music passed through the door. Ivy felt herself plummeting into a dark hole.

"It's already started." Ivy slumped against the wall. For a moment, she'd managed to forget about the young men, and the giant video screens, and the champagne and the slaughter and the blood.

Piper shook his head. He was lost in his thoughts. "What? No, I don't think so." He bit his lip and poked his head around the door. "That's just pre-show music. There's still time." He cleared his throat and tapped his foot.

A minute passed. "What happens now, Piper?" Ivy spoke from the very top of her head. She flashed to her morning levitation and imagined she was floating away.

"We wait for the wounded, like all the other times," he said, again absentmindedly. To offer an explanation would be to risk being overheard by a goon, or Mariko. Ivy understood this, and fought the urge to interrogate. Frustration lapped at her toes. She closed her eyes and rubbed her temple with her free hand. *Maybe Victor was supposed to be here already. Maybe Victor isn't coming tonight. Maybe he'll never come.*

"Merchuk."

"Victor."

He had entered the hallway through the far exit without making a sound. Dressed head to toe in black. A sword in a black lacquer sheath hung from his belt. His dark eyes shimmered in the harsh white light. He hadn't shaved in weeks and his face sported a light beard and shadows. He blinked as if he doubted his eyes. His sudden appearance had taken Ivy's breath away. She felt her heart break and swell at the same time. *How could I ever doubt him?*

Ivy raced towards Victor. He took long strides to meet her. Her palms seared hot and she glowed with brilliant happiness. As she ambled down the hallway, she wondered if his lips tasted as she remembered. Wondered how much she'd changed during her captivity, if they would still fit together, if he would find her cold, damaged, tainted. *Shut up and just be.* Poor Piper scrambled to keep up. Ivy knew she should ask him to unlock the handcuffs and spare him the awkwardness of being quite literally the third wheel, but she had no more time to waste.

Victor and Ivy collided. Their lips met for a moment and then her head was pressed against his shoulder. His arms wrapped around her. He pressed his lips against her hair. "I never thought we'd…" She placed her free hand against his chest and flooded his body with a low-level wave of healing energy.

Finally, Piper fumbled at Ivy's wrist, freed himself, and scampered down the hall.

Ivy's wandering fingers found the Saint Michael medallion around Victor's neck. Slowly, she raised her eyes to meet his. Love, grief and relief shone from the pools of green. Ivy began to laugh and weep. "This is surreal."

Victor took a step back and ran his eyes over her body. Ivy blushed. She was suddenly shy. Finally, he smiled broadly, and she knew it had been weeks since he'd last smiled. "Still luminous." She averted her eyes from his intense gaze, and for the first time noticed the all-access key card he clutched in his hand. "I'll hold you all night but first I need to get you home."

"What's this talk of home? You're already home." A caramel voice sang out from the end of the corridor. In an instant, ice coursed through Ivy's veins. Mariko stood twenty feet away. A nightmare in a red satin suit. One hand on her hip, the other wrapped around a small pistol. Piper cowered behind her. "Welcome back to the family, Victor." A sneer on her painted face.

"Mariko." There was danger in Victor's growl. Immediately, he was in front of Ivy with his hand on his sword.

"And what exactly do you intend to do with that sword? Charge at me like a samurai? Come now, Victor. Drop the sword and slide it over to me or I'll bury a bullet in your girlfriend's face." She raised her arm slightly so that Ivy's forehead was in her line of fire.

"Stop!" Victor quickly removed the sword from his belt and slid it towards Mariko. It skidded to a halt beside her shiny red stilettos. "This was never about her anyway. You've hurt her enough. Leave her out of this."

"Says the man with no sword and no chance of escape. But I wonder: have I hurt *you* enough?" Mariko's chin quivered slightly and once again Ivy glimpsed fragility and powerlessness. Even though Mariko was the one with the gun. Even though her goons were only a shout away.

"Why do you want to hurt me, Mariko?" Victor delivered his words with a measured calm that bordered on the saccharine. "What happened to you? You were always smarter than Joji. You were the one who had a heart."

"You broke my heart." Mariko's eyes were far away. She seemed to be shrinking.

"What are you talking about?" Victor took slow steps towards Mariko. Ivy realized he intended to disarm her, and her heart froze. She doubted her powers extended to bullet fragments. "You were the one person in the family who seemed human. That's why I reached out to you a few weeks back. I didn't realize…"

"What didn't you realize?" Ivy heard the suffering beneath Mariko's question.

"I didn't realize you were in charge." It was not what Mariko wanted to hear. Her eyes clouded over. She teetered on her stilettos. *Victor, speak to the woman in her. Say whatever you need to say.* "I didn't realize how far you'd risen." He was now within arms' reach of the gun. "Mariko, if I hurt you, I'm sorry."

Mariko's eyes were crazed. She didn't seem to be processing Victor's words. "I heard it in your voice when you called and asked for a meeting with Joji. You were so fucking happy. Why should you be happy?" She bared her teeth. "I wanted to hurt you. I wanted you to be without her, to live each day knowing she was alive but unable to touch her. I could have killed her like Joji wanted but I knew this would hurt you more." Her voice broke. It was clear she'd reached her limit. "I want you to know my emptiness." Mariko fired the gun before Victor had a chance to snatch it away. The gunshot was no louder than a pop. Victor smacked the pistol out of Mariko's hand and sent her tumbling to the floor.

For a couple seconds, Ivy couldn't understand why Victor was running towards her, why his mouth was forming words she could not hear, why she was stumbling backwards. She hit the wall. It was only when Victor reached her and guided her down towards the floor that she registered the fact that the blood gushing all over her white jumpsuit was her own.

"You're going to be okay, baby." Victor's eyes didn't seem nearly as confident as his words. He ripped the sleeve off her tracksuit. Above them, the fluorescent tubes flickered. Her arm was hot and icy. Victor dabbed at the wound with the torn fabric. "See? Only a flesh wound."

"No!" Mariko charged down the hall towards them. Now the barrel of the pistol was inches from Ivy's face. "You're not leaving alive." Suddenly Mariko's eyes widened. The pistol fell from her fingers and clattered against the concrete. She opened her mouth to scream but could only issue a gurgle. She staggered forward and fell to her knees. Soon she was prone on the floor. A few muscle spasms before absolute stillness. A puddle of blood took shape beneath her. Victor's sword was lodged in her back.

Piper stood tall above her. Blood had spattered across his face. He stared at Mariko. Her blood pooled around his shiny shoes. "Can you fix her?" His voice was hollow.

Victor checked Mariko's wrist for a pulse. "She's dead, Piper," he said gently.

Ivy felt a wave of despair. *Piper will relive this moment every day for the rest of his life.* She steeled herself against the white pain in her arm. "You saved my life, Piper." *I need to be part of this memory.* Piper did not seem to hear her. On instinct, she raised her hand to her flesh wound and was momentarily shocked when she saw past the torn skin and into the violated nerves and crisis-ridden cells. She flooded her arm with healing energy. The corridor filled with light and wind. In seconds, she was regenerated, rejuvenated. Victor's relief was palpable. Ivy jumped to her feet.

"You have to go." Piper's eyes remained locked on Mariko's corpse.

"We're all going together, Piper. There's no way I'm leaving you behind now." Ivy smiled through a sudden mist of tears. "We'll get you to Kyoto. You'll ride the bullet train."

"They're going to blame you for everything, Piper." Victor pulled his sword from Mariko's back and wiped off the blood on the scrap of torn sleeve. "You're going to lose a lot more than your little finger."

For a moment, Piper's eyes drifted up to Victor's. He blinked a few times, as if unable to recognize the man in front of him. Soon his gaze returned to the red satin suit. "Ivy, I need you both to leave. Victor knows the way out." His voice cracked. "If you don't go, this will have been for nothing."

"Piper…" Ivy sighed. Piper's resolve was intractable. She threw her arms around his neck and kissed his cheek. "Thank you, Piper. For everything, from the very beginning."

"I'm free now. So are you." Piper gently extricated himself from her embrace and squeezed her hand. He offered her a sad smile, an echo of his previous grins. "Go and live."

Victor nodded at Piper, who bobbed his head solemnly in return. As Victor pushed open the exit door, Ivy stole one last glance at the heartbreaking tableau behind her. Piper had aged. Perhaps from the moment he'd picked up Victor's sword, felt it heavy in his hand and chose a course of action that placed one human life above another. His life was no longer simple. She hoped he would find his way back to his canary, and his cat, and his mathematical equations and wide smile. She left him in his cloud.

The door led into another bright corridor, and then another. Victor and Ivy raced through the maze in silence. At last, they peeked into a giant warehouse and faced another arm of Joji and Mariko's multi-faceted business in full-swing. Dozens of men stacked crates, lugged boxes between unmarked trucks, and operated heavy loading machinery. *I don't want to know what they're hauling.* The only way in and out of the warehouse appeared to be through a massive garage door. Victor shot Ivy a knowing glance. Ivy nodded. She would wait for his signal, and together they would make a run for it. Within a hundred heartbeats, there was a break in the human activity. Ivy and Victor darted between the crates and trucks, taking cover only once behind a large box when a man in dirty coveralls paused to fire up a joint a couple feet away. Finally, they broke free into the open air.

The night was clear. The stars were out in full force and Ivy had to restrain herself from lifting her arms to the sky and embracing the night. They kept to the shadows. All around them, gun-toting goons patrolled a well-lit dockyard. Ivy did her best to keep pace with Victor, but after weeks of limited use, her limbs were soon sore. They crept along an unlit portion of chain link fencing. Ivy's nostrils catalogued fish, mildew, and other glorious scents of freedom. Waves lapped along the unseen shoreline.

Victor paused in his tracks and produced a small flashlight. For a split second, he illuminated a tear in the chain link. "Your truck is less than a hundred feet away." He peeled back the fencing. "Ladies first."

But Ivy could not move. Suddenly she was in the midst of a cavalcade of swirling colours, sounds, and faces. Wen Li's terrified eyes on the giant video screen. Diluted blood running off her body and down the drain. Cigar-chomping spectators poring over programs, wallets, smiling women. Piper standing motionless by Mariko's cooling corpse. *I'm free now. So are you.* It was all a lie. She was as much a slave as the fighters, because the slaughter would continue on without her, and she was complicit in its continued existence. There would be no escape.

"Do you know what I was doing down there?"

A long pause. Ivy wished she could read Victor's face. "Piper told me about the sword-fighting. I had no idea this place existed."

"They're using your swords."

"It makes me sick when I think about it." Ivy heard a spark of rage in Victor's whispers.

"Those men are slaves."

Ivy discerned Victor smiling through the darkness. He knew her thoughts. Again they were one person. He pulled her to him. She felt his breath against her cheek. "The odds are against us, Merchuk."

He's right. We could die.
I could lose the baby.

Suddenly she wondered why she hadn't yet discussed the pregnancy with Victor. The truth kicked her in the gut. *I don't want anything to prevent him from charging back in behind me. I have to end this war for the baby.*

"You said you'd follow me into battle." But Ivy knew she didn't have to twist his arm.

Victor chuckled. "I hated leaving Piper like that. He's a good guy. I'm sorry I hit him."

"You did that?" Ivy's voice was incredulous but her heart was light. "Poor Piper."

"What would you do if your enemy shows up on your doorstep? He's lucky I didn't slice off his head."

Ivy frowned. "Are we crazy? Should we call the police?"

"They're probably in on it. An operation this big wouldn't be able to operate unnoticed." He gritted his teeth. "No, we'll have to do it ourselves. And yes, we're crazy."

"Do you have a plan?"

"I've got a sword on my hip and another in the truck," Victor replied. "Between that and our audacity, we're as good as gold."

"Sounds perfect." And it did. For a moment they stood in silence. Ivy felt Victor's heart beating against her chest. A gust of ocean breeze toyed with Ivy's curls. She longed to press his hand to her belly. *There will be time enough for that.* She sighed heavily.

"You've changed, Merchuk." Victor's quiet words sent Ivy reeling. *I'm damaged. I'm tainted. It's over.* Victor continued on, unaffected by Ivy's inner violence. "You're ferocious. Ready to charge back into battle. I've got your back." Ivy felt her cheeks flush.

"I do not know my own strength," she whispered into his ear. "That's why I need you."

CHAPTER 21

Alarms sounded. The word was out. The armed men were visibly ruffled. They scurried to and fro and shouted into walkie-talkies in search of instructions. On the other side of the building, a mass exodus of nervous spectators swept out of the Cutting Room and into waiting limousines.

The boss was dead. Her witchy murderer was on the loose. The men prowled the perimeter fencing and illuminated every shadow. Dozens of goons poured out of the warehouse to assist with the search. "She could be anywhere," barked out a goon who seemed to fancy himself more important than the others. "Work those flashlights." But their efforts would be fruitless. While Joji's men were scouring the dockyard for Mariko's killer, Ivy and Victor were creeping back into the building.

The hallways were deserts. Victor and Ivy retraced their steps with little deviation. Back in the corridor outside the Cutting Room, Mariko's body remained untouched. *The entire organization is up in arms because she's dead, and yet they've left her out here like trash.* Ivy half-expected Mariko to rise from the floor and saunter towards them with her stilettos tapping against her own shed blood.

Piper was nowhere to be seen. His bloodied footsteps led towards the door to the Cutting Room.

"Piper better be alive or I'm going to decapitate Joji myself," Ivy seethed. She clutched her unsheathed Tomoe sword in her hand. Victor had retrieved her sword from the Jeep. Already the blade vibrated with heat. She had no idea how to use it, or whether she'd even be able to use it when pressed, but holding it lightened the fear she carried on her back. She feared that Piper had already martyred himself.

Victor smiled wryly. "So the healer is out for blood, eh? Remind me to stay on your good side." He paused with his hand on the door to the Cutting Room. "We might be seconds away from a bloody confrontation. What's our goal?"

Ivy mulled over Victor's earnest question. Again she saw Wen Li's frightened eyes. Piper frozen over Mariko's corpse. Bill's kindly smile. Their pain lived heavy on her chest. The images dissipated. "I want Joji to know pain," she said quietly. She was unnerved by the uncharacteristic bitterness. But she had no other wish for Joji. An execution would be too easy. She heard Joji's voice in her head. *I'm going to push you right to the edge and bring you back so I can do it all over again.*

"I think that can be arranged." As Victor moved to open the door, Ivy's instincts shrieked out their objections. "Wait!" Ivy cried. She grabbed his wrist. "I'm not a murderer. I can't be like him."

"You're not like him, baby." He brought her fingers to his lips. "Trust yourself." He swung open the door.

Ivy and Victor paused for a moment behind the stack of crates and surveyed the arena. The unoccupied stands were littered with programs and broken champagne glasses. The only sounds came from the ventilation system and the fighters, who had been abandoned in their cages during the hysteria and ensuing exodus. They muttered to themselves, and laughed, and shouted. The frustrated cries of caged animals.

"Jesus," Victor muttered as his eyes darted around the arena. "All that's missing are the hotdog vendors and the mascots. I knew Joji was a sick fuck, but this is unreal."

"What's even more unreal is how many people bought into it." Ivy tightened her grip around her sword. "It ends tonight. Let's free the fighters."

They passed out of the shadows and into the main thrust of the Cutting Room. Immediately Ivy was floored by the sheer size of the cavernous space. The arena could accommodate thousands. Ivy wondered just how big Joji intended to grow his extreme sword-fighting league. Victor climbed into the fighting cage. He peered into one of the cameras and his perplexed face filled the giant screens. Again he shook his head in disbelief. Ivy passed a cursory glance over a mobile sword rack as she moved towards the cages that held the fighters.

When the fighters noticed Ivy inching towards them, they ceased their muttering and shouting. They stood motionless with their eyes locked on her face, and Ivy, surprised as she was by this reception, gazed back at them warmly. She'd long thought that they hated her. Blamed her. It was only in this moment that she realized that they'd grown to revere her.

Victor leapt out of the cage and plucked a discarded bottle of champagne from the floor. "French. Expensive stuff."

"It flowed like water." Ivy was in front of the first cage now. Sergei pushed past the other fighters and stood directly in front of her. He passed his hand between the bars. Gone was the crazed warrior who cackled like a hyena when he sliced into his opponents. As the pre-fight stimulant drugs wore off, there was only sadness. Ivy placed her palm over his and sent healing energy racing into his body. The other fighters watched in silent amazement. Sergei smiled. It changed his face. Ivy saw that he was younger than she'd first thought. Handsome. *He should be dating, studying, hanging out with his friends.* She spun to Victor. "They need to be free."

"You want to toast your success over the corpse of my sister?" Joji's voice filled the arena. He emerged from the shadows clutching the wireless microphone in his four-fingered hand. "First you kill Mariko, and now you want to kill my business?"

Victor smashed the champagne bottle against the concrete floor. "Don't give me the heartbroken brother routine, Joji," he spat. "I'm sure you've been thinking about all the ways you're going to renovate this shit hole ever since you found your sister dead on the floor."

"Victor, Victor. You talk a big game but what have you ever accomplished? Once a loser, always a loser." Joji advanced further into the arena. His alligator shoes clicked against the concrete. Ivy fought a wave of nausea. "As for me, I've built something big here. I'm a creative thinker, and I'm raking in big money. This arena"—he spread out his arms—"is a symbol of my genius."

Joji and Victor were less than fifteen feet apart now. Victor's sword was tight in his hand but the blade tip remained on the floor. He seemed to be biding his time. "But what's the point of all that money and genius when you've got a face like that?" Joji winced. Victor saw the flicker in the cocky façade and pushed on. "You really should thank Ivy, you know. She brought out your true beauty."

Joji tossed the microphone onto the floor. "What do you want here, Victor?" Suddenly Joji bared his teeth in a hideous smile. "I know what it is. You want to kill me. Do you really think you can defeat me, loser? How many times have I left you bleeding?" He spun to Ivy. "Do you have anything to say, little girl?"

Ivy thought carefully before she spoke. "You can't hear anyone but yourself," she said finally, and pulled herself up to her full height. No longer would she cower in Joji's presence. "These young men"—she gestured to the fighters—"need to walk free."

Joji snorted. "Yeah, good luck with that." He pulled a sword off the mobile rack. "First I'm going to massacre your loser boyfriend, and then I'm going to slit your throat. How's that for a happy ending?"

"You're pretty arrogant for someone who's outnumbered," Victor observed. Ivy saw the fire in his eyes, and knew there would be blood.

"Outnumbered? I don't count your witch as an opponent, and I never stroll into a battle without backup." A giant thug emerged into the light. It was Yuki, the goon who'd overpowered Ivy in her bedroom. Yuki's gun was trained on Ivy. Victor bristled, and though Ivy felt her confidence falter slightly, she listened when her instincts piped up. *It will not end like this.*

"I'm here, too, Joji." Piper's voice sent chills racing up and down Ivy's spine. Ivy had assumed that Piper had been imprisoned or killed after alerting the masses to Mariko's murder. But when he emerged from the shadows, his eyes sparkling and a strange smile plastered on his face, Ivy knew that he had been skulking unseen ever since he'd dragged his bloodied boots into the Cutting Room. He gripped Mariko's pistol in his hand.

"Well, if it isn't my sister's moronic little lapdog," Joji mocked. Piper's sudden appearance clearly delighted him. "You must be devastated that your friend is responsible for the death of your mistress. At least we can agree on that."

"No, Joji." Piper's delivery was measured and bright. The crazed smile remained on his face. Ivy worried that he was lost to her. "I grew to hate Mariko as much as I hate you." He raised his arm and pointed the small pistol at Yuki. He held the gun as if he knew how to use it.

No longer a child at play. "Drop your gun, Yuki, and walk away from here. This isn't your fight."

Yuki was visibly floored by this turn of events. Joji flared his nostrils. "You spineless weasel." He thought for a moment and his face visibly relaxed. "I forgot who I was talking to. Piper doesn't have the guts to fire a weapon." He turned his back on Piper and waved him away. "Scurry back into your hole and leave the adults alone."

"I killed Mariko," Piper said quietly. He pulled the safety on the pistol. The blood drained from Joji's face. "I will think nothing of killing you. So drop your gun, Yuki, and scurry back into your hole." The final words were soaked in venom. Yuki swallowed. The gun shook slightly in his hand.

"Don't even think about it, Yuki," Joji seethed through clenched teeth. "Remember who you work for."

"The fact is, Joji, none of your men care enough about you to sacrifice their lives," said Victor. "You're not running a crime family. You're running a failing business." Yuki dropped his gun to the floor, turned on his heel, and hurried out of the arena with his eyes downcast. Piper strode over to the abandoned gun and scooped it up. "And it looks like Yuki just got a better offer." Now Piper's gun was trained on Joji.

Through all of this, Ivy stood with her back pressed against the cage of fighters. A spectator to a Shakespearean drama. The love she felt for Piper was monumental. He was forever changed, it was clear, and she mourned the death of his innocence. But she also knew at that moment that he was no longer conflicted. He'd picked a side. *I'm free now. So are you.* And she finally understood what he meant.

"So what now, loser?" Joji was enraged. "Are you going to hide behind the weasel and the witch, or are you going to make a move?"

Victor grinned, but his eyes were frosty. "We're going to fight like warriors, Joji." He gestured to the cage with his sword. "You've been hiding behind your sister and your thugs for a long time now. Do you even know how to fight your own fights?"

Infuriated, Joji brushed past Victor and stomped up the ramp and into the fighting cage. He whipped off his oversized sunglasses. "Oh, I get it," Joji squealed as he bounced on the balls of his feet. "This is about your mother. You blame me for what happened to your mother. That was your own fault, loser."

For a moment, Victor locked eyes with Ivy. She couldn't read his thoughts but she saw a glimmer of doubt in his eyes. She knew the malice behind Joji's taunts had long rung true for Victor. Victor was his own biggest enemy. *You saved my life. That counts for something. Don't let him shake you.* Without thinking, Ivy's hands went to her belly. The doubt vanished from his eyes. He smiled and winked. Ivy inhaled sharply.

Victor shrugged off his leather jacket and tossed it onto the floor. "Joji, I understand you, and I forgive you," he said as he strode up the ramp. "And now I'm going to make you feel pain."

"Ever the philosopher," Joji retorted. The men were circling each other now with their swords extended in front of them. "You've become very boring, Victor. You were more interesting when you were a drunk."

Piper padded over to Ivy. He cast a wary glance at the caged fighters before coming to a halt beside her. "I told you to stay away," he mumbled.

"I'm finished with people telling me what to do," Ivy replied lightly without looking at him. Her eyes followed Victor and Joji around the ring. She rested one hand on Piper's arm. "You're full of surprises, Piper. Thank you."

"I keep surprising myself." Piper's laugh was measured.

Victor and Joji continued to circle each other like wild dogs. Suddenly Ivy's palms seared hot and she pulled her hand away from Piper's arm. The outcome of the fight was not clear. Joji and Victor were equally matched. *There's no guarantee that good is going to win. And what will it mean to win? To kill Joji? Is that a victory for us?*

"You shouldn't have come back," Piper scolded. He peered into her anxious face. "This is too stressful for you."

But Ivy barely heard Piper's words of concern. Her attention had drifted to the young men behind her. Despite the gaps in language, despite the fog of drugs, despite the months of torture and imprisonment, the young men were following the events playing out on the giant video screens with unbridled interest. They knew precisely who Joji was. They knew that his defeat could mean a changed life for each and every one of them. They were daring to hope.

"Whatever happens here, Piper, make sure these young men are returned to their families," Ivy said. Piper opened his mouth to say something, reconsidered, and nodded.

Joji's bravado began to falter. He would not be able to maintain his posturing dance much longer. He stumbled slightly. His misstep seemed to fill Victor with new confidence. Victor now prowled around the cage with a cat-like swagger. His eyes narrowed. Ivy saw him in the field outside Bill's cottage, his katana glistening in the sun. She saw his razor-sharp precision and focus. Again he'd found his centre. He was ready.

Joji threw back his head and roared as he struck out at Victor. Victor cast off Joji's angry move with little effort. Their duelling swords shone brightly under the white lights as they collided again and again. Joji, driven by desperation, his inner ugliness naked on the video screens. Victor, cool and sharp, his jabs and strikes thoughtful, elegant. The harsh screech of metal on metal rang through the air. Now Ivy was dizzy with anxiety. It was clear to Ivy that Victor was the better fighter. And equally clear that Joji was determined not to die.

Minutes passed. "Getting tired, loser?" Joji was nearly out of breath. Sweat poured into his eyes.

"You can't beat me, Joji." Fast as lightning, Victor cut the air in front of him. It was a dazzling display of his mastery. "I have something to live for. What do you have?"

"You sound like a woman." Joji spat onto the floor. "You're spineless. I killed your mother and you never did anything about it. Did you know your mother was a slut?"

"Coward!" Ivy cried out. Throughout the fight, she'd struggled to remain silent. The last thing she wanted to do was pull Victor's mind out of the ring. But Joji's rhetoric could prove fatal. *If Victor loses his confidence, we could lose everything.* She raced to the foot of the ramp. Energy coursed from her hand and up the sword. Sparks shot out from the tip. "You're a monster!"

But Victor did not lose his confidence. Instead, as Joji shot a gleeful, victorious smirk in Ivy's direction, Victor dove towards Joji and thrust his sword deep into his abdomen. Immediately, Joji was on his knees. He pressed his hands against his wound. Blood poured out over his fingers. His mangled face reflected sheer agony. "Oh shit! Shit! Help me!" His yelps were greeted by raucous laughter and jeers from the caged fighters.

Victor yanked his sword out of Joji's abdomen. His eyes were fixed on Joji's writhing body, as Piper's had been fixed on Mariko's corpse less than an hour previous. "It hurts, doesn't it?" Ivy could only just discern Victor's quiet words over Joji's shrieks and whimpers. "And yet even now, there's no way you could ever know my pain." A sudden storm erupted on his brow. He glanced at the tip of his katana. Droplets of blood fell from his sword onto the cage floor. "No fucking way."

Ivy moved as if directed by a force outside her tired body. Her Tomoe sword fell from her hand and clattered against the floor. Victor's eyes were now on her. She floated up the ramp and into the cage. Victor observed her actions with little surprise or judgment. She knelt beside Joji and raised her hands to his abdomen. Her instincts were in full control.

"What… what are you…" Joji sputtered. Ivy looked past his sleazy suit and into his torn abdomen.

"I'm a healer," Ivy proclaimed with breathless pride, as the wind began to whip around them and the white light poured out of her eyes, chest, palms. "This is who I am. This is what I do. Even for someone like you."

Joji awoke with a start. He was alone in the fighting cage. He pulled himself up, inspected his healed abdomen, and glanced at the puddle of blood under his feet. "Where've you gone, loser?" Joji hollered. "I'm ready to fight again." He strained his eyes against the bright lights. The loser and the witch were nowhere to be seen.

Joji snorted and took a few steps towards the ramp. "They've wasted enough of my time," he muttered. Suddenly he froze. The cages were empty. The fighters were free. Twenty-four young men were now moving up the ramp and into the fighting cage. Each with a sword in his hand and fury in his eyes. Frantically, Joji searched for his own sword. It was gone. He staggered backwards until he could go no further and his back hit the cage.

"Boys," Joji stammered and raised his hands in front of him. "I'm sure we can work something out. I'm a businessman. I'm rich. I can offer compensation."

"Welcome to the Cutting Room, Joji." It was Piper's voice on the public address system. Joji scanned the arena and saw nothing except his own scared, scarred face on the video screens. "This battle is going to be epic, folks." Now the ring was completely filled with young men. They faced Joji, unspeaking, as still as statues. Sergei stood proudly at the head of the pack. Suddenly Sergei threw back his head and issued a spine-rattling cackle. The laugh of a bloodthirsty hyena. Joji began to scream at the very moment that electronic music began to blare from the speakers.

"Mariko and Joji weren't really Yakuza. They were a pair of spoiled brats who paid for loyalty," Victor said. "It's over."

It was nearly dawn by the time they'd pulled into the parking lot at Jericho Beach. Ivy had asked Victor to make this their first post-imprisonment stop. They watched from the Jeep as the November sun slowly illuminated the deserted beach. Slabs of driftwood, their ends curled like desiccated fingers, were scattered in unlikely piles by forces of nature. Beer bottles were abandoned around fire pits. A lone sandal, a relic of bygone summer days, poked out of the sand. And in the distance, there was the city of Vancouver, a collection of tightly packed glass-fronted condominiums and people, hundreds of thousands of people, with no clear concept of the violent underworld that existed just below the surface. *I hope they never know.*

"I want to feel the sun on my face," Ivy said after twenty minutes of silent rumination. She was unable to focus on a single thought or emotion. Victor nodded. His eyes had been on her face since he'd pulled into the lot. Outside the car, the chill swept straight through Ivy's torn jumpsuit, and though the morning sun was devoid of warmth, she threw her head back all the same and invited the sun to bathe her face in natural light. Victor slung his jacket over her shoulders. "It's shining just for you, Merchuk," he said. Ivy knew there was grief behind his breezy delivery. "We've had nothing but rain for weeks now."

They were the only souls on this long stretch of wild beach. They held hands and walked to the water's edge. The tide was in. The grey water was frantic and alive. The waves crashed at their feet and Ivy began to laugh. "It's perfect," she said at last, and rested her head against Victor's shoulder.

It's over. The constant surveillance. The numbing boredom and terror. The powerlessness. The commercialized slaughter. All over. No one would come after them. They could begin their lives anew. But Ivy knew the whole truth. There would be a part of her that would always be a slave. It was impossible to forget what she'd witnessed in that arena. She would never be completely free of Mariko and Joji's surreal world, and she knew it. "I want to burn what's left of this jumpsuit," she announced after five minutes of silence. Victor pressed his warm palm against her abdomen. "Whatever you want." She heard everything he didn't say and laid her hand above his own. "I'm at your command."

Ivy's eyes followed a pair of seabirds gliding high overhead. They swooped towards the water, and rocketed up into the cold sunlight. Their calls were mournful. She thought of Bill and felt the sting of tears. Victor had delivered the devastating news. Bill was dead. He'd lived long enough to provide a statement to the Tumblestone police. He'd reported that armed assailants from Vancouver—led by Joji—had invaded his home, shot him down, and abducted his young friend. Despite this, Victor had been held as a suspect for three days before his alibi—sitting in a Tumblestone diner, staring into a cup of coffee—was verified. Upon his release, Victor had made a beeline to the hospital, and had held Bill's hand at the very moment that Bill passed out of this life and into the next. Ivy closed her eyes and saw the smile that had once reminded her of a dolphin. She lifted her face to the sun and allowed a few tears to slide down her cheeks. Her anger was renewed. *We made the right decision.*

Ivy did not regret healing Joji's wound. Victor was not an executioner. He would not have to live with Joji's blood on his conscience. And in the end, universal justice had been served. She flashed to Sergei's relaxed smile, and hoped he walked free. He and the others were part of her past now. She wondered if they'd haunt her dreams. *At least they will have satisfaction.* She shuddered.

"Ivy, I'm sorry." Victor choked on his words.

"For what?"

"For all the pain you've suffered because of me."

"Victor..."

"Do you regret walking into that alley?" Clearly it was not a new question. For a moment, she stared at him, her face blank. This left Victor visibly unnerved. His eyes fell to his feet. He kicked a stone into the water. She studied his face. In the month since she'd been carted out of her bedroom, Victor had suffered an unbearable burden of doubt, hurt, and blame. Her heart swelled. *I'm free now. So are you.* She threw her arms around Victor's neck. He lost his footing and they crashed to the damp ground. She kissed his eyes, cheeks, mouth. "Never apologize," she said firmly. A small wave lapped at their shoes.

I'm going to burn those white sneakers, too. "We're the same person. And now, we're actually growing a person." Here Victor's eyes filled with light. He hoisted her back up and onto her feet.

"Let's get back to the car," Ivy said, smiling brightly. "We've got a lot of planning to do. Tomorrow is ours."

THE AFTERMATH

CHAPTER 22

"Everything looks good."

Ivy clumsily manoeuvred her feet out of the metal stirrups. It had been years since she had last suffered through the indignities of a medical examination and she felt like a violated turkey. A few seconds passed before she realized that the doctor was addressing her. "Excuse me?"

The doctor pulled off her latex gloves and tossed them into a bin marked "hazardous waste." "I said everything looks good," she said as she scribbled on her prescription pad. "Were you expecting bad news?" She ripped off the top sheet and handed it to Ivy. "I'm recommending a stronger prenatal vitamin. Otherwise, keep doing what you're doing. You're right where you should be. Let's chat again in three weeks." She walked towards the office door.

"Doctor?" Ivy was surprised by the tension in her voice. She fidgeted with the hem of her paper gown and pictured Victor nervously flipping through outdated magazines in the waiting room.

"Yes, Ivy?"

Ivy sighed. It was impossible to verbalize her actual fears without sounding demented. *I'm terrified that living underground for a month and witnessing unspeakable violence damaged my baby.* "I've been under a lot of stress lately." Her eyes fell to the beige floor tiles. *That's as close to the truth as I can get.* "I was worried that I'd harmed the baby."

The doctor smiled pityingly. *She thinks I'm weak.* "Our bodies are more resilient than we realize," the doctor declared with patronizing authority. "Women have been giving birth for millennia. Sometimes our bodies know what to do even when we don't." The doctor paused, and Ivy realized it was her turn to speak.

"Oh. Uh, thanks," Ivy replied finally. Though much had changed within Ivy during her captivity, her social awkwardness remained intact. "I didn't think of it that way. That helps a lot." The doctor nodded, clearly convinced that she'd helped Ivy negotiate through a treacherous psychological minefield, and left Ivy alone to dress.

It had taken Victor a week of gentle prodding before Ivy would agree to meet with a doctor. "I know how you feel about doctors," he would begin, and Ivy would cross her arms in front of her and scrunch up her face. Her mistrust of the medical profession was deeply ingrained. She had little confidence that a doctor would be able to contend with the likes of her. "I've managed just fine without the help of doctors," she would retort, and silently scold herself for sounding like a child. She read the concern in Victor's eyes, and she knew that her objections were threadbare.

"I'll do it for you, but I'm not going to mention anything that'll land me in a psychiatric ward," she'd said after Victor had broached the subject for the third time. "The minute it gets weird, I'm out of there. I just want to make sure the baby is okay." She'd made her announcement at dinnertime. She'd been perched on a stool at the breakfast bar and toying with her spicy spaghetti. The novelty of eating hot, fresh food had not yet worn off and Victor delighted in preparing filling feasts for her. Victor had cleared his throat and continued eating, but she'd heard the triumph in his grin without looking at him.

Since Ivy's return to the world, Victor had successfully tip-toed the line between doting lover and suffocating protector. He gazed at her, and held her tightly, but he did not treat her like a victim. He did not press her for the grizzly details of her imprisonment, or beg her to remain indoors. Instead, every morning, Victor asked Ivy how she wanted to spend the day. On the first morning, she was at a complete loss.

"I want to eat pancakes, and then I want to take a long bath," she'd said finally after many minutes of frenzied thought. She'd been disturbed that what should be a simple question was so difficult to answer. Victor had smiled and assembled the ingredients.

When Victor had pressed this same question the second morning, Ivy stammered and, after a desperate glance out the window, answered that she wanted to take Milo—who had survived his encounter with Joji's henchman and now lived blissfully in Victor's shadow—for a long walk. Again Victor smiled, and they spent two hours watching Milo chase invisible rabbits alongside the tracks. On the third morning, she'd been prepared for Victor's question, and she announced that she wanted to scour thrift shops for baby furniture, and so they visited a dozen antique shops and returned to the loft with a sturdy old rocking chair and a stack of vintage picture books. Each morning she worried that her plan for the day was the wrong plan, and each night she wondered why she'd been so worried in the first place.

Finally it dawned on her that Victor was subjecting her to this daily exercise to remind her that, just as she was in control of their day, she was also in control of her life. *I can go wherever the wind takes me. I'm free.* The realization was liberating. When Victor next asked her how she wanted to spend her day, she'd laughed and replied, "I want a routine. I want to rebuild my life." And so Ivy turned her attention to figuring out what it meant to be a happy pregnant woman.

As Ivy peeled off the paper gown, her eyes fell across a framed photograph on the doctor's desk. Ivy peered in for a closer look. A cherubic infant with dimpled cheeks smiled up at her. Ivy could almost hear the baby's gleeful squeal. She gasped. "I'm going to have one of those." She smiled, placed her hand against her abdomen, and flooded her body with a burst of healing energy. She vibrated with contentment. *Life is the true miracle.*

Ivy's second week of freedom began with five minutes of uninterrupted barking. Milo barked at almost every little noise and shadow that befell his path, and Ivy and Victor had quickly learned to turn a deaf ear to his constant chatter. Ivy's heart ached whenever she looked at Milo. She wondered if he remembered the violence he'd suffered in the cottage, or if he noted the absence of his oldest friend. For his part, Milo seemed to have adapted well to loft living, and remained completely enraptured with his urban samurai.

Ivy was floating in the warm, fluid space between sleep and consciousness when Milo's barking pierced into her dream. "Oh, Milo, five more minutes and then I'll take you for a walk," she moaned with her eyes still clamped shut. "I'm strolling down a beach right now." But Ivy's words failed to silence Milo's tongue.

"Merchuk?"

"Hmm." Ivy could feel hot sand between her toes. "Seriously, Victor, I would love a vacation in the sun. I think we deserve a vacation after everything we've been through." She spotted Milo down the beach, frolicking in the waves. *Even Milo needs a vacation.*

"You seem to be on some kind of trip right now." Victor sounded alarmed. "You're floating five feet above the bed."

Ivy snapped open her eyes and saw that she was indeed much closer to the ceiling than she should have been. The sheet hung from her body like drapery and she felt like dozens of invisible hands were pressed against her back. Beneath her, Milo's barks turned to low growls. Ivy panicked, and fell a couple inches into Victor's waiting arms.

"Am I going to have to strap you down before bedtime, Merchuk?" Ivy saw through Victor's jovial tone. He set her down on the mattress. Milo padded forward timidly and sniffed her fingers. Evidently satisfied that all was in order, he waddled off towards the door.

"Well, it's better than morning sickness," Ivy replied lightly. Victor furrowed his brow, and Ivy knew that he was more worried than amused. "Look, we can't get stressed about every little thing. I don't know what to expect from this pregnancy, but I'm not particularly worried so long as you're around to catch me." Here Ivy smiled confidently, and the tension in Victor's face receded. He whistled for Milo and the pair slipped outside for a morning walk. Ivy rubbed her temples and wondered whether she actually believed her reassuring words. She yearned to return to the beach.

Ivy spent the remainder of the morning wielding her measuring tape and scratching numbers into a small notebook. She had realized quickly upon her return that hefty doses of creativity and ingenuity would be required to baby-proof their post-industrial palace. Neither she nor Victor wished to leave the loft, but neither were they blind to the challenges of raising their child in a giant concrete box.

"Our baby should have a nursery," Ivy had sighed as her eyes travelled over the tall bookshelves and muddy motorcycle and dormant metal-working tools. "A room of his or her own. That's going to be difficult if we stay here."

"The second loft," Victor had said suddenly, which resulted in a long, uncomprehending stare from Ivy. "Let's break down the second loft into two rooms."

"But what about your sword workshop?"

For a brief moment, a cloud had passed over Victor's eyes. "I won't be producing swords on a mass scale anymore." *We'll always be slaves.* "I'll confine my work to the main loft," Victor had continued. "Let's build a nursery for Baby Morgan, and a studio for you." Again Ivy had stared uncomprehendingly. "You said you always wanted to learn to paint, right? Let's give you space to do that." Ivy could only reply by pulling Victor into a tight embrace. Soon after, her mind was teeming with design ideas, and each hour she spent bringing her dreams to fruition made the pregnancy feel more real.

Victor poked his head into the second loft. "You got a minute, gorgeous?" Ivy sat cross-legged on the floor poring over her notebook. *As soon as the walls are up, I want to cover them with bold colours. I'm finished with white walls.* It took Ivy a few seconds to register that Victor's voice held a playful lilt. Her head snapped up. "You have a visitor."

Immediately Ivy's heart began to pound in her chest. "Who would visit me?" she asked anxiously as she jumped to her feet. Her palms burned and she heard that familiar buzzing in her ears. But Victor winked and retreated into the flash freezer. She heard him shifting boxes and realized he wasn't going to accompany her out into the main loft. Ivy pushed back her shoulders, took a deep breath and charged through the door. Within seconds, she skidded to a halt with her jaw on the floor.

Piper crouched next to the motorcycle. Milo lay sprawled out at his feet. "Hi, little buddy," Piper said cheerfully as he rubbed Milo's head. His efforts were greeted with satisfied snorts and groans. "Victor, you never struck me as a dog person." Piper's eyes wandered over to Ivy's shoes, and he leapt to his feet. For a moment, they stared at each other without speaking. Piper was dressed in a crisp blue suit. The bruise on his cheek had vanished and he radiated positivity and youth, as he had when they'd first met. *How much we've both changed since then!* Ivy replayed their last meeting in her mind. He'd squeezed her fingers, even though they were still covered with Joji's blood. "Be happy," he'd said quietly with an uncharacteristic gravity that brought tears to Ivy's eyes. At that moment, she'd assumed that she'd never see him again.

Piper shifted nervously and giggled. "This shouldn't be awkward." His words pulled Ivy back to the present. "Aren't you glad to see me?"

"Oh, Piper," Ivy gushed as she strode towards him and grasped his hands. "Of course I'm happy to see you. You caught me off guard. I didn't think…" Ivy's words trailed off and, once again, she was in the arena, and she was saying goodbye. She shook off the memory.

"I know," Piper said quietly. "I didn't think I'd ever see you again, either."

They sat on deck chairs on the rooftop patio. Though the thermometer hovered around freezing and the wind was aggressive, the skies were clear and the sun was shining, and Ivy thought it was perfect. She had been away from the sun for far too long.

The young men—the former fighters—were safe. Ivy didn't even have to ask. Piper filled in the blanks as soon as he settled on his deck chair. "At first I thought about calling the authorities, but I didn't want the guys to get lost in the system. I wanted them to be back with their families as soon as possible." Here Piper sighed, and it was clear to Ivy that the stress of Piper's life had not disappeared with the deaths of his employers. "That proved difficult. I had twenty-four undocumented people to move across international borders. But then… I was inspired." He paused dramatically and leaned forward. "Jiang Chen."

Ivy frowned. Jiang Chen was cut from the exact same cloth as Joji. He was remorseless, narcissistic, and obsessed with his own coffers. "Jiang Chen owned some of those men, Piper," Ivy objected. "Why would he help return them home?"

Piper laughed heartily. "Oh, Jiang Chen asked me that very question when I visited him with my proposition." Piper took a sip of the hot coffee that Victor had served them before returning to his work. "But I told Jiang Chen that I was in possession of certain documents that would land him in jail for decades, should they fall into the wrong hands."

Ivy leaned back in her chair and smiled. "Impressive." She didn't want to know what the materials were, but she had no doubt that they had the slime of violence and greed all over them. "And exactly how does your sneaky scheme benefit the fighters?"

Jiang Chen owned a fleet of ships that were in the process of smuggling the men back into their home countries. Piper had divided the bulk of Mariko and Joji's tainted fortune between the surviving fighters before bidding them adieu. The first of the men had already reunited with their families.

Despite the fact that Piper seemed perfectly confident in his plan, Ivy was wary. "But how do you know Jiang Chen is going to honour his word?" Ivy asked. "His word means nothing. He's a criminal."

"I've asked the men to contact me the moment they return home," Piper replied. "If I hear that they've been mistreated in any way, the deal is off and Jiang Chen goes down. Same thing goes if I hear that Jiang Chen revives the league. This ends now."

"What about your safety?" Ivy could not shake the feeling that Piper's plan seemed too good to be true.

"I've entrusted all of the incriminating evidence to several lawyers. If I'm killed or disappear, or if Jiang Chen comes within 500 feet of you and yours"—he glanced at Ivy's abdomen—"the lawyers will pass the evidence onto the authorities, and Jiang Chen's entire organization will crumble." Piper beamed, and Ivy finally relaxed. Piper had kept his word. The young men were free. Ivy gazed out over the inlet for a few minutes. Just over two weeks ago, the contentment of this moment had seemed impossible.

Piper said he was going away. He'd booked a one-way ticket to Japan. It was time to make new memories that didn't involve violence or crime or recycled air. "I hear they have mountain retreats where you can soak in hot springs and wash your cares away," he said dreamily. One of his first trips would be to the Golden Temple in Kyoto. "I'm not sure when I'll be back. I guess I'll know when it's time to return. I've earned a vacation." Piper snorted, and Ivy sadly noted a whiff of bitterness. He jumped slightly. "I almost forgot." He reached into his jacket pocket, retrieved a long red envelope, and handed it to Ivy.

"What's this?" Ivy stared at the envelope. It was as light as a feather and appeared to contain a single slip of paper.

"Reparations." Piper licked his lips nervously, as if he'd been dreading this moment. "It's a cheque for a big sum of money. Enough to make your dreams come true. I'm sure you can find some use for it."

Blood money. Every cent soaked with the blood of the fighters. Ivy shook her head emphatically and thrust the envelope back into Piper's hands. "No. Absolutely not. I refuse to take their dirty money."

"I know how you feel, Ivy," Piper said gently. "But it's not from them. It's from me. If you don't want it for yourself, then do some good with it." Suddenly Ivy envisioned herself as an urban Robin Hood, anonymously donating wads of much-needed cash to rape crisis centres and animal shelters. Victims of violence, the hungry, the elderly, the disenfranchised, the forgotten—many would benefit from Mariko and Joji's anti-social behaviour. She nodded and retrieved the red envelope from Piper's open palm.

"You're my brother, Piper," Ivy blurted, at which Piper immediately turned a deep shade of crimson. "We were orphans, but we found each other." She managed a small smile. "Even Victor says he'll never hit you again."

"I'm glad to hear it." Piper's voice was thick with emotion. He cleared his throat. "Man, I could use a cigarette." His expression brightened. "So, sister, will you look after my pets while I'm away?"

Ivy chuckled and squeezed his shoulder. "Sure. And as your sister, might I also suggest that you quit smoking? It's a nasty habit, and you're going to be an uncle."

CHAPTER 23

The stench of rotting food bowled Ivy over the moment she swung open the door. Immediately she recoiled and stopped in her tracks. *Could mouldy vegetables harm my baby?* A variation of a question she asked herself a hundred times a day. Eventually she collected her wits and soldiered over the threshold. "Jesus," she muttered as she tossed her keys on the kitchen table and disturbed the thick blanket of dust clinging to its surface. "Maybe I should just throw the key in the ocean and call it a day."

A lifetime had passed since Ivy had last entered her West End domicile. The tiny apartment that she'd once considered so safe and cozy now seemed to belong to a stranger. A stranger had regularly fallen asleep on the futon with a book open in her lap. A stranger had prepared simple single-serving meals in the cramped kitchen. A stranger had stared at the mirror and yearned for invisibility. Ivy surveyed the stranger's domicile. Everything remained precisely as she'd left it, save for the dust, the rot, and the occupant. Ivy felt no sadness, no loss. She intended to pack up the few belongings that were suited to her new life, donate the rest to charity, and say goodbye to the stranger once and for all.

Victor had offered to assist her. "Four hands are better than two," he'd said. "You shouldn't be doing any heavy lifting. That's what I'm here for."

"I'm pregnant, not sick," Ivy had quipped in reply, at which Victor had narrowed his eyes and Ivy realized she was in danger of hurting his feelings. His ever-present concern for her well-being was comforting, but she was determined not to play the victim. Besides which, this was a journey she wanted to take alone. She'd taken a deep breath before continuing. "If it's too heavy, I'll leave it. I promise. And anyway, these two hands"—here she squeezed his fingers and sent a wave of healing energy careening into his palm—"have a floor to install in the nursery."

Victor had looked her squarely in the eyes and she'd suddenly felt quite naked. "Asking for help doesn't make you weak. We're in this together." To which Ivy had dove in for a deep kiss. *He'll get it eventually.* Soon Ivy was out the door and driving a route she hadn't ventured in months.

As Ivy had manoeuvred the familiar streets, she'd reflected on this past month of domestic life. After years of living alone behind thick walls, Ivy was learning what it meant to be in a relationship. Any kind of relationship. She'd escaped from Joji and Mariko's world into her own happily ever after, but she was learning that the prince and princess didn't just stroll into the sunset; a fairytale ending was followed by an incredible amount of work. Constant communication. Accountability. And this ilk of work made Ivy very happy, because it meant that she could truly take pride in their shared life, and that it would never, ever be stagnant.

But now that Ivy was alone in her old apartment, faced with several months' worth of dust and a fridge full of rotting food, she reconsidered her decision to face this alone. *Such is the price of stubborn independence.*

It did not take long for Ivy to isolate the items she wanted to haul over to the loft. Some clothing (*how much longer will this stuff fit me?*). Beloved books. A crate of cooking utensils. Ivy would formally close the door on her old life with no more than three suitcases.

Once Ivy had packed up her crates and cases, she flipped open her little notebook and consulted her to-do list for direction. She phoned her landlord and explained that she'd be vacating the apartment at the end of the month. Ivy had never missed a rent payment—her post-dated cheques had been deposited during her absence—and the landlord was chagrined to see her go. She shuffled through her bills and watered the surviving geranium plant (*I'll take better care of you now, I promise*). With her healing hands encased in yellow gloves, Ivy confronted the gurgling contents of the fridge. *A carton of stinky old milk isn't quite as horrifying after you've pressed your hands against someone's bloody abdomen.* She shuddered and pushed the thought to the outer reaches of her consciousness.

Eventually Ivy completed all her housekeeping tasks. She collapsed onto the musty futon and gazed out the window. For the first time, she was struck by how quiet and colourless her apartment truly was. *This was never an oasis. I'm ready to go home.*

Soon a blinking light in her peripheral vision caught and held her attention. The answering machine. Ivy groaned. She could think of no casual acquaintances from her former life who would call to check up on her, and so a blinking light on the answering machine could only mean Janet from the library demanding to know her whereabouts. Reluctantly, Ivy pushed herself off the futon and shuffled to the machine.

But there was only one message.

"Ivy, this is Dr. Oliver. Vivian Oliver. I hope you remember me. I was your doctor, and your mother was a dear friend of mine." The throaty female voice paused and took a deep breath before charging ahead. "Ivy, I'm calling about your father. I know you haven't spoken in years but he needs to speak with you. Nick won't call you of his own accord, of course, so I've taken the liberty, because..." Again Dr. Oliver hesitated. "I don't know if you remember this or not, but I know how... how *special* you are, and I think it would be beneficial to you both if you saw each other again. I believe you're the only one who can help him. You can give me a call if you'd like." Then Dr. Oliver rattled off a Toronto-area number and hung up, leaving Ivy alone in the resounding silence with her mouth slightly open and her finger on the delete button.

Ivy's first response was contempt. *How dare she call and ask me to do anything for him?* Her father was little more than a sperm donor. He'd dwelled in Ivy's past for years, and she was perfectly content with the status quo. *All I have to do is press this button and he'll be gone forever.*

But still she could not bring herself to apply the pressure necessary to delete the message and consign her father to the past. Suddenly her mother's tinkling laughter filled her head. Ivy rewound the message, searched for a pen and paper, and jotted down Dr. Oliver's number.

By the third ring, Ivy was wondering what in Hell she was thinking.

"Hello?" A voice from out of the past sounded in her ear.

Ivy opened her mouth to speak but could only manage a strangled gasp. *It's not too late to hang up.*

"Hello?" Ivy detected a kernel of impatience in Dr. Oliver's voice and for the umpteenth time regretted making the call without analyzing all the angles and implications.

"It's Ivy, isn't it." Not a question. Ivy could hear a smile spread across Dr. Oliver's face and she felt a knot forming in her stomach. "Thank you for calling me back. It's been more than a month. I was beginning to doubt I'd ever hear from you."

"I've been tied up," Ivy replied defensively, then sighed. Once upon a time, Dr. Oliver had been her mother's best friend. For this fact alone she deserved more than a modicum of courtesy. "And my father isn't a favourite subject."

"I understand, Ivy."

Ivy rolled her eyes and wondered if Dr. Oliver could detect her disgust. "Do you?"

"I know there's been some tension since Amrita died."

Ivy flashed to the last time she'd seen Dr. Oliver. A graveside meeting the afternoon of the funeral. Dr. Oliver had grasped her by the arms and whispered into her ear. *"I'm here for you."* At the time, Dr. Oliver's words had failed to cut through Ivy's tough emotional armour. It had fused to her skin, with good reason. Her father had ignored her since the hospital. He'd planned the funeral without her input. Even at the burial, she was invisible to him. She knew he hated her, and so she hated him in return. By the time Dr. Oliver had reached out with her niceties, Ivy was fully immersed in grief and hate. *It's taken so many years to shed the baggage.*

Ivy fought to maintain an even tone. "He was never much of anything to me."

"I know you see it that way. Relationships are hard, but they're a two-way street, Ivy."

Ivy twisted the phone cord around her finger and pictured Dr. Oliver sitting at her desk surrounded by hundreds of photographs of smiling kids. In Ivy's youth, Dr. Oliver's office walls had been papered by colourful photos of happy children in bathtubs, in party hats, in wading pools, in tacky department store portrait studios. Young Ivy had wondered if Dr. Oliver could remember all their names.

Ivy's palms began to burn. So many years had passed but now the hate and grief were rushing back and she was a teenager again. "Why did you call me, Dr. Oliver?" Ivy asked through clenched teeth. "I'm not interested in dredging up the past, and I'm pretty sure my father feels the same way."

"That's just the thing, sweetheart," Dr. Oliver replied in her smooth tone. *I'm not one of your patients anymore, lady.* "He needs to speak with you."

"You said in your message that he doesn't want to talk to me," Ivy objected.

"He would never call you himself, but he does need to speak to you."

"Why?" Ivy felt her knees buckling under the weight of the dread.

"Something is happening to him."

"What?"

"Things I can't adequately explain over the phone." Here Dr. Oliver paused, and after ten seconds of dramatic silence, Ivy cleared her throat impatiently.

"What kinds of things?"

Ivy was surprised when Dr. Oliver snorted. "Isn't it obvious, Ivy?"

"What, is it cancer?" Ivy could hear Dr. Oliver fuming on the other end of the line and she felt her own frustration mounting. "I'm sorry Dr. Oliver, but you're not being clear and I can't read minds…"

"But you can do other things, Ivy," Dr. Oliver said breathlessly. "Things I can't explain. Amazing, magical, wondrous things. And so can your father."

CHAPTER 24

"What do you think I should I do?" Ivy clung to Victor with her eyes clamped shut. Her conversation with Dr. Oliver had left her uncomfortable in her own skin. Victor's arms provided a safe haven. She heard Milo's snores from across the loft space and felt a pang of envy.

Dr. Oliver had not ventured far beyond her initial revelation. "You never know who could be listening," she'd explained cryptically when pressed for details. "Just know that you're the only one on this planet who is in any position to understand. Will you see him?"

Ivy hadn't said no. She hadn't slammed down the phone. "I'll think about it." She'd been stymied when the words first tumbled out of her mouth. And hours later, in the relative security of night's confessional, she struggled to understand why she'd left it open.

Ivy was angry, and had been from the moment she'd slid behind the wheel for the journey home. At first the anger was formless, a mere spark of discontent, but soon it grew to blinding proportions and the headlights of the Jeep shattered from a sudden surge of wild, black energy. She'd pulled over to the side of the road to rein in her rage.

It wasn't that she was angry at her father—at least, she had no new anger to hurl in his direction. She wasn't even all that angry at Dr. Oliver for reaching out to her. Dr. Oliver was an old friend of the family. She believed she was doing a good deed.

"Should I see him?" The confusion formed a lump in her throat.

"I can't tell you what to do, Ivy. This is about your family."

"But you're my family." Ivy gripped Victor's hand. *Pass your clarity on to me.* "Tell me something. Tell me why I'm so angry."

Victor kissed her shoulder. "You're angry because you thought your past was behind you, and it's not."

"I guess that's part of it." But it wasn't everything. Ivy groaned and pushed the blanket off her body. "I feel like I'm suffocating."

"And you're angry because as much as you'd like to put it all behind you, you're curious."

This too was true. Ivy sat up, rubbed her eyes, and sighed dejectedly. "You got anything else?"

"Well…" Victor pulled himself up onto his elbows. Ivy heard his gentle smile through the darkness. "Of all the people in the world, it's your dad. Maybe the thought that you could possibly share some sort of special bond with your dad is most disturbing of all."

Ivy felt the sting of tears behind her eyes and knew Victor had touched on the truth. She pressed her hands against her abdomen. She had only just begun to show. She longed to share the experience of pregnancy with her mother. The futility of the yearning was a source of daily pain. And now, in this joyous moment of her life, she was drawn back to the very last person she wanted to see.

"I'll go," Ivy said quietly with her eyes on her hands. Victor rubbed her fingers. "I'll go and hear what he has to say. And I'll do it for her."

"Is this your first visit to Newmarket?" Ivy groaned inwardly. She recognized all the signs of a chatty cab driver.

"No." Ivy did not venture further. She wanted to stew in her discomfort. The driver took the hint and switched on the radio. A disco version of Silent Night filled the car.

T-minus two weeks until Christmas. Once upon a time, Ivy's mother had reigned over the holiday season. She'd made all her cards by hand. She'd bake shortbread cookies and honey cake. The house would be fully decked out with lights long before all the others on the block. Mrs. Merchuk had been the Christmas Queen, and it had been years since Ivy had celebrated Christmas. Since moving West, she'd spend her mandatory vacation reading and sleeping while her colleagues immersed themselves in wrapping paper and festive frivolity. For the first time in years, Ivy had actually been looking forward to Christmas—even though Milo had eaten her first sorry attempt at a gingerbread house—until Dr. Oliver had dragged her into the past.

Ivy had not flown cross-country alone. "I respect your independence, Merchuk, but we've spent enough time apart this year," Victor had announced. "I'm going with you." Clearly he had expected an argument, and he seemed surprised when he'd received none. In fact, Ivy was relieved that Victor had accompanied her on her gruelling trek. He'd wanted to meet her father, and see the house she'd grown up in, but she'd asked him to remain at the hotel. Ivy wanted to be able to return to him, and she didn't want to expose him to her father. She didn't want to taint all that was good in her life with all that was rotten. If it had been at all possible, Ivy would have left her unborn child at the hotel, too.

They passed the five minute mark. Soon the cab would be in front of the house. Ivy felt a rock forming in her chest and she shifted uncomfortably in her seat. Never in a million years had she expected to return to that house. She hated how familiar her hometown still seemed, even after a fresh dumping of snow, even after years and years of exile.

The cab sped past the elementary school that Ivy had attended as a child. A large group of kids were hard at work building a snow fort. *I never built a snow fort. I was never invited to join in.* Suddenly Ivy was stricken with the poisonous thought that she had no clue how to raise a well-adjusted child, and once again she pulled at a loose thread in her gloves and wondered how she was going to get through the next hour.

It's hard to stay in the moment when the ghosts keep pulling me back.

Ivy didn't know if her father was expecting her. When pressed, Dr. Oliver had danced around the issue. "Just know that I'll be there." This was hardly reassuring. Now that Ivy was minutes away from the confrontation, she could not decide which option—to be a surprise visitor or an expected guest—she preferred. *I wonder if he's dreading this as much as I am.*

Ivy thought about her father. For as long as she'd known him, he'd been frenetic, manic, and prone to ridiculous whims. He'd fire up the barbecue in the middle of winter and burn all the burgers beyond recognition. He'd announce that he was going to reduce the heating bill by using the fireplace more and soon the house would be full of smoke and firemen. In the aftermath of such catastrophes, Ivy's mother would clean up the mess and soothe the bruised ego, and her father would return to the world with his confidence intact.

Ivy's mother had belonged to her, and her parents had belonged to each other. She had not fit into his equation, and he had not fit into hers. *Lord knows I tried.* But young Ivy had taken comfort in the fact that she didn't need her father. Her mother had been enough, and when her mother had died, Ivy had chosen to be an orphan. The arrangement had long suited both father and daughter.

And now Ivy was rushing to provide aid to a man who was likely to slam the door in her face.

The cab rolled to a stop at the foot of the driveway. Ivy stared up the house. It seemed unchanged in every way—her father clearly spent money on upkeep—but an acute bleakness seemed to radiate from every shingle, brick, pane of glass. *I can't go back there. I can't feel that sadness again.* The driver moved to stop the meter but then hesitated and turned around in his seat. For the first time she noticed that his eyes were as blue and kind as Bill's had been.

"Do you want me to wait?" Evidently even the driver sensed Ivy's reluctance to proceed. "Is it going to be a short visit?"

Ivy grimaced. "It might be." She reached into her wallet and passed over enough to cover the first leg of the journey. "Please wait. If I'm not out in twenty minutes, just knock on the door and I'll pay you for your trouble." He agreed and restarted the meter. *At least I'll have a getaway car on the curb if I need to leave in a hurry.* The thought brought a small smile to her lips as she willed herself out of the car and up the shovelled walkway.

Dr. Oliver flung open the door before Ivy could raise her hand to knock. Dr. Oliver was far more handsome than Ivy remembered, with high cheekbones and chiselled features and silver hair swept up into an elegant bun. "Thank you so much for coming," Dr. Oliver exclaimed as she ushered Ivy through the door. For a long moment they faced each other in silence. Ivy sensed apprehension behind Dr. Oliver's smile. Ivy surveyed the front hall. There was no indication that anyone else was in the house. The air was heavy and oppressive. The furniture was unchanged. The same photos hung on the wall. Ivy had entered a crypt. *No one lives here.* Ivy's attention drifted back to Dr. Oliver's anxious face and it dawned on her that Dr. Oliver's interest in the Merchuk household might be more than that of an old chum. *Better women than you have tried to change my father.*

"Where is he?"

Dr. Oliver glanced over her shoulder. "In his den," she said quietly. "He spends all day in there."

"Doesn't he work?" Ivy couldn't imagine her father taking early retirement. "The man never even took a vacation."

"He's changed, Ivy. Everything has changed since you last saw him." Dr. Oliver opened her mouth as if to continue but the words seemed to catch in her throat and her eyes dropped to the floor.

Ivy sighed and pulled off her boots. "So you still won't tell me anything, Dr. Oliver? Even after I've come all this way?"

For the first time, Ivy saw a shadow of fear pass over Dr. Oliver's brow. She stared at Ivy for an eternity before turning on her heel and heading down the corridor. "Some things you have to see for yourself."

The pair stopped outside the closed door of Ivy's father's home office. As a child, her father's private room had been shrouded in myth and mystery. Often Ivy would loiter outside the closed door and imagine that her father was a secret agent with a direct line to world leaders. But as an adolescent, she'd come to view the room for what it was: a place where her father could avoid family life. Only her mother had possessed the power to lure him out.

"I told him you're coming but he might not remember," Dr. Oliver whispered as she cracked open the door. "I'm hoping you'll be able to break through the fog. He's in sad shape. You'll see it yourself."

Ivy walked slowly into a dark room. There was no light save for the last remnants of the afternoon sun limping in through the open blinds. It was almost a full minute before Ivy managed to locate her father. He was slumped far down in his armchair with his elbows on his desk and his head in his hands. She could not make out his face and was struggling to see whatever it was that Dr. Oliver wanted her to see, until she began to notice the incongruities. The room was silent. In Ivy's childhood, her father's den had never been silent. The phone had always been ringing. The television had always been broadcasting the latest stock news. The room had always been awash in the light from two imposing lamps, as if her father was allergic to darkness and stillness. But now it was clear to Ivy that much had changed since her childhood.

Her father sat in the middle of a graveyard of burnt-out electrical devices. What was once a top-of-the-line computer was now a blackened mess of twisted shards. Small piles of broken glass lay at the base of each of the darkened lamps. Ivy could only assume that the gnarled, blackened pile of glass and metal that sat in the middle of the floor had once served as the television. What had once been ivory walls and ceiling were covered by a thick layer of soot. Bits of sharp plastic jutted out of the wall as if they had been lodged there by a bomb blast.

"He won't let me clean up in here," Dr. Oliver said softly as if her words provided some sort of reasonable explanation. "He won't let me touch anything. He spends all his hours staring at the mess."

"Why won't you leave, Vivian?" Her father sounded so small and defeated that Ivy was surprised when she experienced a surge of pity. "I don't know why you keep coming back. I don't want you here. How do you even have a key?"

"But you have a visitor, Nick. Someone has come a long way to see you."

The years had not been kind to Mr. Merchuk. The tough hide of a tired ghost hung from his lean frame like loose clothing. He was dishevelled, twitchy, dirty, pale, a bum. The swaggering attorney was gone and replaced with a nervous, shaky shadow.

"Hello, Nick." Ivy had never called him by his first name before. *It would be a lie to call him Dad now.*

Mr. Merchuk lifted his eyes to Ivy's face and reeled back as if he'd been smacked. "God in Heaven!" he cried as he cowered against the back of his chair. "Amrita!"

Ivy winced. "No, Nick, it's Ivy." Mr. Merchuk blinked but his face remained contorted in horror. Ivy took a deep gulp of air. "I'm your daughter. Ivy. Do you remember me?" His bloodshot eyes flashed recognition.

"Ivy," he repeated slowly. "My daughter." He jerked in his seat and slammed a fist down on the desk. A big chunk of burnt-out machinery clattered to the ground. In that moment, Ivy realized that no closure would be found here. "My daughter with Amrita."

Dr. Oliver gave Ivy's arm a gentle squeeze. "I'll wait in the hall."

She closed the door behind her, and father and daughter were alone amongst the wreckage.

They stared at each other in silence. Ivy saw the mist behind Mr. Merchuk's eyes and suspected he spent his days and nights floating between past and present.

"What happened here, Nick?"

"What?" Mr. Merchuk brought his hands to his face and examined them for a moment before laying them down on his desk. His eyes remained transfixed on whatever he saw therein. Ivy glanced down at his dirty palms and remembered a time when she too had stared at her hands and wished with desperate futility that they were connected to someone else's arms.

"Nick… Dad." Ivy sighed. *What the Hell? It's only a word.* She wondered what her mother would think of this pathetic spectacle. "What's happened to you? Dr. Oliver called me and said…" Here Ivy floundered. Dr. Oliver hadn't said much of anything. "Well, she said we share something in common."

"Vivian is trying to be Amrita." Bitterness dripped from every word.

Ivy brushed a handful of ash off the desk and hoisted herself up. "She's worried about you," Ivy replied. "You're lucky."

Mr. Merchuk snorted angrily. "Lucky." His eyes shot up to hers and she was surprised to see tears mixed in with the rage. "Do you feel lucky, Ivy?"

A small smile began in Ivy's heart and surfaced on her lips. She thought of Victor, and Bill, and Piper, and the young men she had liberated from slavery. She thought of the sunny art studio where she spent long hours splashing paint on giant canvasses, trying to capture the beauty that enveloped her. She thought of the new life growing inside her, and the love she still felt emanating from her mother despite the years that had passed since her death. "I feel incredibly lucky," she said quietly, and paused. "Are you a healer, Dad?"

Mr. Merchuk clamped his eyes shut against a sudden rush of tears. "I'm a destroyer." The tears could not be stemmed. Mr. Merchuk fell over his desk as his entire body trembled and fought a losing battle against an inconsolable pain that Ivy recognized but no longer shared.

Suddenly the desk began to shake and creak as if rocked by a powerful earthquake, and Ivy tumbled onto the floor. She watched wide-eyed with amazement as her father leapt to his feet, howled as wounded animals do, and the massive desk split in two.

"Stand back, Amrita!" Mr. Merchuk cried as his eyes shone silver and bright light shot out of his overstretched palms. An all-too-familiar wind whipped around them. He clearly wasn't in control of any of it. The light ricocheted from wall to wall, illuminating all that remained of this once-proud den, until it hit a blackened bookshelf and Mr. Merchuk collapsed in a heap on the floor, still wracked by sobs. Again they were in darkness.

Ivy rose from the singed carpet, stepped around the pieces of broken desk, and knelt down beside her father. She placed her hand on his convulsing shoulders and saw into his pain. His energy was wild, black, and angry. A volatile cancer had infested his soul. *I can't help him. No one can.* She sent a burst of warm energy into his body and hoped he would find a moment's peace.

After a few minutes, Mr. Merchuk pulled himself up onto his haunches and rubbed his eyes, before seeming to notice that Ivy was beside him.

"Do you need any money?"

"Money?" Ivy blinked, disbelieving. *This is as close to a declaration of love as it gets.* "No, Nick… Dad. I'm fine."

Her father had died with her mother. He would never return from his grief, would never harness the energy that flowed through them both. She knew he was not long for this world and suddenly hoped for an afterlife so that he could reunite with his wife. She wanted him to be happy. *I will live life for all of us.* She planted a kiss on his forehead and left the den without looking over her shoulder. She felt lighter. She'd forgiven him. She knew she would never have a real relationship with him. She knew she would be a good mother.

Dr. Oliver loitered in the hallway. She grabbed at Ivy's arm the moment Ivy stepped into the light. "Did you help him? Do you know what's wrong with him?" Ivy glimpsed a desperate love in Dr. Oliver's eyes. *Maybe she'll help him. Maybe she'll draw him out. But he needs to want to be helped, and he's not there.* Now she felt a pang of pity for Dr. Oliver, and she placed a warm hand over that of her mother's oldest friend and sent forth a low-level wave of healing energy.

"It's nothing to be afraid of," Ivy said confidently. "I think it's caused by anxiety."

"Have you experienced it yourself? I mean, have you ever…" Ivy knew that Dr. Oliver had no words in her medical vocabulary for cases such as hers.

"I have, but he's not in control of the energy."

"So he might even be… like you?"

"A healer? Maybe. Probably." She thought of her mother and father together in happier times, and smiled sadly. "I'm his daughter, and look what I can do." She called the light to her hands and lit up the foyer. Dr. Oliver's face erupted in terror and awe. Ivy permitted herself a moment of satisfaction before switching off and moving toward the front door.

"You're leaving? So soon?" Dr. Oliver seemed so disappointed, so desperate, that on instinct Ivy turned back and folded her into her arms. *I have to leave here and be happy.* "I'll be in touch," Ivy said as she pulled herself from Dr. Oliver's embrace. "I promise. I'm having a baby. I'll send you pictures." And Ivy knew that was exactly what her mother would want her to say and do.

The afternoon light was gone. Night had descended. The cab idled at the foot of the driveway.

"Was it a good visit?" The driver inquired as Ivy settled into the backseat.

"Yes," Ivy replied without thinking, and then she thought about it, and she knew that it had been.

CHAPTER 25

Ivy went into labour during a deafening rainstorm. Rain alone was not unusual for Vancouver, but thunder and lightning most definitely were, and the streaks of lightning and thunderous booms commenced shortly after Ivy, ten days past her due date, experienced her first contraction.

Each contraction hurt more than the last, and certainly more than Ivy had ever anticipated. At first Ivy tried to ride each wave of pain gracefully using breathing exercises—as the obstetrician had advised during one of her monthly appointments—but she soon realized that deep breathing wasn't going to alleviate pain of this magnitude, and so she screamed through each contraction in a most undignified manner. Despite the agony, Ivy was determined to labour at home as long as possible. For months she'd known that it would be virtually impossible to explain any of the strange sights the doctors and nurses might see during labour—and as labour progressed and Ivy became feverish and delirious, her grasp on the energy grew increasingly tenuous. By the end of the first hour, most of the light bulbs in the loft had exploded. The wind whipped around her so frantically that books toppled off the shelves and dishes crashed to the floor, sending both Milo and Piper's cat Stanley scurrying under the bed for safe haven. But despite the danger to his person, Victor was by Ivy's side the entire time, whether she was tossing and turning on the bed, or pacing frantically around the kitchen, or writhing against him in some sort of crazed maternity tango.

"We should head to the hospital now," said Victor for the fifth time.

"Not yet," seethed Ivy through clenched teeth.

"When?" Ivy detected a hint of impatience in Victor's even tone.

"Soon."

But they would not make it to the hospital in time. After many hours of repetitive contractions with no end in sight, everything accelerated at once and before Ivy knew it, she was crouched at the foot of the bed and Victor—who as a young police officer had delivered a couple babies and so was not at a complete loss—was telling her he could see the crown of the baby's head.

"It's got brown hair!" Victor cried. "We're almost there!"

One final push, one burst of silver light and Ivy—exhausted and dazed and thirstier than she'd ever been in her life—pushed with everything she had. Immediately she had nothing left to give. She desperately hoped it had been enough.

"Victor?" The name barely made it out of her throat.

But Victor didn't make a sound. Outside, the storm had ceased. There was only stillness. Suddenly Ivy was hit by a massive wave of panic.

"Victor!"

"She's... beautiful." And with that, Willa Amrita Morgan opened her mouth and screamed, and her parents laughed.

"Mommy, meet your baby," said Victor, his voice thick with unshed tears. Ivy knew a father had just been born.

"Somehow I knew I'd have a little girl," she whispered as she peered into her daughter's face. The baby's eyes were clamped shut and her indignant cries filled the loft. "I love you, Willa." The name had been selected in honour of Bill, and now that Ivy had laid eyes upon her daughter, she thought it suited her perfectly. Overcome with love and countless other emotions—relief, joy, fatigue, even grief—Ivy decided to send a nice wave of soothing healing energy through Willa's tiny frame. *It's time to introduce her to the light.* She placed one palm on Willa's little hand, and—nothing. For the first time in nearly a year, the energy eluded her. She couldn't see the light. She couldn't hear the rush of the universe, couldn't call it to her hands, couldn't send it careening into her daughter despite the umbilical cord that still connected them.

"I must be tired," Ivy said dismissively, but somehow she knew it was over. She gently stroked Willa's fingers and realized that she would have to soothe her baby using other means. The energy was no longer hers to wield as she saw fit. As inexplicably as it had appeared, it was gone. She was no longer a healer.

After decades of constant self-loathing and anxiety, Ivy now faced each day without the suffocating burden of her secret. She revelled in her lover and her daughter, in splashing paint on canvasses and losing herself in thick books, in Victor's home-cooked meals and walks along the train tracks, and in lengthy phone chats with Piper (who, within weeks of his arrival in Kyoto, had announced he loved Japan so much that he planned to remain there indefinitely), and once Willa was past the not-quite-terrible twos, Ivy picked up some shifts in a used bookstore. Though she could no longer send waves of warmth through Victor at the end of a long day, or call upon the energy to treat a torn ligament or a scraped knee, she could trust a new set of instincts—those of the maternal kind—to guide her when pressed. Sometimes she would gaze down at her palms and experience a loss that surprised her, but she'd shove the sensation aside and attend to her happiness. Her daughter—with Victor's green eyes, an abundance of curly brown hair and a confidence that Ivy lacked and admired—was a bottomless source of joy.

Willa Morgan was an explorer. Once she started walking, it was virtually impossible to confine her to a crib or playpen, and so her parents spent a great deal of time clamouring to keep up. Willa's curiosity was unquenchable, and by the time she was four years-old, she dedicated every waking hour to understanding all the ambiguities she observed in her universe.

"Why does Milo have a tail but Daddy doesn't?"

"Do the Sun and the Moon like each other?"

"What do flowers dream about when they nap?"

Ivy and Victor didn't always have the answers to Willa's insistent inquiries, and when their knowledge failed them, they invented fantastical answers and Willa was satisfied. Sometimes the only time they were able to catch a breath was when Willa was fast asleep in her bed and they could gaze down at her gently snoring and grasp each other by the hand. It was not difficult to be happy.

One sunny Saturday afternoon in mid-June, the family—three humans and their portly canine companion—strolled along a winding path near Jericho Beach. Victor carried a basket filled to the brim with intricately constructed submarine sandwiches, chocolate milk and apple crumble—the traditional picnic feast of the Merchuk-Morgan clan. With Willa and Milo in the lead, the quartet headed towards their final destination: a secluded clearing in the midst of a patch of blackberry bushes, beloved by the family for its rabbit population and million-dollar view of the inlet.

Willa twirled and chattered on to Milo about fairies and elves and marshmallow clouds. Ivy remembered being five-years-old, and the magical world she inhabited. *My life is more magical now than it ever was.* She linked her arm through Victor's and, with a pang of melancholy, prayed that her daughter would never lose her sense of wonder.

"Look, Mama, a bunny!"

"I see it, baby," Ivy called out as Willa and Milo darted between two blackberry bushes in pursuit of said rabbit. "Stay on the path. Willa!" She turned to Victor and grinned wryly. "She's getting more stubborn every day."

"Doesn't get it from me," Victor chuckled. "Just wait until she's a teenager. I might have to go back to drinking."

They were five steps away from the clearing when the shriek of a child—*her* child—turned Ivy's blood to ice.

"Mama! Daddy! I found a hurt bunny!" Again Willa screamed, but this time her scream was accompanied by a blinding flash of light and the crackling of electricity.

Not Willa.

The picnic basket clattered to the ground as Ivy and Victor ran past the bushes and into the clearing. *Not my daughter. Maybe it's…* But there was no other explanation. Willa was now as Ivy had been, and as Ivy skidded to a halt a few feet from where her daughter knelt at the centre of a whirlwind—her hands pressed against a bloodied rabbit and silver light pouring forth from unseeing eyes—she sank to her knees in despair. *I can't protect her from this.* She felt Victor's hands on her shoulders. They watched and waited.

Finally the spectacle ended and Ivy rushed to where Willa now slumbered on the grass next to the healed rabbit. She stroked Willa's left hand. Freezing to the touch, as she knew it would be. Immediately her eyes shot up to Victor's. The pools of green rippled with concern. "Don't be afraid," Ivy said resolutely. "She will own this."

"I have no doubt of that." Victor's soft smile was tinged with sadness, and despite her declaration to the contrary, Ivy knew that Willa faced a long road. "She'll have a great teacher by her side." Milo sniffed the sleeping rabbit and Ivy thought of Willa's namesake and vowed to embody Bill's sense of calm.

Ivy pressed her sleeping daughter to her chest and caressed her icy hands. Willa's eyes seemed to be dancing under her eyelids. For a moment Ivy longed to be with her daughter in the white light, and wondered if her mother was there with her now. Victor knelt beside her and pulled them both into his arms. Ivy sighed. They would manage the rocky times ahead. No one was better prepared.

Beside them, the rabbit stirred. It blinked a couple times before seeming to notice the little family and scampering into the undergrowth.

"Ingrate." Victor chuckled. "Didn't even both to thank her."

"Mama." Willa's weak voice floated up from the centre of the family embrace. "Ouch." With her bottom lip stuck out in a pout so melodramatic that Ivy knew immediately that all was well, Willa presented a cut finger to her mother.

"You'll be okay," Ivy cooed as she brought Willa's finger to her lips to kiss it better, as her own mother had done for her countless times before. But this time, she felt a familiar buzzing in her palms, and as an unexpected torrent of relief and delight bore down upon her, she realized how much she truly loved the luminescence, the wind, the power—and that there was nothing wrong with loving any of it. Finally she was complete. She called the energy to her hands. *This is the moment.*

ABOUT THE AUTHOR

Sabrina Furminger spins futuristic yarns from an antique secretary desk in Vancouver, Canada.

Born Sabrina Rani Mehra in the dying days of disco, Sabrina studied English Literature at Queen's University and edited The Reader, the monthly literary supplement published by the Queen's Journal; later, she honed her craft as the Journal's news editor and spent one glorious summer interning at the Kingston Whig-Standard, where she covered the raucous opening of Wolfe Island's first public toilet (complete with ribbon cutting, a blessing, and a toilet-shaped cake), and visited a men's penitentiary during its annual Sports Day.

After many years penning feature articles and marketing columns for a diverse roster of trade and consumer publications, Sabrina has returned to her first loves: creative non-fiction (in which she often explores her biracialism), historical narratives, and speculative sci-fi. To follow Sabrina's ongoing literary escapades, visit http://www.sabrinafurminger.com.

CPSIA information can be obtained at www.ICGtesting.com
Printed in the USA
LVOW030003231211

260735LV00005B/2/P

9 781462 040759